RIPPLE EFFECT

N.A. COOPER

BLOODHOUND
— BOOKS —

www.bloodhoundbooks.com

Print ISBN 978-1-914614-66-8

To Rex and Kit
For filling my heart with love and our home with laughter

Ripple Effect – the continuing and spreading results of an event or action.
'The ripple effect is huge when something like this happens.'
Oxford University Press

NORFOLK 1996

I'm sat on my dad's knee. The wind is blowing through the grassland, dandelion seeds flying weightlessly through the air – a storm is on its way. Clusters of clouds crowd the sky, a patchwork of greys, hostile and intimidating. Crows circle overhead, a series of loud caws piercing through the howls of the wind. I'm worried about them. 'Poor crows. They'll get blown away.' Dad pulls me close, his grip strong around my waist. 'They'll be okay. Their feet are special – when they relax, they grip. They'll find somewhere safe and they won't let go.'

1

FIFTEEN YEARS AGO

I'm waiting where he told me to, in the space between the trees and the abandoned manor house. It's half past nine but still light, the low sun casting long shadows that are playing tricks on my mind. It's been an unbearably hot day and the humidity is still clinging, determined to make it into the night. I stand in the shadow of the old east wing, graffiti covering the entirety of the wall, a collage of garish scrawls trying to pass for art.

Feeling vulnerable and exposed, I check my watch again. He's late. The excitement of sneaking out of the house has waned, replaced by a sense of foreboding, the stirring of doubts that have remained hidden until now.

I'm starting to think it's a bad idea, a fantasy that should have remained in my head, when I hear something – the soft crunch of leaves; the snapping of twigs underfoot; the faint rustle of the trees as they're disturbed.

I'm hit by a sudden wave of fear: what if it's not him? Then I see him. He emerges through an opening in the trees and hurries down the forgotten footpath snaking out towards the house. Towards me.

I run to him, the excitement returning – boundless, reckless. I throw my arms around his neck and he lifts me off the ground, pulling me close to his chest and kissing me hard.

"You're late, Mr Miller."

"I'm here now aren't I."

"I thought you'd changed your mind."

He smiles. "Never! But what did I tell you, outside school it's Danny. Mr Miller makes me feel old."

I laugh. "You *are* old!"

"Oh is that right?" He picks me up and lifts me over his shoulder, carrying me back towards the house. I fight at first, playfully thrashing around and giggling, then I let myself go, my arms hanging towards the floor as he carries me effortlessly over the dry hard ground.

He bends to put me down against the graffitied wall and part of me wants to hold onto him, to not let go of the moment. I could stay like that forever, caught in his grip, going wherever he goes. I feel him push me into the wall behind me and take my face in his hand. His palm is warm and smooth and I lean into it, savouring the contact, the feel of his skin on mine. "You looked so good at school today."

I kiss him again and he responds eagerly, his hands slipping under my dress and caressing my body. I let him, enjoying his greed, the feeling of being desired.

"Come with me." He puts his hand out for me to hold and I take it, following his lead to the other side of the wall, a space afforded some degree of privacy by the old manor. Empty bottles of Smirnoff Ice and Bacardi Breezers litter the floor, broken glass protruding awkwardly between the weeds.

He takes his rucksack off his back and opens it, pulling out a blanket and lying it on the floor, kicking a couple of empty cans out of the way as he smooths it down. I watch him, the way he moves, his self-assuredness. He goes back to his rucksack and pulls out a bottle of champagne, uncorking it and taking a drink straight from the bottle.

"Here," he says. I take it and drink, suppressing the urge to spit it out. It's warm and bitter, a distinct tang to it which makes my eyes sting. I take another drink and he smiles, approving, the corners of his eyes creasing as he does. He sits down on the blanket, looking up at the sky through the stark remains of the dilapidated roof. I join him. He's changed since school, swapping his shirt and tie for a plain white T-shirt and cut-off jeans. His hair is messier too, no longer brushed neatly to one side. He looks different and I can't help but wonder if I'm seeing him the way his wife sees him – the casual Danny, the husband and father.

"What did you tell her?" I ask, though I know he doesn't like to talk about his family.

"Erin," he warns. "That doesn't matter. What matters is I'm here." He puts his arm around me and pulls me into him. I pass him the bottle of champagne and he takes a drink before setting it down next to the blanket. He looks at me and for a moment I think he's going to tell me he shouldn't be here, that it's wrong – but he doesn't, he just pushes me to the ground and kisses me once more. It feels different. There's an urgency to it and I understand that it's going somewhere, to the place where this has all been leading – two months of unspoken possibilities all resulting in one inevitable end.

"It'll get better," he says afterwards. "You're inexperienced. It takes a while."

Shame washes over me at the thought of my comparative naivety.

"Hey," he whispers, sensing my embarrassment. He puts his

finger under my chin and lifts my head up until our eyes meet. "It was nice." He kisses me softly then tilts his head to one side, his expression apologetic. "I've got to go, wait here for half an hour in case anyone sees me leave, okay?"

"You're going already?" It's dropping dark but he seems to have been here for no time at all. My heart tightens at the thought of him leaving.

"It's late, Erin. And it's a school night. Shouldn't you be getting some sleep?"

"I'm fifteen not five," I snap.

Disappointment flickers across his face and I instantly regret my childish response. I stroke his face with my hand, tracing the outline of his jaw. "Sorry, I understand." He raises his eyebrows. "Honestly, I do."

"Good, because I don't want to be with some kid. I was drawn to you because of your maturity."

"I know, I know. I'm sorry."

"Apology accepted." He gets to his feet. I stand and watch as he folds the blanket and stuffs it back into his rucksack. "Remember, half an hour, okay?"

I nod. "Okay. When will I see you again?"

"Tomorrow."

"Not at school, I mean when will I see you again... properly?"

He slips his rucksack onto his back then sighs. "I've got a lot on at work this week before the holidays. But..." He pauses, thinking about what he's about to say. "Melissa and the kids are visiting her parents for the first week of the holidays so I'll have some free time, maybe you could come over." He notices my excitement and quickly adds: "It will have to be very discreet though, Erin."

I throw my arms around his neck and jump onto him, my legs clinging around his middle. He holds me there, suspended in a moment which feels too good to be true.

"I take that as a yes?" He laughs.

"Yes! Yes! Yes!"

He pulls away from me, loosening his grip until my feet touch the floor again. I want to reach out for him, to pull him towards me, but I realise he's already gone. I can see his loyalties shifting back towards his family, his eyes failing to meet mine and the distance between us growing, the empty space filling with uncertainty.

"I'll text you," he says, "but remember to delete it afterwards."

He kisses me briefly on the forehead and turns to leave, walking along the overgrown path and disappearing into the trees. I check my watch: 10.20. The darkness has swept through the forest without me realising but now I'm alone it's all I can think about. I walk unsteadily, feeling my way around the wall and into the sheltered space where I'd left my bag. Inside, my hand finds a small torch. I turn it on, the narrow beam highlighting fragments of the space – tree roots; litter; graffiti; the champagne bottle, still half full. I pick it up and drink, letting my back slump down the wall until I'm sat on the dry dirt below. I shine the light on my watch and wait.

2

NOW

There's a difference between being alone and being lonely. It's subtle, but it's there. Each can exist independent of the other, or they can be woven together so tightly that it becomes impossible to separate them. In my dream I am alone, but it's peaceful – I'm not lonely, I'm happy – an island among the rough seas. I feel powerful, unassailable, the solitude is comforting. I hear waves crashing against rocks, a thunderous to and fro, the ocean dancing with the land. I'm mesmerised by the transcendent beauty of it, the waves that have travelled countless miles to end up at my feet.

The noise becomes louder and louder, increasing in intensity until it no longer sounds like waves at all but a shrill and threatening echo. The vibration of my phone pulls me from the waves, rhythmic bursts of energy hammering against the glass top of my nightstand. I want to sink back into sleep, to return to the comfort of the water, but the noise continues and I reluctantly pick up the phone and check the display. *John*. I check my watch, 5.08am. I put the phone back down and listen as the vibrations fade to silence, content in knowing he won't try calling again. I toss and turn for a while, sleep just out of reach, until I'm satisfied that enough time has passed.

He answers on the third ring. "Hello?"

"Hi," I say, stifling a yawn.

"Sorry it's early, I'm waiting to go to bed."

It will be just gone one in the morning in New York. I wonder what couldn't wait.

"Happy birthday," he says. I look at my watch, checking the date, my mind still foggy with sleep. "Listen, can you be around this morning for a parcel? I'm expecting some legal documents that I need to get over to the office ASAP." It annoys me – probably more than it should – that he uses the acronym as a word.

"What time?"

"Earlyish." He over pronounces the *ish* and I realise I could be waiting around all day.

"Okay, I'll run early. I'll be back for nine." I try to make it sound like a statement but I realise, to my annoyance, that it's a question.

"That's fine. Can you drop them at the office for me?"

"Sure, but why don't you just get them sent straight there?"

"They're... sensitive. I don't trust the receptionist with them. Leave them on my desk."

I decide not to ask anything further, caught between not caring and knowing it will annoy him if I probe. "Fine, I'll drop them off."

"Thanks. Then go and treat yourself – get yourself something nice, whatever you want."

I bite my lip, preventing myself from saying things that can't be unsaid. "You'd better get some sleep."

"One more thing – I've got to stay in New York longer than I'd planned. Three, maybe four days."

"Okay," I say, my mind already wandering.

"Right, I'd better get some sleep, I've got an early meeting."

"Night." I hang up.

The sun has begun to rise by the time I step outside, a deep orange glow breaking the horizon and seeping into the cloudless sky – a world in suspense, stuck somewhere between night and day. There's been a frost overnight and patches of it still cling to the ground, reflecting under the glow of the street lights. I start my watch and run, turning right at the end of the paved driveway onto the sleepy crescent, then another right onto the main road into town. I run against the wind, a couple of miles of steady downhill gradient until I reach the outskirts of town. On my left, Oakwood Park sits behind huge, black, wrought-iron gates, quiet at this hour but well lit. I run along the central walkway, flanked on either side by large English oaks, their leaves rotting on the ground beneath them. Uplighting pierces the path, guiding the way as I pick up my pace past the old stone war memorial still covered in a blanket of red poppies.

At the north side of the park a narrow footpath opens up into the dense woodland. I have to move over to one side to make way for an excitable Labrador bounding towards me, tail wagging, its owner apologising in its wake. I stick to the main footpath once I'm inside the woods, aware of a subtle change in atmosphere, the outside world unable to penetrate the buffer of trees. I usually feel safe here – protected – but there are times I feel like an intruder, an unwelcome guest in a revered space. The silence is so absolute, so haunting, that it seems artificial somehow.

I run past an old wooden bench where a fresh bunch of flowers has been left. Pink roses today; a different flower each week. They weren't here yesterday – a wilting bunch of lilies had stood before them. Last week a teddy, propped up against the back of the bench, left to endure the elements. When I went back the following day, it had gone. I wonder about the person leaving them, the offerings made to a life already lost. A tragedy, maybe, someone consumed by grief, returning to that old wooden bench that has started to rot, to leave gifts for someone who's probably doing the same. There's no plaque or markings on the bench, nothing to indicate who it stands for, just a long line of flowers and the occasional gift. Last Christmas there had been a wreath, but no card; no words of sorrow or regret, love or loss. It's a funny thing, grief. It can make you do things a happier version of yourself would have considered quite absurd.

I reach the end of the footpath and take the unmarked trail to the left which forms a semicircle back round to the main footpath. The first part of the trail is uneven underfoot and I have to take extra care not to trip over, navigating around fallen branches, tree stumps and marshland, the earthy smells of the forest thick in the air. Light is filtering in through the trees, narrow beams dissecting the ground as the sun rises.

Eventually, the trail opens out into a clearing strewn with empty bottles and cans – the local kids resorting to drinking in the middle of the woods to flout their parents and escape the boredom of living in a small town. Bursts of bright green leaves pierce the otherwise dull browns left by the passing autumn, rare but welcome, and I allow the tranquillity of nature to wash over me, trying to push everything else out of my mind.

A bird interrupts the silence, its song startling me from overhead. A robin – its red breast standing out amongst the barren landscape. I listen to it singing, its voice carrying through the trees. A memory comes to me, vivid and unexpected: I'm watching a robin hop around in our garden, so close I can almost touch it. My dad is smiling. He's happy. 'The robin is special, Erin. He's one of the few birds to sing all year round.'

I am so lost in this moment of simple happiness – lost in the love I feel for my dad – that I don't hear footsteps from behind, ones catching up with my own. I don't hear him until after I feel the warmth of him; his breath, his body, the stench of smoke and sweat. Before I know what's happening I realise I'm on the floor, shouting and flailing my arms and legs, trying to get him off me.

"Be quiet," he says. "I won't hurt you if you're quiet." His voice is low and hoarse, a stark contrast to the high-pitched singing of the robin. He pins my arms down with his hands while he straddles me. I try to use my legs to kick at him, but it doesn't work – the angle is wrong, my hips too immobile under his weight. I try to twist and turn my back against the floor to unbalance him, but he is too strong. He has size on his side. "Be quiet," he repeats. "I don't want to have to hurt you."

I feel like I am being slowly compressed, the air being forced out of me, my life being extinguished. I fight against it, gulping at the air and thrashing around hopelessly.

"You're pissing me off now," he spits. "I have a knife, I don't want to have to use it." He's speaking in an urgent whisper, forcing an unnatural quietness to words that should be shouted. I hear them but my body is acting independent of thought – I am no longer in control, instinct has taken over. I hear myself shouting but I can't work out what I'm saying and I wonder if I'm having an out-of-body experience, my soul escaping the horror that I'm being subjected to. I make the terrifying conclusion that I'm dying. What a tragic end to a tragic life.

The sense of unfairness overwhelms me and I begin to cry, a childlike sob, guttural and all encompassing. But my tears are not for this man, they do not belong to him. I want to shout and tell him that he is not allowed my tears, they belong to regrets in my own life – if you can call it that. A half life, maybe. A life unlived. An avoided life.

He puts his gloved hand over my mouth with force and I realise I've stopped moving, my legs are still and my eyes are closed. I don't remember closing them, and I don't remember deciding to stop fighting. The man takes this as a sign that I have given up – decided to comply – but I realise that isn't the case. I'm waiting for my moment.

"I'm going to tie your hands together. Be a good girl and it'll soon be over." He lets go of one of my arms briefly while moving my wrists together and I take the opportunity to lash out at his face and lurch to one side; some primal survival instinct I didn't know I had taking over. He loses his grip, the shock unbalancing him, and I'm able to flip over onto all fours. My adrenaline is pumping and I try to use it to my advantage, leaping to my feet ready to make my escape.

The punch catches me off guard. His fist comes from my right and connects with my face with such force that I'm propelled backwards and into the base of a tree, my head smashing into a cold, hard root protruding awkwardly from the ground. "Bitch," he snarls, his voice louder, hatred tinging his words.

This time I don't try to get up; I can't, my head is spinning and my ears are ringing, the world suddenly unstable.

"You shouldn't have done that." He's scowling, discoloured teeth visible through gaps in his black balaclava. He's on his feet, looking down at me through squinting eyes – cruel eyes that have begun to lose their colour, the blue diluted by milky streaks, all brightness fading to grey. He stands so large above me that it seems there is nothing else, just this man and the threat of what he is about to do to me; all goodness and hope in the world has been replaced only by this man.

"I didn't want to have to hurt you," he says, then he kicks my side with such force I feel my body momentarily leave the ground.

The pain makes me retch and I feel myself at a tipping point, a choice between pain and unconsciousness. I try to choose pain, to resist the temptation of blacking out, clinging instead to this hell I have unwillingly run into, but it takes a huge amount of effort. I'm crying again, loud primal sobs.

"Quiet," he growls, saliva clinging to his lips. But I can't, no matter how much I fear him or how much I believe he will hurt me, I'm unable to stop. I close my eyes and sob into the void, hoping my cries are carried like the song of the birds. I try to go to a place in my mind where I can pretend this isn't happening, a safe place no one else can reach, but it's inaccessible, no matter how much I need it. He's pulling at my leggings, his breathing fast and shallow, his eyes full of hunger.

Then I hear something out of place. I can't align it with the situation, it feels almost otherworldly. A dog barking and then a voice. A man's voice, but not this man's. I wonder for a second whether I'm imagining it or whether I have blacked out and slipped into a dream. I listen for the welcoming sounds of the waves, but then I hear it again, closer this time; definitely a man's voice. Hope rises cautiously in my heart, beating wildly against the agonising pain in my side.

The man above me looks startled, he's heard it too and he's panicking. I see a rush of golden white and suddenly a dog appears. He's barking at the man, relentless barks which echo between the trees. The man seems to be frozen in indecision as he tries to work out what to do. Then he makes up his mind; he jumps to his feet and runs through the woods, clumsily dodging the low-hanging branches, further and further out of sight until he is gone.

I try to focus on what he's left behind, forcing myself into the present. My ribs ache with a ferocity I haven't experienced before, it consumes my mind and overshadows the dull throbbing coming from my head. The pain comes in waves, gaining and receding in intensity, but never disappearing. Then without warning a sudden, violent urge to be sick takes hold and I retch, my body no longer able to hold onto the contents of my stomach. I wipe my mouth on my sleeve.

I'm aware of a presence drawing closer as I try to stand, wincing at the pain and pulling my hands instinctively to the source. The man approaches me cautiously – I'm not sure whether he's scared of me or whether he is worried that I'll be scared of him. Maybe both. But I'm not scared of him. I know he's not the man who attacked me, the man in the balaclava and gloves who smelled of cigarettes and sweat. This man has come to help.

3

NOW

"Are you okay?"

He appears concerned, looking first at me then over my shoulder, checking for signs of anyone else lurking nearby. I don't respond. I can't – I'm in shock, shivering from the adrenaline and the cold. Am I okay? I'm aware of the dog sniffing around at my ankles and wagging its tail.

"Here, boy," the man shouts with a whistle. The dog responds, moving away to stand obediently at his master's side. They're both watching me. The man gets his phone out of his pocket.

"Do you want me to call the police?"

"No. No thank you, I'm okay," I lie.

"You don't look okay, you're bleeding." He gestures to my head then plunges his hands into his pockets and rummages around. He pulls out some tissue and hands it to me. I take it, but I don't know what I'm supposed to do with it – I don't know where exactly I'm bleeding.

"For your head," he says, touching his own head at his hairline.

I hold it to my forehead then pull it away, looking at the

blood it has found. We stand in silence for a moment, concern etched on this stranger's face.

"I really think you need the police here," he tries again. "Do you know who that was? Did you recognise him?"

"I don't need the police." Memories of long ago, vivid and intense, swarm my mind and threaten to overwhelm me. I slow my breathing down and fight against the feeling of impending doom. The weight of the past is always lingering, threatening to suffocate me.

"Okay," he relents. "What about an ambulance? Or the hospital?"

I attempt to think clearly but the more I try to force logical thoughts the harder they become to grasp, the pain pushing everything further and further away and distorting whatever is left. I touch my fingers to my head. The wound feels superficial. "I don't need the hospital. It's just a cut."

"Is there someone you could call at least?"

I think of John in America. He wouldn't come home – an unavoidable truth that hits me with unexpected sadness. "No, I don't need to call anyone."

"I can't just leave you here. Let me at least walk you home, or to a safe place, and then you can decide what to do."

I want to tell him this was a safe place, now tainted by one man spreading his evil and leaving a trail in his wake. There are no unsafe places, just unsafe people polluting the world around them. I realise I'm nodding, accepting the suggestion of this stranger, but I feel unable to move. He takes a step towards me, the dog at his side, and places a hand on my shoulder to gently guide me forward.

"Come on," he says. "I'm Nick, and this," he gestures to his dog, "is Bear. He heard you shouting and bolted." He's guiding me slowly back to the footpath, a gentle pressure with solid intentions – good intentions, I think. "He never runs away so I knew something was wrong. Watch your step." He points to a thick tree root protruding from the ground. "Do you live nearby?"

"Yes," I reply, but I don't elaborate. I feel as though I'm in a dream, my eyes transfixed on a spot in the distance. I'm shaking, a relentless tremble throughout my body, my teeth rattling against one another. I don't know which is worse; the cold or the shock. The man, Nick, stops and removes his coat as though he's read my mind.

"You must be cold. Were you out for a run? Here." He holds out his coat to me and I reluctantly slide one arm inside. "You need to warm up."

When I try to put my left arm in I almost double over in agony, the motion of lifting my arm causing the pain to shoot through my ribs.

"Where does it hurt?" he asks.

"My ribs." I'm slowly getting the coat on properly, the warmth from his body transferring with it. I look at Nick, stood in just a hoody, jeans and hat. It's barely above freezing. Somewhere, a thought occurs to me that he must be cold and the selflessness of this simple gesture makes my eyes sting.

"You really need to go to the hospital. I can take you if you want? You might have broken them."

"I think they're just bruised," I lie. The pain is excruciating. We walk in silence for a few minutes and I get the feeling that he's weighing up his options, deciding how far his good intentions should stretch.

"What's your name?" he asks eventually.

I consider lying – my usual urge to remain invisible bubbling beneath the surface – but I don't, I owe him the truth. "Erin."

"Erin." He pauses. "Where do you live? Are you local?" When I don't reply, he tries again. "Look, I want to help you get home safely, but I can't do that if I don't know where we're going."

"Park View," I tell him.

I feel him glance at me, a shift in his perception – an affluent area, familiar to the locals. "Do you live alone?"

"No," I reply, but I don't say any more and he doesn't ask.

We walk slowly through the woods, weaving our way around the unmarked trail, Nick's hand connecting with my back every now and again, a reminder that he's still there.

When we eventually leave the thick canopy of trees I'm hit by an overwhelming rush of relief. I feel as though I've been holding my breath, compressed by the constricting grip of the woodland, and now I'm out I can finally breathe. I suck in the air, filling my lungs.

The sun has risen above the treeline, continuing its journey despite my distress. A cluster of blackbirds fly low overhead, the pale contrails of an ascending aeroplane visible in the distance. Life carrying on, regardless.

Nick looks over at me and I can see he's checking the wound on my head. "You okay?"

"I'm fine." I realise I'm still holding the bloodstained tissue and I press it to my head again as if proving a point – the bleeding has stopped.

"The guy," he says cautiously, "did you get a good look at him?"

I shake my head. "No. He had a balaclava on. He was white. Blue eyes. Not young, not old. That's about it."

"That's something," he says encouragingly, "you know, if you report it to the police – which I think you should." He bends to pick up a stick and hurls it into the open space in front of us. Bear gives chase but doesn't bring it back. Instead, he lies down and begins chewing it into small pieces. Nick and I walk on across the park, Bear occasionally coming over to my side.

As we reach the gates I have to stop, the pain threatening to overwhelm me; I feel nauseous, the sharp stabbing sensation radiating through my ribs every time I breathe. Nick puts Bear on the lead, his attention diverted for a second. When he looks at me again his expression changes. "You're really pale."

I feel dizzy and I'm worried I'm going to faint, my vision blurring and the ground beneath me suddenly feeling unstable. I hold onto the cold iron bars of the gates, clinging to their strength and sturdiness. I look over at Nick and notice he's got his phone out. "No, don't. I just... I just need some help getting home. Please." I feel guilty for putting him in this position, for asking for more when he's already done enough. I think of the walk to my house, the steady uphill climb – the thought of it feels daunting.

Nick sighs. "My place is on the corner." He points towards town then scratches his head over his hat. He seems to be debating whether he should continue. "I have a studio on the high street and I live upstairs," he explains.

I try to work out whether this is an invite but before I can say anything he adds, "Why don't you come back with me, I'll make you a drink, get you some painkillers, then I can drive you home. Save you walking up there." He gestures to the long uphill road stretched out to his right. "And if you change your mind at any point," he holds his phone up to me, "we can call someone."

I nod, relief washing over me. The high street is a few hundred metres away, I can manage that. Nick no longer hovers behind me, he links his arm underneath mine and wraps it around my back. He feels solid – strong – and I allow myself to weaken in his grip.

4

NOW

"This is me," Nick says, carefully letting go of me and pulling a bunch of keys out of his pocket. His studio is a classy-looking place on the corner of town, I must have walked past it countless times before but never really registered it. The sign says 'Nick Kerr' in black against a plain white background. Underneath, the tag line says 'Commercial Photography Studio'. He unlocks the door and stands back to let me in. "After you," he says.

Inside is one long rectangular room with a door at the back. Everywhere is white with flashes of dark blue and yellow. There are shelves full of carefully labelled files against the wall on my right, and to the back of the room boxes are stacked neatly into a storage unit. The rest of the room comprises of a couple of desks full of lots of screens, a dark-blue sofa with yellow cushions and a bright, white corner which looks almost clinical, cameras on tripods pointing towards it. Nick heads to the door at the back of the room.

"I've got to take Bear upstairs. Sit down and I'll bring you a drink."

I do as he says and lower myself carefully onto the sofa. The pain sears through my side but eases slightly once I sit back. I use a pillow to prop myself up and for the first time I notice other injuries. My left hand is cut from my forefinger to my wrist. The blood has dried but it looks red and swollen. I'm also aware of the cut on my head, as well as a throbbing around my temple and the side of my face.

I listen for Nick upstairs but I can't hear him. The occasional car or pedestrian passes outside but it's still relatively quiet in town. After a few minutes I hear footsteps on the stairs then the door quietly swing on its hinges. Nick walks in carrying two large mugs.

"Here you go." He hands me a yellow one. "I went a bit mad with the sugar."

"Thank you." I take the mug from him, trying to move my left side as little as possible.

"Here, take these." He hands me a packet of paracetamols. "Sorry I don't have anything stronger."

I pop two out and swallow them down with the tea. The warmth soothes me and I wrap my hands around the mug to take it all in. Nick grabs a chair from one of the desks and wheels it over to the sofa, positioning himself in front of me. He gulps at his drink and I realise he has taken his hat off. His hair is darker than I'd expected, almost black with a few strands of grey around his temples. In the distance I can hear the dustbin lorry making its weekly trip down the narrow cobbled street, the sound of bins being loaded and unloaded, the shrill beeping growing slowly closer. The cut on my hand stings and I notice fresh blood trickling out. Nick notices too and quickly gets up again.

"Wait here, I'll go and grab a first aid kit from upstairs."

Moments later he is back and carrying a dark-green first aid kit which he wastes no time in opening and unloading all over one of the desks. He tears open a small square packet and takes out its contents. "Sterilising wipe," he explains. "Give me your hand."

I clutch my mug with one hand while I hold out the other. He kneels down in front of me and gently wipes the cut. When he's satisfied, he goes back to the desk and unwraps a bandage and a pad. "I don't think a plaster would be enough," he says, placing the pad on the wound and then wrapping the bandage around it. When there is none left, he grabs some tape and sticks it down. "That should do it," he says, checking out his handiwork, "but I'm not sure what to do about your head."

"Don't worry, I can sort that out when I get home."

He looks sceptical and thinks for a moment before grabbing another sterilising wipe and repeating the same process with my head. This time, he applies a plaster.

"I'm not a doctor," he says, sitting back down on the chair in front of me. "I really think a doctor would do a much better job." I go to protest but he cuts me off. "Look, if you're in some kind of trouble, there are people who can help."

I don't know what to say. I sit thinking for a moment, unable to express the thoughts whirling around my head, misplaced anger rising to the surface. "Trouble? Someone attacked me!" I'm shouting, but I don't mean to. The emotion has caught up with me and I can no longer keep it inside. Tears escape my eyes and I feel them fall down my cheeks and onto my bandaged hand.

"I'm sorry," he says. "I didn't mean to offend you. It's just, you didn't want to call the police. Or go to the hospital."

I sit trying to compose myself, clutching onto my mug of tea. Nick gets up and comes back with a box of tissues. I take one and wipe the tears away, but more fall in their place. They can't be contained. He sits back down on his chair but moves it closer, the box of tissues balancing on his knee. After a few minutes he reaches out and gently takes my bandaged hand. I close my eyes and sob.

I don't know how long I cry for, but when the tears dry they are replaced with a sense of embarrassment so painful I impulsively stand up to leave. The sudden movement catches my breath and I double over, momentarily incapacitated by the violent waves of pain.

"Hey, where are you going? You need to take it easy," Nick says, standing up beside me.

"I have to go, I have to go home."

"There's no rush," he says, bewildered.

"There is, I need to go." I realise I'm being incredibly rude and ungrateful to this kind and compassionate stranger, this Good Samaritan whose quiet morning walk has been turned upside down.

"Okay. I'll get my keys and drive you home." His voice remains calm and patient, unaffected by my unpredictability. He heads out of the door at the rear and returns minutes later wearing a coat. It's only now that I realise I'm still wearing his.

"Your coat," I say, beginning to unzip it.

"Don't worry about it," he says, opening up the front door. "I'm parked just around the back."

He points to a little parking area where there is a white van and a black Toyota Rav4. He presses the key and the Rav4 flashes and unlocks. He opens the passenger door for me and I carefully climb inside, slowly clipping the seat belt in place. He gets into the driver's seat and reverses out onto the road. The traffic's light and we're soon out of the town centre and travelling smoothly up the snaking hill.

"How far had you run?" he asks.

"Around four miles, I think."

"Do you run a lot?"

"Most days, yes."

"Ever run round the reservoir?"

"No, I've always stuck to the park and the woodland." *Until now*, I think. Will I ever feel safe running there again?

"Try the reservoir. When you're better, I mean. It's all open and there are always a few people walking round there. Safer," he adds.

"I've never been." I don't really go to new places, but I don't tell him that. I want to ask him if he runs, or whether he's familiar with it because of walking Bear, but I don't get the chance.

"Which one?" Nick asks, pulling into the crescent.

"I'm the second one on the left."

He pulls the car slowly onto the driveway. He keeps the engine running but gets out and comes round to my side to help me. He opens the door and I unclip my seat belt.

"Here." He holds his arm out. I take it, allowing him to support me as I get out. "Got your key?"

I feel around my leggings, unable to recall where I put it. I locate it in my back pocket and take it out, showing it to Nick.

"Got it," I say. "Thank you."

"No problem. You take care."

I watch him get back in the car and drive away, leaving me alone, a sinking island among the rough seas.

5

FIFTEEN YEARS AGO

I wait until after dark, and then I wait for another hour – just like he said. It's almost eleven when I leave, sneaking out on tiptoes, avoiding the floorboards that creak on the landing. It's another warm night and I leave without a jacket, not wanting to hide the new dress I've bought for the occasion – short and yellow, with buttons down the front. He's told me which route to take, cutting through the outskirts of the forest to avoid town, minimising the chance of being seen.

After almost half an hour I arrive on Rutland Road, a quiet street in the suburbs full of double-fronted detached houses that all look the same – the kind of place Dad would say lacked character, a world away from our old Tudor house. They're all sat in darkness, the only light coming from the orangey glow of the street lamps overhead which only seems to enhance the sticky heat that still lingers. I check the numbers on the houses as I pass... seventeen, nineteen, twenty-one.

When I come to twenty-three I slip straight down the side without hesitation, through a little gate and on to the back garden – a large rectangle with a lawn and decking area, a solitary swing in the far corner. He's waiting for me, sat on a wooden chair with a can of beer in his hand.

"There you are," he says. I see his eyes wander up and down, taking me in as I walk slowly towards him. I stop just out of his reach, letting his eyes linger and enjoying the power I feel I hold over him. He can't help himself, he finishes his drink and tosses the empty can on the floor. "Get inside," he demands, his voice barely audible but his intentions loud and clear.

~

At three in the morning I begin to fall asleep, exhaustion setting in, the comfort of Danny's king-size bed proving too hard to resist. I feel his hand on my bare shoulder, rousing me as I begin to drift.

"Erin, wake up. You should get dressed."

I open my eyes though it takes significant effort. "Why?"

"You need to go, you can't stay here. Your dad will notice you're missing in the morning."

I groan. "I'm so tired."

"Worn you out have I?" He traces his fingertips down my spine, still damp with sweat.

I move closer, trying to hold him, but he resists. "No, no, we both know where that will lead. Come on, sleepyhead, get up." He gets out of bed and pulls both my hands, trying to lift me up. I watch him, the contours of his muscles, the hair on his chest and the manliness of his stature as he pulls against my dead weight. I giggle, watching as his eyes wander up and down my body. He gives in, biting his lip. I love the effect I'm having on him, it gives me a false sense of control over a situation that usually leaves me feeling powerless. I move my hands above my head, lying stretched out before him.

"God damn you," he says.

~

I wake to the sun pouring in through the gaps in the blinds and it takes me a minute to realise where I am, the sudden panic quickly fading when I see Danny lying next to me asleep. He looks peaceful, devoid of that flicker of worry he usually carries when we're together. I check my watch – just gone six. I shake his shoulder, trying to stir him. His eyes open slowly, squinting against the sunlight. I speak softly while stroking his arm. "It's okay, it's only six. I'm going to go."

"Shit." He rubs his eyes. "I can't believe we fell asleep."

"I can." I laugh, getting out of bed to dress.

He watches, his eyes never leaving me. "You're trouble, Miss Knight."

"Is that right?" I kneel on the bed and lean over to kiss him.

"Yes, that's right. And you're going to end up getting me in trouble."

"How can that be, when no one knows?"

He laughs. "Get out of here, before the whole world knows."

6

NOW

When I get inside I stand with my back to the door for a long time; thoughts wash over me but nothing settles, nothing but a numbness so dense I am unable to feel anything other than the presence of physical pain. I force myself to do something – anything. I need to feel clean, to wash away the stench of the man. I head upstairs to the bathroom, one implausibly slow and laborious step at a time. I run a bath, hoping the water will wash away more than just the physical evidence of what happened; I need it to penetrate my skin, to cleanse me from within. I catch a glimpse of myself in the mirror and double take, the reality of the situation facing me head-on, battered and bruised.

Around the plaster on my head there is a ring of dried blood and a bruise is starting to form, angry and red. My right eye has begun to swell, the redness trailing over the bridge of my nose. I look a mess. Remnants of dry dirt cling to my skin and my hair hangs loose and knotted over my shoulder. I undress, my limited mobility combined with the relentless pain making it a slow and difficult process.

I wipe a section of the mirror with my hand, removing the

steam that's gathered, and look at my ribs – blues, greens and purples beginning to form. I take a step closer and gently remove the plaster on my forehead; the cut is over an inch long, running almost parallel to my hairline, but it doesn't look too deep and the bleeding has stopped.

I step into the bath and submerge myself in the hot water. The warmth is soothing but the effect soon wears off, leaving me wondering how I was ever able to lie in the bath for longer than five minutes. The angles feel wrong and the bath feels smaller, my battered limbs bending to fit. I try to lie back and wash my hair but the task seems overwhelmingly difficult. I settle with turning on the shower above the bath and standing under a steady stream of hot water, watching it run down my body, discoloured by the mud and the dried blood. I turn up the temperature and stand there for as long as I can bear, until my skin is red and I feel as though I am disintegrating, on the brink of disappearing along with the steam cascading around me.

Once I'm dry I can think of nothing but sleep, exhaustion consuming my mind and body. I'm about to get into bed when I hear the doorbell ring. I check the security monitor in the bedroom; it's the delivery John asked me to sign for. I sigh heavily, heading back downstairs in my dressing gown, one hand grasping my side while the other clings to the bannister. When I open the front door, a short chubby man thrusts a small device at me to sign which I take without saying a word. He makes no mention of the state of my face and I am simultaneously thankful and alarmed. I hand the device back to him and he swaps it for a large brown envelope, thick and unimpressive. I feel a sense of irrational resentment towards it.

"All done," he says, adjusting his cap and turning to leave. His van is parked on the driveway, the door open and engine still running. I stand and watch him climb back in, the driver's side dipping under his weight as he sits. As he leaves I notice him turn to look at me, his eyes only briefly meeting mine but so clearly filled with pity.

I wake in a cloud of confusion which is quickly overshadowed by a pain so intense I scream just to try to release it. Everywhere aches. It's dark out and I can see the moon through the open blinds, the milky white light casting shadows into the room. It takes me back to being a child: I'm lying on the garden looking at the night sky. 'Look at the moon, Dad, look at it!' He's too busy watching me. It feels like a waste when there is such a beautiful moon. 'It's a Beaver moon,' he says. I giggle. 'The full moon in November is called the Beaver moon.' He looks up at the sky. 'It's when all the beavers begin to take shelter, preparing for the long winter ahead.' I turn to him, propping my head up on my hand. 'That's called hibernation, silly.' I feel clever for using such a grown-up word. He turns and smiles kindly, the moonlight reflecting off the rims of his glasses. 'Not quite. They don't hibernate, they just get their house in order and hunker down. They've stored their food for the long winter ahead, they've fixed their lodges and dug pools that are too deep to freeze. They prepare, then they ride out the tough times.'

I press the backlight on my watch looking for the time to anchor me, to bring me back to the present – 6.05pm. I've slept all day. The house phone is ringing and I realise that's what must have woken me.

"Hello?"

"Erin?" John snaps. "Where have you been? I've been calling your mobile all day."

"I... I've been asleep."

"Asleep? All day?" He places a particular emphasis on the

word *day* and his exasperation annoys me. I don't want to have to explain everything. "Erin?" he prompts. "What's going on?"

"Nothing," I lie. "I wasn't feeling well, that's all."

There's a pause on the line and I can tell he's trying to make the switch to caring husband, but he's struggling.

"What's wrong?" he asks.

"I'll talk to you properly when you're home," I say, hoping to move the conversation along.

"Is everything okay? You sound... off."

"I'm fine. What did you call for anyway?"

"The documents." He sighs. "Did you get them? I called the office but they said they haven't received anything."

"Shit, yes. I signed for them this morning then I went to bed and I've just woken up."

"Okay, okay, someone will drop by to pick them up this evening."

"This evening? Is that really necessary?"

"Yes, I need the legal department to look over them ASAP."

"Right."

"Sorry, but it's really important."

"What time will they be here?"

"Within the next hour. Do you think you've picked up a bug or something?"

"I'm not sure."

"On your birthday as well. Did you get my gift?"

"Gift?"

"Yes, I sent you something. Have a look outside." I can tell by his voice that he's smiling. I go over to the window and look down to the front of the house but I can't see anything obvious.

"I can't see, it's dark and I'm upstairs. I'll go down soon."

"Okay. Get back to bed once Ian's been."

My stomach turns. "Ian?"

"He's only picking up the parcel, you don't even have to speak to him."

"But he makes me feel uncomfortable."

The silence hangs between us, the murky area we've frequented countless times before but never resolved.

"Erin, please, he was pissed and it was years ago. He's with Trish now."

I don't say anything, letting the uncomfortable silence stretch out. I'm flitting between anger and disappointment but I don't have the energy for either.

"Erin?"

"Fine," I snap. "I've got to go." I hang up the phone and head downstairs. I need to find some painkillers. I go into the kitchen and rummage around in the cupboards, finding some ibuprofen. I gulp them down with a glass of water, check the brown envelope is ready and waiting next to the door, then go into the lounge and wait.

Twenty minutes later, Ian is standing at the door with a huge bouquet of red roses.

"You must have an admirer!" he says cheerfully, thrusting the bouquet at me.

He's dressed in a black suit and a long beige trench coat, traces of his dinner on the collar of his white shirt. He's smiling broadly, holding the flowers out for me to take.

"What?"

"They were on the doorstep."

"Oh. They're from John," I say, then immediately regret explaining myself.

I take the bouquet with some difficulty and sit it on the sideboard next to the door. I pass the envelope over to Ian who takes it, a look of curiosity on his face.

"Get in a fight?" he asks.

He runs his hand through his greasy black hair, his pointy features twisting as he smirks.

"I fell," I reply tersely.

He raises his eyebrows. "You... fell?"

"Yes, I fell. I'm tired, Ian, so if there's nothing else..."

"No, nothing else. You know where I am if you need anything." He winks, turning towards his car.

I shut the front door and lock it, listening as the sound of his engine disappears.

The flowers are a mass of red and green, wrapped in an elaborate gold bow. I pick out the small envelope from the middle. The note reads: *30 roses for 30 years – Love, John.* The handwriting is in cursive, neat and graceful – not at all like John's. I recognise it instantly as being his father's. I leave the roses on the side and head back up to bed, eager to find the sweet relief of sleep.

7

FIFTEEN YEARS AGO

I arrive home just after half past six, horrified to see my dad standing at the open front door. He watches me as I walk down the street, leaning against the door frame with his arms crossed. I can't read his expression.

"Good morning," he says. "Out for a morning stroll, were you?"

"I'm sorry, Dad."

"Let's go inside, shall we?"

I follow him into the kitchen and sit at the table. He takes his time making us both a drink, the silence hanging between us. The wait is painful and I wonder if he's doing it on purpose, dragging out the inevitable. Eventually, he sits opposite me, resting his elbows on the table and clasping his hands in front of him. He's ready for work but I sense he's in no rush to leave.

"So," he says. "Where have you been?"

My mind flits between different responses, none of them the truth but all seeming fairly plausible to my exhausted brain.

"I'm sorry, Dad. I wanted to go to a party but I didn't think you'd let me."

"So you snuck out?"

I nod. "I snuck out."

"And where was this party?"

"Holly's house."

He sticks his bottom lip out, a habit he's had for as long as I can remember. He does it when he's deep in thought, concentrating on something.

"And were you drinking at this party?"

"No, Dad." He raises his eyebrows. "Okay yes, a little. But I wasn't drunk, I promise. I didn't even like it."

"And were there boys at this party?"

"A few, but I *am* friends with boys, you know?" I realise I'm actually beginning to believe my own story, defending a scenario I've made up. I can imagine it in my head, a party at Holly's not unlike the one she had for her birthday earlier in the year. Some of the boys from our tutor group were there and we'd drunk a little of her mum's vodka. I hadn't liked the taste, no matter what we tried mixing it with.

"Friends?"

"Yes, Dad, friends."

"I know you're not a child anymore, but you're not an adult either, so I need you to help me out. What should I do? Do I let you sneak out of the house at God knows what hour without being punished in the hope that you'll have enough respect for me to not do it again? Or do I ground you? Take away your privileges?"

I suddenly feel very guilty – the last thing I wanted to do was upset my dad. I sit in silence, riddled with shame.

"Erin, if there's something you want to tell me, I'm here. Okay?"

"No, Dad, there's nothing. It was just a party I wanted to go to and it won't happen again."

"You know, I was your age once – as hard as that may be for you to imagine. I went to parties." I look at him in mock horror.

"Yes, your old man partied and drank and snuck out to meet girls. But one of those girls was your mother and she ended up pregnant and scared. I don't want that for you."

"Jesus, Dad, I'm not going to end up pregnant."

"We've never had the talk, have we? Maybe that's a failure on my part. But if you need anything – whether that be advice or birth control – you can come to me."

I'm mortified, embarrassed in equal measures for both of us. "Dad, it was just a party with my friends."

He puts his hands up. "Okay, okay, I get it." He takes a sip of his tea. "You could have asked me, you know. You might not have got the answer you were expecting."

"Really?"

"Really. You're fifteen, I know I can't treat you like my baby forever."

"Thanks, Dad. I'm going to go to bed for a bit."

"Sweet dreams, party animal."

I laugh. As I'm walking away, he calls my name. I turn but he remains seated with his back to me.

"Yes?"

"Do not make a fool out of me."

8

NOW

I wake surrounded by darkness and in a moment of panic I try to grasp for the lamp next to my bed, only to be overcome with pain. When I finally manage to find it, I switch it on and look for my phone but can't recall where I left it. I check my watch: 2.10am. I try to go back to sleep but I know within minutes that it's pointless; I'm wide awake, my body clock completely out of sync. I feel confused by my lack of routine, my anchor dangling.

I slowly get out of bed and search the room, focused on finding my phone. I head downstairs and find it sitting on the worktop in the kitchen. I realise I haven't eaten for over twenty-four hours and my stomach aches with the emptiness. I open the fridge and pour myself some orange juice then grab a croissant from the bread bin. I sit down and unlock my phone. There are two messages from John:

How are you feeling?
Erin?

I type out a response:

Just woken up, feeling a little better. Thanks for the flowers.

There's also a message from John's dad Ray wishing me a happy birthday. I go to reply then remember the time and decide to wait until tomorrow. There's a soft beep as I get another message from John. It will be 9.15pm in New York and I wonder whether he is back in his hotel room or out being wined and dined in Manhattan.

I spoke to Ian. He said you have bruises? What happened?

It didn't take Ian long to report back to John. I hit reply.

I did it while out running. I'll talk to you properly when you're home.

A few seconds later, I get another reply:

Ok, will be home in a few days.

I curl up on the sofa and flick through the channels absentmindedly, but I find myself unable to concentrate on anything. My mind keeps wandering back to the woods. I keep seeing distorted flashes of the man in the balaclava, followed by clearer images of the Good Samaritan, Nick. I take the laptop from the coffee table and decide to google his name. His business page comes up, Nick Kerr, Commercial Photographer.

There is also a LinkedIn profile, some articles about his work, and a mention of him running a photography course. I click on his business website. The home page is simple and says very little about him – he has twenty years of experience working in the sector, and he specialises in product and property photography. There some photos from his portfolio, I scroll through but they're all of projects he's worked on. I click on the header labelled *About Me* and a photograph of Nick himself appears.

He isn't looking at the camera but away into the distance, through a camera lens. He looks different, smarter, his hair shorter and with just a hint of stubble – not the messy beard and longer hair that I recall. I scroll down. He set up his own business eleven years ago, and it looks as though he's doing well. There is no mention of how long he's been living and working in Kestwell.

I go to the *Contact Me* section and see the address for the studio and a telephone number listed. I look at it for a moment – it's a mobile number. I close the laptop, lying down on the sofa to disappear back into the darkness.

The next couple of days pass by in a blur. I get into a routine of sleep, medication and the occasional bite to eat, the pain easing at times but never disappearing. I wake on Monday to the sound of the doorbell ringing and it takes me a moment to come back to reality, not wanting to lose sight of my dream. I'd been dreaming about my dad; I was chasing him on the beach, the waves crashing, the sand warm between my toes. I tried to reach out and touch him but I couldn't, he was too quick, always slightly beyond my grasp.

The doorbell rings again and I reluctantly pull myself out of bed, careful not to move too quickly. I look at the security monitor and see that it's Ray, then quickly realise I forgot to reply to his message. I put on my dressing gown then look in the mirror and consider whether there is any way to hide or at least minimise the bruising that has grown steadily darker over the weekend, but there is not much I can do.

My forehead is now a tie-dye of blues and purples, ugly and

dark. The bruising across my nose and under my eye looks insignificant in comparison, but the overall effect is alarming. I head downstairs and unlock the front door, standing aside to let Ray in.

"Morning, I was..." He stops, his eyes taking in the bruising on my face. "What the... what happened?"

"Long story." I close the door behind him.

"I have time, let me put the kettle on." He takes off his coat and heads into the kitchen. "Have you eaten? I'll make us some eggs." He makes himself at home, pottering around the kitchen, cracking some eggs and whisking them while the kettle boils. I sit at the kitchen counter and watch him work, effortlessly multitasking. It's been a few weeks since he was last here, but he slips back in and it's like he's never been away. "Talk to me, kid. What happened?"

"I... was attacked." And there it is. The truth I couldn't bear to tell John.

Ray stops what he's doing and rests his hands on the counter, taking a minute to process what I've told him. "Where?"

"The woods. I went for a run Friday morning and a man... he grabbed me."

Ray looks down, avoiding eye contact, and a part of me wishes I had lied, protected him from my reality. "Do you know who it was?"

I shake my head.

"Do the police have any leads?" His question carries a certain urgency, an expectation that the police will have all the answers. I look away. "Erin, tell me you reported it."

"I just want to forget about it, put it behind me."

"Erin, kid, you've got to report it. Did he... were you..."

"No, no," I say, understanding that he can't ask the question he needs to know. "Someone came along and scared him away. It's just cuts and bruises, nothing else."

A look of relief crosses his face but it's brief. "You can't let him get away with this, what kind of monster..."

"I didn't see him, he had his face covered. I don't want to involve the police when I can't tell them anything."

"What about the person who disturbed him? Did they see anything?"

"The back of his head maybe. Nothing of significance. Nothing the police could use. Honestly, Ray, I need to put it behind me."

"There could be witnesses, CCTV..."

"Ray, please. I've made up my mind."

"Does John know?"

I shake my head.

"No? Erin, come on, you've got to tell him, he's your husband. He would want to be here with you."

We look at each other for a moment and something unspeakable passes between us, a silent acknowledgement that what Ray said was because he has to say it – it's his duty as a father – and not because he believes it.

"I'll tell him when he gets back. I didn't want to worry him while he's away. He's been really stressed with work lately."

"When is he due back?"

"Wednesday night."

"Right. Okay." He nods, then goes back to whisking his eggs.

We eat in silence but I can feel him watching me, his eyes lingering a little too long on my bruised face. I make an enormous effort to hide the pain I'm in, not wanting to add to the upset I've caused him already. When we finish eating he tidies up, stacking the dishwasher and making me another cup of tea.

"Want to watch a movie?" he asks.

"Sure."

I lie on the sofa and he takes a seat on the chair next to me, picking up the TV remote and flicking through the films. I smile to myself – sometimes it's just nice to know there is another heart beating nearby. I slip in and out of sleep while the film plays in the background, Ray simultaneously watching the movie and me. When it ends, the title music rouses me and I see Ray sat on the edge of his seat.

"I need to go soon. You're welcome to come back with me, stay with us until John gets home."

"Thanks, Ray, but I want my own bed."

He nods. "You can call me anytime, day or night. I'll keep my mobile next to my bed."

"Thank you."

He gathers my collection of empty cups and glasses from the coffee table.

"You don't have to do that, I can clean up tomorrow."

"I'm happy to. Only, don't tell Agnes how good I am at it or she'll get me doing more around the house." He winks and chuckles but it seems hollow and, not for the first time, I wonder whether he's happy. I've always got the impression that he feels trapped, stuck in a loveless marriage by the binds of time and shared history, and I wonder whether his kindness towards me has something to do with a sense of solidarity; maybe he can see a part of himself in me.

"Thanks," I say. "And not just for today, but for the roses too."

He walks into the kitchen and I follow.

"Oh, well, it was all John really, I was just the facilitator."

I smile at him, but inside I want to shout: *He doesn't appreciate you!*

Once he's finished he puts on his coat and kisses me briskly on the cheek before leaving. As he's getting in his car he turns back to me and asks: "Did you get my card?" He must read the puzzled look on my face. "For your birthday. I sent you a card?"

"I haven't opened any mail yet," I say, not wanting to tell him that his was the only card I received. "But I will. Thanks, Ray."

I stand and watch him go, the emptiness he leaves weighing more than ever before.

9

NOW

By Wednesday I feel suffocated by the walls around me. I'm perpetually tired and my mood is low, made worse by the sense of dread caused by John arriving home this evening. I have to pull myself together, to hide the extent of the situation from him. I need to get some fresh air and start to eat again, my tummy feels hollow, my ribs protruding awkwardly – I didn't have weight to spare to begin with.

I have an uncomfortable shower then try to blow-dry my hair but give up halfway through, the pain becoming too much. The thought occurs to me that I'm probably in no fit state to leave the house considering I can't even complete this simple task, but I push it out of my mind, my need to be outside overriding any logic.

I leave the car and decide to walk into town for a coffee. I take my time, enjoying the sting of the cool air on my cheeks, the crispness stimulating my senses – I feel as though I'm coming alive. It's a bright day, cold but sunny, and I'm thankful to be outside despite the discomfort.

As I near the high street I pass an elderly couple walking arm in arm, lost in conversation, mirroring each other's footsteps as they climb the steady incline out of Kestwell. They look happy and at ease in each other's company and I can't help but wonder how long they've been married.

The town centre is alive with the hustle and bustle of lunchtime. A group of mums head into a new vegan café that's popped up recently, their toddlers strapped inside buggies, babies tucked safely in slings. I carry on down the cobbled street, passing the quaint little bookshop, the greengrocers and butchers.

Halfway down I come to Mimi's coffee shop – small but stylish – tucked neatly between a children's clothing shop and Live Well Herbal Store. I decide I'd better sit in today, aware that I need the break and the chance to rest my throbbing ribs. When I get to the front of the queue Mimi smiles warmly at me before noticing the cuts and bruises on my face. She gasps audibly, her hand shooting to her mouth.

"Erin, darling, what happened to your beautiful face?" She leans forward across the counter to get a closer look at me.

"Oh, it looks much worse than it is," I lie. "Just a coffee please, I think I'll sit in today, Mimi."

"Sweetheart, you sit yourself down. I'll bring it over." She pats my hand away as I go to pay.

I sit down on a small two-seater table by the window where I can watch the comings and goings of the town outside. Mimi soon arrives with my coffee and a slice of chocolate cake, a concerned look in her eyes.

"You look too thin, honey. You must eat, put some meat on your bones."

"Thank you. It looks delicious." And it does. Chocolate sponge with chocolate frosting and a single piece of Terry's chocolate orange on top. I take a long drink of my coffee, savouring the warmth of it. Mimi stands watching me, leaning against the other chair with one hand on her hip. She's a short and stocky woman with shoulder-length curly brown hair and a permanent application of red lipstick. She speaks with a heavy Polish accent, her words animated and vibrant. I've worked for her in the past, a few catering events she's hired extra staff for, and she's always been kind and warm towards me. She is, I realise, the closest thing I have to a friend.

"You'd tell me if you're in trouble, yes?" Her eyes remain fixed on me as I take a sip of my coffee. "You tell me if someone did this to you, honey. You don't carry things like that by yourself."

"Oh, no, no, Mimi, I'm fine, I just had an accident, that's all. But thank you."

She stands looking at me. I'm certain she knows I'm lying, but she's too kind to say.

"You can come here anytime, our door is always open to you," she says sincerely, and she leaves it at that, returning to her position behind the counter. I sit and enjoy my coffee and chocolate cake and watch as people go by outside, everyone lost in their own lives. Every now and again I feel Mimi watching me, her eyes burrowing into me, looking for the truth I'm not willing to share. When I've finished I pull a ten-pound note out of my purse and leave it on the table, shouting a hasty goodbye to Mimi as I leave.

Once outside, I zip up my coat against the chill. Christmas lights sparkle in a window across the road and a large festive wreath hangs neatly on the door. I look left and right, wondering whether to go home or walk further down the street. Kestwell is an old market town set in an L shape with a large town hall at one end and a church at the other. The cobbled streets are filled with shops, cafés and a few bars, almost all independently owned. The park and woodland run parallel to the centre and a lot of people use it as a cut-through.

I don't often venture further than Mimi's, I've never had any need to before, but now I find myself wanting to turn left, to the outskirts of town and to the corner where I know Nick lives and works. I've been thinking about him, wondering whether his concern that day has flowed over into his life. Would he be pleased to see me? Would it help him file away that day as a good deed? Give him closure? I tell myself I want to see him for his benefit, but I'm not entirely sure I believe myself. I turn left.

As I reach the corner I see his car is parked behind the studio, but the blinds are down in the windows. I walk straight past, towards the church, my embarrassment from that day still too fresh.

John was due to arrive home around eight but an hour later I'm still waiting. I've long since accepted punctuality is not one of his strong points. Eventually, I hear his car pull up outside and he walks through the door minutes later, suitcase in one hand and a holdall in the other. He looks tired, his suit crumpled and hair dishevelled.

"Sorry," he says. "Took ages to get my car." He puts his bags down and locks the door behind him before his eyes settle on me, taking in the damage. "Jesus, Erin, what the fuck?"

I step away from him, my hand automatically moving to my head, blocking his view. He steps towards me and pulls my hand away, getting a better look. There's no plaster anymore, just a half-healed cut and the accompanying bruising, in varying shades of purple and green.

"What happened?"

"I didn't want to worry you."

"Erin, what the hell happened?"

I feel as though I'm at a crossroads, unsure which route to

choose. I take a deep breath before I speak, my mouth revealing a lie I hadn't realised I'd decided on.

"I was running in the woods and I tripped on something. I think I cracked a rib."

He stands with his hands on his hips, taking in the cuts and bruises on my face. I can't work out whether he's waiting for more information or deliberating my honesty.

"You tripped?"

I nod, trying hard to maintain eye contact, to resist the urge to look away in shame.

"You shouldn't go running in there by yourself. What if you'd been knocked out? It's too quiet in there."

I shrug.

"I got you a present," he says, changing his tone and smiling. He unzips his holdall and takes out a small wrapped package. "Happy birthday, sorry it's late." I take it from him and unwrap it, revealing a dark-blue box which I open. Inside are a pair of square-cut diamond earrings. "You like them?"

"I love them, thank you."

It's the third pair of diamond earrings he's bought me – if they're different, it's not in a way I'm able to notice. I close the box and try to hug him but the movement stretches my torso and I retreat in pain.

"Go and sit down, I'll order us some food." He grabs a menu from the drawer beside him and looks through it. I stand watching him, lost for a moment in the mundanity of the situation – the old familiar – thoughts of Ray and the secret we share turning in my head, protected, safe, but troubling.

10

FIFTEEN YEARS AGO

I'm desperate to get back to school, the summer holidays seeming more like torture than a break. I need to see him, to ask him why he hasn't been in touch. I've gone over and over it in my head, analysed everything we did, everything we said – but I'm missing something. Why else would he have been ignoring me?

The morning drags in a haze of paperwork and formalities. As soon as I get my new timetable I scan it looking for his name.

Wednesday. I won't see him until Wednesday. My stomach sinks, misery taking hold once more.

At lunchtime I break away from the crowd and head into the south block, taking the stairs to the second floor. I can't wait until Wednesday, I need to see him now. The geography department is limited to a single corridor with two classrooms positioned opposite each other and Mr Miller's office at the end – the perks of his recent promotion to head of geography. The classrooms are empty and his office door is shut. I check the hallway, listening for footsteps, but it's quiet. I knock. A minute later, he opens the door.

"Get in," he whispers, pulling me into his office by my arm.

He looks shocked to see me and I suddenly find myself wondering whether I've made a mistake – I should have been more careful, more respectful of his request to stay away from each other at school. The room is small and cluttered – boxes of paperwork balancing on the desk and chairs; shelves packed with disorderly books; empty, coffee-stained mugs scattered everywhere.

"What do you want?" He scowls, but he doesn't give me the chance to answer. "What are you doing coming to my office?"

There's an anger in his voice that I haven't heard before and it catches me off guard. I'd been expecting him to sweep me into his arms and explain away all my concerns. He looks dishevelled, not his usual groomed self. His shirt is creased and his tie loose, and there is a hint of stubble I haven't seen before.

"I wanted to see you, you haven't been replying to my texts."

"You shouldn't have been texting me in the first place. I text you first, remember?"

"But I hadn't heard anything from you and I... I missed you." I feel pathetic even as I'm saying it. "I don't understand."

"You left your fucking bracelet in my bedroom." He spits at me as he speaks, hushed but menacing, as though there is a rage in him that he is desperately trying to suppress. "My wife found it." He raises his eyebrows. "Now do you understand?"

"Oh God, oh God." I put my head in my hands, horrified by my own stupidity. I hadn't even missed it – just a cheap piece of costume jewellery, one of many hung on my stand. "I'm so sorry, Danny, I didn't mean to. I was in a rush to leave, remember?"

"Ha! You're sorry? You've fucked up my marriage and all you can say is you're sorry?"

I'm crying, tears streaming down my cheeks and onto my clean white shirt.

"Danny, please, I didn't know... I didn't mean to..."

He interrupts, his tone cold and full of anger. "It's Mr Miller to you. Now get the fuck out of my office." He sits down heavily behind his desk, on the only available space in the whole room. I want to stay. I want to beg him for forgiveness, plead with him to let me make it up to him, but I know it's futile. I can tell from the way he's looking at me that the only thing he feels for me now is hatred.

I spend the rest of my lunch break in the toilets reduced to an emotional weeping wreck. I feel broken, shattered beyond repair – I can't believe I have no wounds, no gaping hole in my chest where my heart used to be. I look at my red blotchy face in the mirror and wonder how I'll ever fit all the pieces back together. I splash cold water on my face and use some toilet paper to scrub away the mascara that's left sad streaks down my cheeks. What a mess.

The afternoon drags by, interjected by sympathetic comments from concerned friends during maths and English who don't seem to doubt my claims that I feel ill.

"You should go and see the school nurse," Lauren tells me. "You look terrible, you really shouldn't have come in."

I shrug. "I didn't want to miss the first day back."

"You don't do anything on the first day, it's a waste of time. Look." Holly gestures to Miss Jackson who's sitting at the front of the class sorting through worksheets and arranging files. "I mean, shouldn't she have done this during her six-week holiday?"

I smile. "I'll be okay."

At the end of the day I walk halfway home with Lauren and Holly before they split off in a different direction, leaving me to continue the rest of the journey alone. I want to shout them back, to confess everything. It suddenly feels like such a huge burden, this secret of mine – a gigantic weight I can hardly bear to carry alone. But I don't. I carry on walking towards home, lost in memories of a love I feel is impossible to ever encounter again.

11

NOW

The next morning I wake by myself, the empty space beside me suddenly appearing bigger. I go downstairs and make some coffee, the tiled floors in the kitchen ice cold beneath my bare feet. On the kitchen table I find a note from John, scrawled on the back of the menu he'd used last night.

Didn't want to wake you, had to go into London early for meetings. Don't wait up.

And just like that, I'm alone again. I throw the menu in the bin and head upstairs to take a shower and dress. I'm missing being able to go for a run, the freedom and clarity it brings, but I know from the pain I'm still in that it'll be several weeks before I can get back to it. I need to clear my mind, shake out the fog that has settled overnight.

I head out into the cold morning, the sun beginning its invisible ascent behind a thick layer of cloud. It's rained overnight and surface water has gathered along the pavements and roads. I walk slowly, taking my time – I have nothing to rush home for. I pass the town hall and head further down the cobbled street, stopping as I come to the library – a beautiful listed building with orange brick walls and an imposing arched entrance. It's perpetually cold inside, but peaceful.

I enter through the heavy double doors at the front and into an entrance area, dark and windowless. A large pinboard hangs from one of the walls, everything from bake sales to lost pets pinned haphazardly to it. Against another wall sits a display stand holding countless different leaflets. I go straight through another set of doors and into the main room – a large rectangular space filled with rows upon rows of books, all arranged on wooden shelves set at different angles. It's enough to get lost in.

I look through the new releases, then the old, reading a few pages here and there and breathing in the familiar mustiness. I find a copy of *Of Mice And Men* and make my way to the back of the room to find the comfy armchairs, tucked together in a corner under the glow of a stained-glass window. I sit down and begin to read the story I already know too well. I try to concentrate on the words, to immerse myself in the characters, but the pain is off-putting, it keeps bringing me back to reality. I try shifting my weight from left to right, trying to get comfortable, but eventually I give up – I need to stretch. I put the book back on the shelf and leave.

Outside, the brightness catches me by surprise, the sun shining through the newly parted clouds. Through squinting vision I catch a glimpse of a familiar figure across the road but it takes me a moment to place him. Then it comes to me with a sudden lurch in my stomach – it's Nick. The Good Samaritan. I stand, frozen in indecision; I can't decide whether to run to him or from him. He's emerged from the bank and is heading in the direction of his studio.

For a brief second I consider shouting to him. *Hey Nick! Remember me?* I quickly quash the urge and instead find myself following him. I'm several paces behind but he suddenly stops – he's seen someone he knows, a man in a black padded coat. They shake hands and begin talking animatedly. I'm walking slowly but they're still talking as I catch up to them. I walk straight past, turning my head away from him, but as I do I hear them saying goodbye. He's on the move again. I glance over to him, trying to be subtle, but he must feel my gaze because he turns to face me. Our eyes meet and for a moment I think he hasn't recognised me, then there's a spark of something in his eyes and he smiles. Relief washes over me.

"Hello, how're you feeling?"

"I'm okay. I've been wanting to say thank you properly, and to return your coat, but I didn't want to just turn up on your doorstep."

He laughs but it's kind and light-hearted and I can't help but smile.

"I'm not bothered about my coat, but it would have been nice to see you and know you're okay. You were in pretty bad shape."

"Sorry, I've only just started going out. I've been in quite a lot of pain."

We walk slowly down the long cobbled street, the sun shining on our backs.

"Where are you heading?" he asks.

I shrug. "Nowhere really, I've just been to the library. I thought I might get a coffee from Mimi's."

"I love Mimi's! She makes the best cakes."

"She really does!"

He checks his watch then says, "I've got an hour before my next client, fancy a coffee?"

"I'd like that," I say, aware of how much I mean it.

We soon come to Mimi's and find it packed full of people. Each table is taken and a couple of customers are hanging around clearly waiting to pounce on the next one that becomes available.

"Coffee to go?" I ask.

"Sure, let me get it."

"No, no, please let me. It might make me feel just a tiny bit better about the whole thing."

He holds up his hands, defeated, then steps to the side to let me into the shop.

"What can I get you?" I ask.

"Black coffee please."

I head in and find Mimi looking flustered behind the counter. When she's finished serving the elderly couple in front she turns to me.

"Erin, sweetheart, your face is looking better. Not so swollen."

I smile at her. "Thank you. I do feel better."

"Coffee?" she asks, already turning to the machine.

"Yes, to take away please, plus a black coffee."

"Oh," she says, raising her eyebrows. "You have a friend today?"

"Kind of."

She looks over my shoulder, trying to see past the queue that's forming behind me, but she gives in and pours the drinks instead.

"Any cakes today, my love?"

I browse the display cabinet, looking over the shelves tightly packed with freshly baked desserts and deciding on a piece of lemon drizzle cake and a coffee and walnut.

"The coffee and walnut is fresh this morning. Tastes delicious," she says, placing them into two cardboard boxes and putting them into a brown paper bag. She retrieves the coffees from the machine and places them on the counter.

I hand her the money and gather my things. "I'll see you soon, Mimi."

"You take care, darling."

I feel her eyes following me as I leave, picking my way through the queue which now blocks the door. Outside the shop I hand Nick his coffee and hold up the paper bag.

"You got cake." He smiles.

"Of course!"

We don't discuss where we're going, neither of us acknowledging the fact we're heading towards his.

"How are the ribs?" he asks, his place coming into view.

"Painful. And blue and green."

"Ouch. And your head? Looks like it's healing well."

"It is. Thanks for the first aid."

"I aim to please." He's smiling but he doesn't look at me, he's searching his pockets for his keys. As he gets them out and approaches his door, I stand back. I'm not sure whether he's expecting me to follow or not. "You're coming in to share that cake, aren't you?"

"Sure, but I'm having the coffee and walnut."

"Deal." He opens the door and walks in, holding it open for me to step inside.

"Come on up," he says, gesturing to the door at the back of the room. He's asking me to go to his flat, to his home, but he's done it so casually that it feels entirely natural. I wonder if I should feel more against the idea. I think of John but the thought is fleeting, passing over my head and never really landing. I follow him. At the top of the stairs he unlocks another door and I hear Bear barking and crying with excitement.

"Take it easy, boy." Nick holds the door open and I walk past him into the room. "Take a seat, make yourself comfy." He points to a large corner sofa and coffee table. "I'll get some plates." He takes the bag from me and I go and sit down, trying to subtly take in his flat.

It's larger than I expected, one big open-plan space with a pale-grey kitchen and an oak-wood seating area, low-hanging lights sitting stylishly over the top of the table. There's wooden flooring throughout and tasteful prints on the otherwise plain white walls. Bear walks over to a large dog bed and lies down in it, watching me.

"Here you go, coffee and walnut."

Nick hands me the piece of cake on a plate with a fork.

"Thank you, did you make this yourself?"

He laughs, sitting at the other end of the sofa and tucking into his own cake.

"This is good," he says.

When we're finished eating we place our empty plates on the coffee table. Bear gets up and comes to sit between us, his eyes on the crumbs left on the plates. I reach out and stroke him. An awkward silence begins to settle; I can't read the signs and I don't know whether Nick's expecting me to leave as soon as I've finished. Before I can say anything, he speaks.

"Have you told anyone about what happened?"

I shake my head. I don't want to go into the complexities of the fact I've told my father-in-law but not my husband. I know how it sounds. I suddenly think of Ray and make a mental note to call him later to prewarn him that I haven't told John the whole truth. I wonder how he'll react.

"You're married." Nick nods towards my wedding ring. A simple gold ring signifying such a significant commitment.

"I am."

"But you haven't told your husband?"

"I haven't."

I know Nick wants me to explain but I can't. Why didn't I tell John the truth? I have run through different reasons in my head – I don't want him to worry; I'm scared he won't worry; I don't want him to look at me differently; I'm scared he will blame me. The list goes on, but the truth is probably a mixture of all of them or none at all. Maybe I just want to keep some things for myself. I change the subject before Nick can push me any further.

"Did you tell anyone?"

He shakes his head. "It's not mine to tell."

I realise I'm relieved. It's a small town, the less people who know the better. I think of Ray again. I trust him, I'm sure he won't have told Agnes.

"Thank you," I say.

He finishes his coffee then takes the plates over to the kitchen. I grab my bag then stand, ready to leave.

"You don't have to go," he says.

"I should let you get back to work. Thanks again."

"Please stop saying thank you," he says, smiling warmly.

I wonder if he feels sorry for me, but there's something else in his eyes, something more than pity. He opens the door for me and follows me downstairs and back into his studio. Before he opens the front door he pauses.

"I think you should talk to someone about what happened. If you can't talk to your husband maybe you could talk to someone impartial?"

"You mean a therapist?"

"Sure, why not? Everyone sees a therapist nowadays."

I clear my throat, caught between saying too much and nothing at all.

"Just think about it," he says, opening the door.

I turn and leave, the words stuck in my throat, unable to explain the panic his idea causes. Some things are better left in the past, unresolved but protected. I head back towards home, alone but unassailable.

12

NOW

I reach home just as a huge downpour arrives, fast and heavy, hitting everything with such force that the water bounces before settling. I make myself a cup of coffee and sit in a chair by a large bay window at the front of the house, immersed in the rain, watching as droplets gather on the windowsill and the plant pots begin to overflow.

I fetch my book and sit reading for a while, but my mind soon drifts to my conversation with Nick. *You could talk to someone impartial.* His good intent holds no weight, he doesn't know me at all. I have endured therapy before, months of arduous conversations with a woman who meant well but achieved nothing. The professional nature of it, the formality, it will never work for me.

I decide to call Ray and tell him about the secret we share; unintentionally, on his part. He won't like keeping something like this from John, his loyalty a fierce facade for the shortcomings he feels he's made as a father.

He answers after a few rings. "Erin, how you doing?"

"I'm good thanks, much better, but I need to talk to you about something."

"Oh?"

"I saw John, but only briefly."

"You didn't tell him, did you?"

"Not exactly, no. I told him it was an accident. He was tired from travelling and work and–"

Ray interrupts. "And he's your husband, he should know."

"I know. I just didn't want to worry him."

He sighs audibly and a moment of silence hangs between us.

"Ray?"

"You're putting me in a tough spot, Erin."

"I know I am. I'm sorry, I wish I'd just kept the whole thing to myself."

"No, that wouldn't be right either. For the record, I don't agree with this, okay?"

"Okay." And just like that, there is nothing more to say. "Thanks, Ray. I mean it."

"I know, I know. I'll see you soon, kid."

I hang up, a weight lifted. I listen as the earlier ferocity of the rain eases into the soft pitter-patter of a light shower, the intermittent *drip, drip, drip*. Then, through the collection of raindrops falling slowly down the window, I see someone approach the house; a man, hood up, dressed all in black.

He's moving around the outskirts of the driveway. I can't make out his face under the shadow of his hood but something about his outline, his movements, makes me move away from the window. I tread lightly, tiptoeing upstairs and into my bedroom to watch from the monitor, but I can't see anyone – the driveway is empty except for cars.

I go to John's office to look out of the side window, but again there is no one there, just an empty driveway leading to the garage. As I begin to question whether my mind is playing tricks on me, I hear something at the back of the house; a creaking sound – the gate. I grab my phone out of my pocket and call

John. It rings twice before I hang up, logic breaking through the panic just enough to realise nothing good can come from calling him. I consider whether to call Ray back then decide against it; if he thinks the situation has escalated there's no chance he'll keep it from John. Before I realise what I'm doing I have Nick's business page up on my phone and I'm scrolling down to his mobile number. I press call. He answers after the third ring.

"Nick Kerr, Commercial phot–"

"Nick," I whisper, interrupting. "It's Erin. He's here, the man, I think it's him. He's at my house." The panic is rising in my voice and I'm shaking, the phone trembling against my ear.

"Are your doors locked?"

"Yes." I'm certain I locked them, it's a force of habit, but with so much at stake I find myself questioning just how sure I am. "I think... I don't know."

"Okay, I'm on my way to your house. Have you called the police?"

I don't reply, I'm listening for sounds coming from outside but I can't hear anything other than the rain.

"Hang tight, I'll be five minutes."

I stand in John's office, my senses heightened and the phone still trembling at my ear. I hear movement as Nick starts his car engine then begins to drive. I'm paralysed by fear, unable to do anything but listen.

"Erin? You still there?"

"I'm here."

"I'm coming up Kestwell Road, I'll be two minutes. You okay?"

"I'm okay."

I'm not okay.

Time seems to slow down and the stillness is stifling. What have I done? Why did I call Nick? I can't answer my own questions, it didn't feel like a choice but a compulsion. I felt compelled to call a man I am already indebted to, a man who owes me nothing, to ask him for help.

The minutes drag but eventually the sound of the engine on the phone merges into the noise from outside and I hang up and run downstairs. It occurs to me that I may have either put Nick in danger or compromised my integrity – will he think I have lured him here under false pretences? I'm suddenly embarrassed and alarmingly hopeful that there is in fact an intruder, an undisputed reason for my call. The doorbell rings and I open the door and stand aside to let Nick in but he declines with a shake of his head.

He whispers, "Which way do you think he went?"

"Round the back." I point towards the side of the house with the gate leading on to the garden.

"Wait here."

He disappears and I stand waiting, raindrops falling sporadically. He's gone for a while, silently absent, and I find myself imagining him stealthily moving around the garden, over the decking area and to the bottom of the lawns. Trees and shrubs line the fence at the far end, a barrier to the rows of allotments beyond.

I wonder if he's checking everywhere, considering all the places someone could hide. I hear the garden furniture scraping against the decking as it's moved around, then I hear footsteps growing closer. I hold my breath, waiting to see who emerges, and sigh with relief when I see Nick reappear.

"All clear."

"I don't understand, I saw someone, I know I did."

He thinks for a moment and I can tell he's trying hard not to offend me.

"Are you alone all night?"

I shake my head. "Not all night, no, but until late."

"You shouldn't be alone. You've been through a lot."

The problem isn't me being alone, I think, it's the opposite – the intrusion.

"I can stay with you for a bit, if you like?"

I have to stop myself from replying without thinking, from telling him to come in and stay, stay until my husband gets home. I have to think it through, consider the implications. If John came home and found Nick in the house with me it would be hard to explain – I can't tell John the truth now, I've missed the window of opportunity, the moment in time where I could have said *I lied, I was scared.* Now it would seem too contrived.

I tell myself I shouldn't complicate things or welcome distraction into my life, but even while I'm telling myself this I realise it has already happened; I am distracted, I am irrefutably complicating my life, decisions seeming startlingly out of my control.

I open the door and step aside, welcoming him in, complications and all.

13

FIFTEEN YEARS AGO

Wednesday comes around with a renewed sense of hope. Maybe he's calmed down, realised I didn't mean to be so careless. Geography is the last lesson before the end of the school day; I can stay behind – tell my friends I want to talk to him about the exams or coursework – then I can apologise, try to make him believe I won't do anything like that again.

I wake early. I shower then blow-dry my hair the way I know he likes it – loose and straight, parted at the side. I put on more make-up than usual, trying to make myself appear older, more worthy of his time. I'm wearing a skirt which I've deliberately hitched up at the waist and a shirt that I leave partially undone, on the brink of breaking the school rules.

Before his class, I make a quick trip to the toilets to brush my hair and apply a fresh coat of lip gloss. I've lost weight over the summer holidays – my stomach in a perpetual state of turmoil – and my cheeks have lost their plumpness. My friends have noticed – a concern they're not always able to hide.

"Where have you been?" Holly asks. I'm a few minutes late, entering the classroom amidst the silence of the register.

"Toilet," I whisper.

He looks at me as I sit down. "Miss Knight, nice of you to join us."

I pout. "Sorry, Mr Miller."

His eyes linger on me for longer than necessary and in that moment I feel it – the chance of forgiveness.

I stay behind after class, feigning a sudden interest in the coursework which seems to astound Lauren and Holly.

"What are you thinking about that for already?" Lauren asks.

"I need the grades to get into college," I say.

They look at each other and shake their heads.

"We can wait, if you want?"

"No, it's okay, I don't know how long he'll be."

He's talking to one of the gifted students at the front of the class – Henry – he's asking him questions which Mr Miller answers animatedly. I roll my eyes.

"Okay, see you tomorrow then."

They leave, the classroom door falling shut behind them. Henry is still asking questions but Mr Miller spots me lingering at the back of the classroom and his focus begins to shift.

"Some interesting questions, Henry, as always. How about we book in some time to discuss in depth?"

Henry beams at the idea. "That would be great, I really want to finalise my coursework title and then get a plan together."

"I will have a look in my diary and get back to you with a date. How does that sound?"

"Thank you, Mr Miller." Henry swings his backpack over his shoulder and leaves the room, nodding in acknowledgement at me on the way out.

We both wait, listening as the sounds of Henry's footsteps echo through the halls and down the stairs. There's a brief pause, a moment of calm where everything seems to hang in the balance. I hold my breath, wanting Danny to let the moment drag out – uncertainty and the hope that it brings is better than his hate. He breaks eye contact, busying himself with tucking in some of the chairs on the front row then moving to the second row, repeating the process until he's at the back of the classroom with me.

"I thought we agreed not to speak at school."

"You've left me no choice, I needed to talk to you."

He perches on one of the tables in the back row and I copy, sitting on the table opposite, our knees almost touching.

"My wife agreed to come back. I told her it was a one-night stand and that it didn't mean anything." He shrugs.

My initial reaction is relief, the suggestion being that there is a chance of things going back to the way they were. It's quickly followed by disappointment, the inevitable gut-wrenching heartbreak at finding out the man you love has fallen into the arms of another woman. It doesn't matter whether that woman is his wife or not.

"I'm pleased for you."

"It's a lie though, isn't it?" he says.

"What is?"

"That it didn't mean anything."

His words catch my breath. Tears prickle my eyes. I can't find the words to explain how I feel – I want to show him. I stand up and step forward, close enough to reach out and touch him.

"Not here," he says. He walks away from me, towards a store cupboard behind his desk. I follow him without hesitation.

The store cupboard is a tiny rectangular room packed full of boxes and props. Rows of rickety shelves line each wall. A globe sits precariously on top, covered in a thick layer of dust. There's a poster pinned to the back of the door – *the rock cycle* written in bold capital letters. There's a picture of volcanoes, lava bursting out of the top, unable to be contained. It smells musty and damp inside and the only light comes from a single bulb hanging overhead, which he doesn't turn on.

When he closes the door behind us, we are plummeted into darkness. I fumble around, feeling for his shoulders to pull him in close, but he pushes my hands away.

"I want you to show me how sorry you are," he says.

14

NOW

Nick stands in the living room looking at an array of photographs hanging on the wall while I fetch us both a drink. I think he's going to move when he hears me coming – hide his curiosity – but he doesn't. He continues to let his eyes roam over the photographs of my life without embarrassment or hesitation. I hand him a mug of coffee.

"Thanks. Your husband," he says, pointing at a photo of John and me on our wedding day – a statement, not a question.

Nick takes a long drink. I know what he's thinking, it's what everyone thinks. An expensive home, an older man with a younger wife. Eighteen years between us, an even bigger gap in wealth and class. I look at the photo. John isn't an attractive man but money has allowed him to make the best of himself; expensive suits and designer glasses, dental work that cost more than my car. But it isn't a magic wand. He's forty-eight and looks every year of it, his receding and thinning hair now almost entirely grey. He's short and broad and carrying a little extra weight with each passing year. I look at myself next to him, wearing my expensive wedding dress and a smile I still can't recall feeling.

"Yes, my husband. John."

"How long have you been married?"

"Six years."

"You have a lovely home." Nick turns his back to the wall, his eyes drifting over the tasteful décor. A show home, never fully lived in. A place to exist.

"Thanks but it's not mine. Not really, anyway." He looks puzzled, his eyes narrowing, and I pause for a moment before explaining. "It's John's. His money, his house."

"But you're married, and you live here."

I sit down on the sofa and he follows my lead, sitting on a chair next to me.

"Yes, but it's not in my name. All of this," I gesture around to the house but I mean so much more, "it's all his." I change the subject. "How about you, are you married?"

"No. Not married."

I've noticed an indentation on his ring finger, a shadow of a former life, maybe. I don't push the subject any further. I see my phone light up on the table and I pick it up and see a text from John.

Sorry I missed your call. I'll be home for 10. Don't wait up, I'm eating with clients.

"It's John. He'll be home around ten."

Nick takes another drink then smiles as though deciding something. "Let's go out." It's not what I expected him to say. "If you feel up to it, I mean. Let's get some fresh air, I can show you the reservoir."

I think for a moment, trying to decide whether it's apprehension or excitement I feel. Then, concluding it's somewhere between the two – nervous anticipation maybe – I reply. "Sure. Let me just get my coat."

I go upstairs and pull out a long grey parka from my wardrobe then hunt around in a cupboard for a pair of wellies which I find hidden at the back. I check my watch – almost 4pm – plenty of time before John arrives home. I zip up my coat and head back downstairs.

"Ready," I shout.

Nick appears in the hallway, keys in his hand and a smile on his face. "Let's go. I'll pick up Bear on the way."

He looks taller in my house somehow, perhaps it's how easily I'm able to compare him to John in here, unintentionally but unmistakeably. The contrast between them is so stark and disarming that he seems out of place, unable to blend into the house like John does.

15

NOW

We drive back to Nick's place amongst the late afternoon traffic, the surface water scattering in our wake. He pulls up outside and I wait in the car while he fetches Bear, who jumps into the back and nuzzles at my arm. I try to turn and stroke him but pain in my ribs stops me.

"You okay?" Nick asks, waiting for confirmation before he starts the engine.

I take some deep breaths. "Yes, I'm okay."

"Has it got any better since it happened?"

"It's not as bad as those first few days."

He starts the engine and begins to drive, manoeuvring slowly down winding country roads and unmarked lanes until we come to the neighbouring town of Heatherton. He bypasses the centre of town and instead takes a right down a narrow lane then a left into an unmarked car park which sits opposite a large reservoir. Ducks crowd the outskirts of the water, taking shelter beneath shrubs and trees. Street lamps flood the area, their light reflecting in the puddles.

There are two other cars parked up and I can see the outline of a solitary runner over on the other side of the reservoir. A couple of ducks venture towards us hoping for food, but when Bear jumps out they turn round and go back to the safety of the water.

Nick opens the boot and pulls out a thick navy coat and a cream woolly hat which he quickly puts on. I can see his breath turning to mist; his inner warmth meeting with the crisp coolness of the evening air.

"We'll go this way," he says, pointing clockwise.

It's a beautiful place, unobstructed and grand. There is a trail which wraps its way around the reservoir, jetties appearing at regular intervals along the rickety wooden fence. It's quiet but it feels calming rather than hostile, the sound of the water lapping at the edges and the breeze dancing with the landscape. I can imagine myself running here, enjoying the peacefulness without trepidation.

Nick whistles and shouts to Bear who has fallen behind; he comes running over to us, his tail wagging. "How long have you lived in Kestwell?" Nick asks me.

I think back to how I came to live here what seems like a lifetime ago. I'd met John in Nottingham where I'd been sharing a flat with three others. I had no money despite working two jobs, and no discernible future. I wanted to live without fear, to be able to enjoy the small things in life without dreading the big. I met John and it was as though everything fell into place.

"Seven years, or thereabouts. How about you?"

"Almost two years. I moved to be closer to my parents after my dad took ill. He's in a home now – dementia."

"I'm sorry to hear that."

"Where did you live before?" he asks, changing the subject.

"Nottingham, then London for a bit."

"So you grew up in Nottingham?"

My stomach sinks, the all-too-familiar response to the conversation that I dread. Every time I find myself avoiding the topic of my childhood with someone it serves to reiterate why it's easier to be alone, unhindered by other people's curiosity. What is it about people needing to know where everyone has come from? Why can't people be satisfied with where we are?

"No, I moved there as a teenager. As soon as I was old enough to leave home."

"That bad huh?"

I look at him questioningly.

"Your parents?" he clarifies.

I correct him, the common mistake. "Parent, singular. It was just me and my dad."

"Oh, sorry. I shouldn't have assumed."

"No, it's okay. My mum died when I was really young. I don't remember her."

"I'm sorry to hear that – that can't be easy."

I shrug. "My dad was always more than enough."

"So why did you leave home?" We walk slowly, the lights overhead guiding our way, and when I don't respond he fills the silence. "You don't have to answer that."

"It's just... it's not something I speak about very often. Some things are better left in the past, aren't they?"

"Hmm." He thinks for a moment, and the moment stretches out into minutes and I wonder whether I have expected an answer that will never come. But then it does. "It depends what it is, and whether it's been dealt with properly. Otherwise the past can spill out into the future and push other things away." He smiles and changes the subject, looking behind him to check Bear is following. "What do you think then, could you see yourself running here? Much safer than the woods, and it's flat."

"Yes, I can. Do you run here?"

"Yes, I'm here most mornings but I come early before it gets busy."

I notice a car pulling into the car park, its headlights doing a full sweep of the reservoir as it turns. My ribs are aching and I realise I'm holding my side.

"Almost back, you feeling okay?" Concern brims in his eyes, the same way he looked at me the day he found me.

"I'm fine, just a little sore."

"Come on, let's get you home."

He shouts Bear over and pulls his keys out of his pocket, ready to unlock the car. I think about going home, about the house, too big for two people, too luxurious to ever feel comfortable. I've always felt like a guest there, surrounded by white and grey, marble and gloss, a place that demands respect. It makes me feel inferior. I don't want to go home alone, but I can't ask Nick to stay.

He opens the back door for Bear then walks round to the passenger side with me. As I'm about to get in the car I sense movement overhead; hundreds of birds flying above the reservoir, swooping and plunging in perfect synchronisation.

"Starling murmuration," I mumble.

I look up in awe, watching, reminded of an evening many years ago. I'd been to the fair with Dad; I'm holding a cuddly blue dog I won on the ring toss and licking the remnants of candyfloss from my lips. A blanket of starlings fly overhead, a silent tune guiding them as they move. The noise makes me jump; a gradual rumbling as though a train were approaching. Darkness descends as other groups join them, blocking out the sun. 'Adaptable birds, starlings,' Dad says. He's resting casually against the bonnet of the car, a sight he's seen many times before, but his eyes are still alight with wonder. 'They have a reputation for being greedy and aggressive, but it's not fair really.

They're resourceful; they can find ways to overcome difficulties. Adapt or die.'

"I've heard about them but never seen one before." Nick's stood looking up, watching as the starlings disperse, scattering into the surrounding trees beyond the reservoir.

"Safety in numbers," I say. "They come together to evade predators."

Nick smiles. "How come they don't bump into each other?"

I shrug. "No one knows."

I turn towards the car and get in, fastening my seatbelt while Nick hovers at the door checking I'm secure. When he's satisfied, he gets in his side and starts the engine. We drive in a comfortable silence, past Heatherton and down the winding country lanes that lead back to Kestwell. Too soon, we arrive back at my house and I notice just in time that there are lights on where they shouldn't be, and a car in the space on the drive that had previously stood empty.

"Carry on!" I shout.

Nick reacts quickly, turning off his indicator and stepping down on the accelerator. "What's wrong?"

"John's home. I don't want him to see you dropping me off. It would raise too many questions."

"Okay. So, where now?"

"Can you drive round the crescent and drop me off at the end? I'll walk back."

He carries on driving to the end then indicates and pulls over.

"Sorry," I say.

"Don't apologise, I get it. Will you be okay walking back?"

"I'll be fine. Thanks. For everything. I could write a list."

He laughs. I unbuckle my seatbelt and go to open the door but he stops me with a hand on my elbow.

"I might be completely out of line here but... you don't seem like you're happily married. Why do you stay?"

I think about his question before I answer. It feels so deeply personal but I realise the lines are skewed in such unusual situations. I look into Nick's eyes. His interest seems genuine, so I tell him the only truth I know. "There are worse things than an unhappy marriage."

I don't give him time to respond or to ask any more questions that I'm not sure I'll be able to answer. I get out of the car and walk slowly back towards home. I hear the sound of his car leaving the crescent and – when I'm sure he's gone – I let a single tear fall. Unhappy might be doing a disservice to my marriage, I think. Perhaps I should have said unfulfilling. John isn't a bad man.

He is sitting at the kitchen table when I walk in, a beer in one hand and his phone in the other. He doesn't acknowledge me, just carries on speaking animatedly into the phone, deep in conversation. I leave my wellies by the door and hang up my coat. He finishes his call and takes a long drink of his beer before turning in his chair to look at me.

"Where have you been?" he asks casually.

"Just for a walk, I needed some fresh air."

"Don't overdo it, you've got to make sure you recover properly."

I shrug off his concern, unable to determine whether it's sincere.

"We've been invited to Graham and Lucy's on Saturday evening. I've said we'll go, you'll be all right won't you?" His tone is neutral, breezy, but I know it's not really a question.

"I'll be fine, but I won't be able to hide the bruising."

"Don't worry, I've prewarned them you look like you've taken a beating."

I shudder. If only he knew. He picks up his bottle of beer, drains it, then goes over to the fridge and gets another.

"I wasn't expecting you home yet," I say.

"Yeah, clients bailed on dinner. I'm starving. I've ordered pizza." He checks his watch. "Should be here in ten."

I go upstairs and shower, trying to wash away the grime left by the lies. I think of Nick. *Why do you stay?* Had I ever been happy with John? At first, maybe. I'd been impressed by his willingness to help me. He'd seemed chivalrous, his self-assurance was magnetic. I was waitressing at a big corporate event, surrounded by people so far removed from my own situation that it didn't seem real. I'd been in a rush, carrying a tray full of drinks that would be emptied within minutes. I'd tripped and the tray had fallen on Ian who'd clearly already had too much. He'd instantly made a scene, drunk and intent on humiliating me in front of everyone there, including John.

Later, Ian had sidled up to me and wrapped his arm around my waist, whispering in my ear. 'I'm in room 205, come upstairs later and we'll forget about the whole thing. Or I could put in a complaint with your manager.' I needed the job, I was already struggling to pay my mounting bills. John came from nowhere, stepping between us. 'Time for bed, Ian.'

Later, after my shift had finished and he'd bought me a couple of glasses of champagne, John asked me if I wanted to spend the night with him – no games or half-truths, just a simple, loaded question. I often think back to that moment, that exact question, and wonder whether this was the moment where I'd chosen my path. I could have declined his offer and carried on working sixty hours a week just trying to get by, but the truth is, I was tired of getting nowhere.

So I spent the night with the stranger who'd helped me, and

I felt free from the worries that had weighed me down for so long. It was a while before I realised it wasn't freedom I'd felt, it was escape, and I'd paid a heavy price for it – my dignity, my self-worth, my respect – for myself and for John. And with the passing of time came the passing of options, the dwindling of any life I could have built on my own. A silent but dangerous contentment began to settle, an acceptance, rotting away like a disease.

16

FIFTEEN YEARS AGO

"Mount Everest," Danny says enthusiastically, "the world's water tower. We all know it's the highest mountain in the world, but did you know that the range of mountains where Everest is located – the Himalayas – supplies water to some one and a half billion people?"

He stands pacing at the front of the classroom, the open windows to the left letting in a much needed breeze. He looks handsome, his white shirt rolled up at the sleeves to reveal tanned arms. I let my mind wander to the skin beneath his shirt, the tan lines across his biceps, the trail of freckles on his right shoulder. I watch him walking back and forth as he talks, trying to make eye contact with him. I resent everyone else in the room for simply existing in this space with us, for providing obstacles I long to tear down. Without them, it would just be us.

"Life revolves around water," he continues. "Lives depend on it. Drinking, cleaning, farming, energy, the list goes on. Now," he holds his finger up as though about to make an important point, "the glaciers on Mount Everest are melting at an alarming rate. Global climate change is having an incomprehensible effect on the watershed – higher temperatures equal rapidly decreasing glaciers, which in the long term could cause a water shortage crisis in the region."

I'm lost in his voice, deep and strong, the conviction and passion in what he's saying, his knowledge and intellect. I could listen to him talk all day. He doesn't look at me, addressing the class as though I were invisible. He turns and walks over to the whiteboard, writing something I'm unable to make out, his broad shoulders blocking it from view. Then he turns back to the class and holds his arms out as though delivering a revelation.

"The ripple effect," he says. "When an initial disturbance causes a series of other disturbances – usually unintentional, but inevitable. Every action has a consequence."

He walks slowly around the classroom handing out worksheets, an almost imperceptible pause behind me as he leans over. I breathe him in: his aftershave, the faint tea tree of his shampoo, the coffee he's had with his lunch. My heart rate quickens, the sense of longing almost unbearable, the dull ache that comes when he is just out of reach.

"Working in groups of three or four, I want you to think about the link between climate change and water security. Consider the implications that might occur many years from now."

As people move, dragging chairs and chatting among friends, I watch him, longing to be alone with him. He sits down behind his desk and takes some papers out of his briefcase, running his fingers down his navy blue tie. He looks lost in thought and I wonder whether he's contemplating the consequences of his own actions, his own ripple effect – unintentional but inevitable.

17

NOW

Saturday evening arrives along with a fog so dense that I can barely see the road ahead as we leave Kestwell, a cloud of grey clinging to the windscreen and clouding the headlights. John drives slowly, hunched forward in his seat trying to make out the road ahead. I feel nervous about driving home – it will be the first time since the incident and my anxiety is exacerbated by the weather – but John's proclivity for too many beers won't change. I feel as though the fog has clouded my mind and I can't shake the uneasiness that's risen to the surface ever since I saw the man at the house – or *thought* I saw the man at the house. We arrive late, the journey taking twice as long as it should, and John doesn't try to hide his annoyance.

"We should have left earlier," he says.

I follow him to the front door and notice the other cars in the driveway.

"Who else is here?" I ask, the thought suddenly occurring to me that it may be more than just the four of us.

"Andy and Olivia, I think. Ian and Trish, maybe." He shrugs, but we both know he has chosen to keep this from me. He isn't oblivious to the way Ian acts around me, he simply chooses to ignore it because it doesn't fit with his narrative. It's easier to think of me as emotional and sensitive than it is to think of his colleague and friend as a pervert.

Graham answers the door and noise floods out of the house, a party already in full swing.

"Johnny boy!"

He steps back to let us in and they shake hands enthusiastically before Graham pulls him into a hug, patting him heavily on the back as he does. He's not only a lot taller than John but fatter too, his gut barely contained by the shirt he's wearing. His red hair is only a few shades brighter than his skin, which has been tinged by his taste for the finer things. Poor health oozes from him, a heart attack waiting to happen – money and success have made him lazy. He's safe in the knowledge that Lucy will never leave him because of their lifestyle so he has let himself go, slipping into a state of decline with no one to please but himself. They walk off ahead leaving me to close the door and immediately be swept into an embrace by Lucy, causing me to cry out in pain.

"What, what's wrong?" She steps back in shock, then her eyes take in the bruising on my face. "Bloody hell, Erin, what happened?"

Lucy hasn't settled the way Graham has, she's fought the ageing process with one surgical procedure after another. She's wearing a red dress, inappropriately revealing. Her clothes always seem like a disguise, an attempt at masking her true identity – her self-loathing and low self-esteem. Ironically, this is all I see, and I can't help but feel hopelessly sorry for her.

"I fell over," I say, carefully taking off my coat and hanging it up.

"John said you'd had an accident but I didn't realise how bad you..." She trails off.

"I'm fine really. It's just my ribs, they're still pretty sore."

"You poor thing, let's get you a drink." She walks me into the dining area where there's a young man wearing a white shirt and waistcoat. He's stood behind a makeshift bar area. "What will you have, Erin? Brad makes excellent cocktails, don't you, darling?" She giggles flirtatiously and flicks her hair over her shoulder. I'm embarrassed for him, she's probably old enough to be his mother.

"I'm driving, just a Coke please."

Olivia approaches but Lucy stops her before she reaches me. "Careful, she's feeling a little delicate after her accident."

Olivia looks me up and down. "Oh my God, Erin, you look dreadful."

Olivia used to be a model, something she manages to fit into almost every conversation I have with her. She's tall and thin with long dark hair – pretty, but an impression tainted so quickly by her personality, her tactlessness and spite masquerading as honesty. What she fails to tell people is that she modelled a range of swimwear for a now bankrupt small business funded by her husband, Andy, the ever tolerant man so eager to please. He's like a chameleon, able to blend in to whatever situation he finds himself in. Graham and John like him because he's a yes-man.

I smile uncomfortably and take my Coke from Brad, slipping away while they discuss which cocktail to have next. I inadvertently find myself standing next to Trish, Ian's wife. The men have gone and sat themselves in the lounge, drinking and laughing, talking about old times. They went to university together, studying different subjects but sharing a flat. John and Ian went into marketing, with John eventually becoming the CEO of his own company and hiring Ian. Andy went to work at his dad's law firm while Graham started a career in banking. They've all come from money and fail to acknowledge the doors this has opened for them, the opportunities they've had because of their privilege.

"Hi." Trish speaks so quietly I can barely hear her over the noise coming from the lounge.

"Hi, Trish." I smile weakly.

"What happened to your face? It looks sore."

"I fell." I wonder how many more times I'm going to have to repeat the lie.

"Sorry to hear that." She's talking to me but her eyes are fixed on Ian in the lounge, through the double doors which have been left ajar. "They get so rowdy together, don't they?"

"Yeah, I guess they do."

"Can I ask you something?" She turns to face me, conspiratorially. I nod without thinking. "Does John have affairs?"

I take a sip of my Coke and look around the room, making sure Lucy and Olivia aren't nearby. "I don't believe so," I lie.

I've always suspected – and accepted – that he has affairs. Nothing regular or meaningful, just the odd fling when he's working away. It's not something that's ever bothered me enough to ask about, which is surprising considering I know more than most the damage they can cause.

"Why do you ask?"

She looks back over to Ian, watching as he laughs at a story Graham is telling.

"There's something going on with Ian."

"How so?" My interest is piqued.

"Late nights, long absences, that kind of thing. I know you don't like him, Erin, but he's usually so attentive, and now he seems to have, well, drifted."

"It's not that I don't like him, it's just–"

She interrupts, but her voice is still quiet and placid. "It's okay, you don't need to lie for my benefit. I know what he can be like. He told me why you don't like him and I can understand, I'd probably feel the same way if I were you. But he isn't like that, not really."

"And what exactly did he tell you?" I ask, curiosity getting the better of me.

"That you were working at one of the corporate events and he drank a few too many. He couldn't remember much the following morning but he knew he'd gone too far."

That's putting it mildly, I think. I stand and process what she's told me, trying to see Ian in another light, but I can't.

"Could it be work? John's been working some pretty long hours."

She shakes her head assuredly. "I try ringing him but his phone's switched off. If he was working his phone would be on."

I nod.

"I'll find out. I won't stand for that shit like they do." She gesticulates vaguely in the direction of Lucy and Olivia. "Sorry," she says, suddenly looking embarrassed. "It's hard, I don't have anyone to talk to about this and it's really messing with my head and interfering with work."

It suddenly occurs to me that I have no idea who Trish is. I have never asked her anything about herself, tarnishing her with the same resentment I feel for Ian. I assumed she was just another rich man's wife, another Lucy or Olivia. Another me.

"You think Andy and Graham cheat?"

She raises her eyebrows, a look that makes me feel as though I have asked a stupid question. "You're kidding, aren't you?"

I shrug. "I've never really thought about it."

"You know why Graham gives you such a hard time, don't you?"

I look at her, puzzled.

"The night you met John, Graham was there. Free night

away, he's not going to say no is he? Obviously Ian was there too. The three of them had a bit of a bet on who could... you know."

I feel repulsed. "Graham was with Lucy then."

"Exactly."

So I was a bet. I feel as though I should be horrified, shocked to the core about my husband's motives, but I'm not. I'm disgusted but not entirely surprised. You get to know a man with the passing of years; opinions you once held evolve over time, experiences erasing who they once were.

"Anyway," she continues, "Graham is used to getting what he wants. They all are."

I change the subject, my skin crawling at the thought of it. "Have you tried asking Ian?"

She raises her eyebrows. "Would you ask John?"

I consider whether I would confront John if I cared enough but I can't make up my mind, unable to imagine myself having those feelings for him. I wonder whether I would be too scared of the outcome if I did.

"He might have a perfectly reasonable explanation though."

She tucks a loose strand of her mousy hair back behind her ear. "He might. Or he could lie."

"So what are you going to do?"

"Nothing, for now. If he's having an affair and I act oblivious he'll get cocky. He'll slip up. I just need to be patient."

I almost mention my own six-year marriage, my own act of obliviousness. I've never had any evidence of an affair in that time, but I haven't exactly been looking. The suspicion has gone on for so long that I realise I've filed it away as something more than that – not quite a fact but much more than a hunch. A conclusion, maybe.

"Do me a favour will you? Don't say anything to John."

"Of course not."

I'm used to keeping secrets.

18

NOW

The rest of the evening drags by slowly, a three-course meal barely touched by Lucy and Olivia who spend most of their time draped over Brad. The rest of the group are either too drunk to care or too stupid to notice. I catch Graham throwing me sideways glances, no longer able to continue with the pretence of civility; alcohol has caused his mask to slip. There is a certain power in being the only sober person amongst the intoxicated, watching as the things they work so hard to hide spill out.

I think back to the first time John introduced us. It was just after Graham's engagement to Lucy, at an over-the-top party masquerading as a celebration. I hadn't wanted to go, I'd given John every opportunity and incentive to go alone or with his friends, but he'd persisted. It had been a disaster from the start, a rooftop bar in London full of faces I didn't know, my internal set of rules screaming at me to leave. I hadn't felt so vulnerable in a long time. There were so many people, so many names to remember as John walked me from one person to the next.

Graham had greeted me with cynicism and the kind of deliberate disinterest that took a lot of effort. He draped his arm over John's shoulder and guided him to the bar, leaving me standing alone. I had waited for quite some time, feeling exposed and vulnerable, wondering why John had been so insistent that I went with him. Eventually, I escaped to the toilets where I spent thirty minutes locked in a cubicle, my absence noticed by no one.

By the end of the night we were among the stragglers, the remaining dozen or so who were being ushered out by the underpaid and overworked staff. I was used to being on the other side and I had a sudden sense of betrayal, as though I had been disloyal to my roots and crossed over to the dark side where wealth made you careless and hollow. They'd all but trashed the place then stumbled outside to their waiting cars, leaving other people to clean up their mess. I was embarrassed to be a part of it.

Outside, I had watched as their true personalities struggled with their public selves, the ones they'd mastered in order to misrepresent themselves. Lucy had been sick in the middle of the street, spitting and hacking as Graham looked on disgusted, contempt and disdain rendering him unable or unwilling to help her. I'd stood next to John, quietly letting my hand find his, looking for the same man who'd offered me protection months earlier. He squeezed my hand – one brief but firm grasp – then let go. There, but on his terms.

Just after eleven I excuse myself from an inebriated Lucy to look for John. I find him in the lounge smoking a cigar, deep in conversation with Graham who sits on the edge of an armchair, hunched over conspiratorially. Ian and Andy are listening in, a glass resting in one hand, a cigar in the other. The smoke stings my eyes. I clear my throat to get his attention, pulling his focus away from Graham. "Are you ready to go?"

He glances at his watch. "The night's still young!" he says, accepting a refill from Andy. They're on the whisky and I know from experience it's a downward spiral from here.

"You're not wanting to go already, are you?" Graham asks. He gets up from his chair and sits perched on the arm of John's. "Stay here, Johnny, stay the night." Graham puts his arm over John's shoulders and pulls him towards him, as though I were about to physically steal him from his grip.

"Leave me here!" John slurs, laughing. His face is damp with sweat and I feel a wave of repulsion. His intoxication is disgusting; he has never known when to stop.

"I can't leave you here, you haven't got anything with you."

"We've got everything he needs!" Graham looks me in the eye, daring me to argue.

I hold my hands up in submission. "Fine, fine, I'll leave you here. Call me when you want picking up tomorrow." I shout a hasty goodbye to everyone else and head to the door to find my coat. Graham lets go of John and puts down his drink, following me as I leave.

"You know, Erin, John's got a lot on at the minute, he needs time to unwind."

"Right." I move to open the door. He rests his hand against it, feigning a casualness that isn't there.

"He takes good care of you, maybe you could show him the same courtesy." He removes his hand from the door. "Don't trouble yourself tomorrow, I'll get him home." He walks away, his distaste palpable in his wake.

The fog begins to lift on the drive home but a smokiness remains, illuminated by the glow of the headlights. I drive cautiously, testing the boundaries of my mobility. My back feels stiff and waves of pain stab at my side, agitated by the steering as I struggle to manoeuvre around the winding country roads that lead back into Kestwell.

Occasionally I can make out the moon shining from behind thick clouds. Trapped. As I drive back up the hill and past the town centre I can't help but glance over towards Nick's place, although I can't see far enough past the church to get a good view. I find myself thinking about him again, wondering what he's doing. I press down on the accelerator as though trying to outrace my thoughts.

As I approach the top of the hill I see a flash of something run out in front of me, fast and low, but it's too late, I'm too close to react in time. I feel a force against the car then a harrowing *crunch* as the wheels take it, crushing it with their weight. I break heavily and come to a stop in the middle of the road, glancing in my rear-view mirror as an afterthought.

There is no one behind me, just the empty road to a sleepy town. I try to determine what I've hit by looking in my mirrors but I can't see anything. I've come to a stop between street lights, the darkness claiming the space in the middle, the shadowy haze of the fog further obscuring the view.

I get out of the car and do a quick turn, assessing the space around me, checking for something I hope isn't there. The shadows move as the wind blows through the trees, their gangly limbs swaying back and forth. I walk a few metres down the hill, looking for what I could have hit.

At first I don't see anything and a naïve hopefulness begins to gather, desperate for whatever it was to not be lay dead or dying in the road because of me. But then I see it – a fox – at the side of the road.

There's no obvious damage that I can see and at first I hover a few paces away, checking for the rise and fall of its chest. It looks as though it's asleep, resting peacefully at the side of the road, surrounded by nothing but the night. But there is no rise and fall; no movement; nothing.

"I'm sorry," I whisper. "I'm sorry, I'm sorry, I'm sorry."

I hear my dad's voice. There's a fox in our garden and we're watching him through the kitchen window – lights out and hushed voices. 'They're solitary creatures, foxes. They hunt and sleep alone unless they have a young family.'

I'm relieved that it's November; the fox has no one relying on it, no one depending on it for survival. Tears gather in my eyes and I blink them away, unsure whose life they're for.

That night I dream of the waves again – they're lapping at my ankles, sometimes warm, sometimes cold. I'm intensely aware of their power, a sense of being faced by something much greater than myself. I watch as bubbles accumulate around my toes; as the sand clings to my skin; as the waves bring in the secrets of the sea – the lies and regrets, the mistakes and remorse.

The ebb and flow of the waves is hypnotic, lulling me into a false sense of calm. All at once, a fox washes up on the beach, far away at first then, defying time and space, suddenly on top of my feet. I'm unable to move it and the waves don't want it, they have given up their offering – but they're not done yet. The fox stays weighted on my feet, anchoring me, my feet sinking further and further into the sand until before I know it I'm waist deep.

There is something on the horizon, moving closer and closer, bobbing with the waves. The sun shines down on it as though it were a spotlight, highlighting the main event, emphasising the importance. Then without warning it's suddenly dark. I am still trapped by the sand, unable to move. Whatever was in the sea seems to have disappeared, the waves deciding to save it for themselves. I feel relieved, but it doesn't last. Out of the sand in front of me, something begins to rise.

I try to scream but there is no sound, just air, no matter how hard I try. I know what it is now. I know *who* it is. The waves have shown me their secrets, and their secrets are mine. I look at the body in front of me, the empty shell of Mr Miller. Then I notice he's not alone, he's brought along his family.

19

FIFTEEN YEARS AGO

I walk through town enjoying the afternoon sun, a McDonald's vanilla milkshake in my hand. I've been on the beach all morning litter picking up and down the length of the shores, along the pier and the coastal paths – all part of Dad's latest initiative to save the oceans. More people turned up than he'd anticipated – everyone eager to do their bit to ease their conscience – and he'd had to start turning people away, no longer able to provide the right tools to carry out the task safely. I'd passed my litter picker to an eager woman in a green anorak who'd stood waiting for her chance to shine, then I'd slipped away unnoticed.

I window-shop to pass the time, eager for Saturday to come to a close – one step closer to returning to school. The weekends seem to arrive all too quickly lately, a vacuum of time to waste while waiting for better things. Lauren and Holly will be on their way to the cinema now, popcorn and sweets stuffed into backpacks, hidden from the prying eyes of staff.

I used to go with them every other Saturday, alternating between that and a Blockbuster movie night. I once managed to sneak a whole Happy Meal in to see *The Notebook*, Holly a large fish and chips from Golden Fry on the corner. I feel nostalgic at the thought of it, the memories – because that's what they are to me now; recollections of a time before Danny. I've started separating my life that way lately – pre- or post-Danny – because it always seems like a choice.

Lauren and Holly would get suspicious if I didn't distance myself from them, they know me too well. It's all for Danny – to protect him and what we have. I hear the sound of church bells ringing; four chimes echoing between the busy streets. They've booked seats to a 5pm showing of *Pride and Prejudice* – if I walk over to the cinema now I would probably bump into them.

I walk slowly down the main road, browsing the occasional shop window as I pass, killing time I no longer want to myself. I'm about to cross over at the traffic lights, still debating whether to walk down to the cinema, when I see him. He's looking in a jewellery shop window, his daughters pointing animatedly at the different items on display. I stand watching them, unaware that the lights have changed, the cars slowing to a halt in front of me.

When the traffic starts moving again, so do they – across the road, three pairs of legs moving quickly away from me. I don't wait for the green man this time, I dart straight across the road at the first sign of a gap and hurl my drink into a nearby bin. I walk briskly, trying to close the gap between us.

After a few minutes they turn left into a corner shop. I stop, unsure what to do or where to go. I don't know why I feel blindsided by seeing him out of school like this, it was always a possibility. I take a deep breath, run my fingers through my hair and neaten my dress, then head towards the shop and go straight inside. It's only small, three narrow aisles filled with household essentials, a fridge against one wall and a newspaper rack against the other. I see them at the back of the shop deciding over pizzas from a small chest freezer.

I walk down the aisle to the right, taking my time, then turn left towards them. He's dressed casually in jeans and a blue T-shirt, a rucksack slung over one shoulder. The girls are stood either side of him. The youngest is in a pink-and-white tracksuit with *Rachel's School of Dance* embroidered on the back, along with her name – Eva.

Her hair is in a neat little bun on top of her head and she clutches a cuddly pink cat in her hand. The older girl is scanning the frozen desserts, dressed in leggings and a denim jacket. Her hair is loose, long and auburn. She slides the freezer door open and pulls out two tubs of ice cream.

"We'll take both," Danny tells her, smiling.

As I approach them he looks up and sees me, our eyes locking momentarily. There is a brief hint of something on his face – recognition maybe, or horror – then his attention returns to his girls.

"Ready?" he asks them.

"But Dad, you said we could get fizzy pop. It's treat night!" Eva whines.

"Yes, yes I did, let's go and choose."

They walk away from me and I let him go; I know the rules and understand the cost of breaking them. I grab the nearest thing to me – a loaf of bread – and take it to the counter to pay. As I leave I glance back over my shoulder to see whether he's looking – maybe he'll give me a half-smile or a discreet wink, some sign that he's at least noticed me – but his attention remains with his girls, unfaltering.

I walk back towards home, away from Danny and away from the cinema – I'm in no mood for company tonight. It occurs to me why I felt so blindsided seeing them: it wasn't seeing Danny that shocked me, it was seeing his daughters – the barrier to our happily ever after, the blatant reality of them. Up until now they were like fictional characters I'd come to think of as his backstory.

He barely even spoke about them – I hadn't even known they were girls until today. I'd imagined him with one of each – Flynn and Ella – and they were both much younger than the girls I saw him with today. The backstory I'd fabricated with details of my own did not add up to the reality. Eva must be eight, maybe nine, but the older one, the nameless, faceless girl with auburn hair – she couldn't be much younger than me.

20

NOW

The next day is shrouded by the aftermath of a sleep plagued with nightmares – a dream hangover – the feelings so fresh and real that I struggle to get out of bed. It feels as though a weight has settled over me, each limb heavier than the day before, beset with emotions that belong to years ago.

The effort is tiring and it takes considerable resolve to keep moving, to not surrender to the gloom. I want to run, to feel my heart beating against my chest and my lungs stinging with the coolness of the air. I want to feel alive, torn from this stupor. I stretch tentatively but immediately concede; it's far too soon. I pull on a pair of jeans and a jumper and grab my coat and bag.

As I get in the car, I consider sending a message to John, but then I remember Graham's words to me. *Don't trouble yourself tomorrow, I'll get him home.* I decide to take him at his word and leave them to it, it's still early and they're probably not even up yet. I drive down the road and past Kestwell town centre, squinting against the sun hanging low in the sky. I drive without thinking, my mind on other things, the waves still consuming my thoughts.

I come to a T-junction and turn left towards Heatherton,

avoiding the town centre and taking the same right turn that Nick had made, down a narrow winding lane. I almost miss the left turn for the car park, the reservoir suddenly appearing amongst the landscape. It's still early, just gone nine, and the fog has cleared overnight revealing an endless blue sky.

There are already several cars parked up, people making the most of the rare winter sun. I pull in between two cars and sit looking out at the reservoir. Ahead, a young mum is helping her toddler feed bread to the ducks, repeatedly pulling him back as he wanders too close to the edge. The ducks crowd round them, hungry for more.

Dog walkers are out in abundance enjoying the clear morning, and as I sit watching I can see why Nick told me to come here; there's safety in numbers. I get out of the car and go in the same direction as the last time I was here but at a brisker pace, pushing myself and my pain tolerance.

Nick's words come back to me as I walk, as clear as when he first said them. *It depends what it is, and whether it's been dealt with properly. Otherwise the past can spill out into the future and push other things away.*

At the other side of the reservoir I pass a small rambling group chatting merrily to each other, hiking boots and backpacks on, ready for a day of walking. A couple of runners follow, but no Nick. Had I been hoping to see him here? I'm angry that I've allowed myself to drift, to begin to think about him more than I should.

By the time I get back to the car park it's completely full, the reservoir a hive of activity. I watch as a family get on their bikes and head off in the direction I've just come from, a baby babbling loudly from the back of her dad's bike. I watch them cycle away, the breeze blowing my hair as they get smaller and smaller against the horizon. My side is throbbing, the discomfort from this morning now a significant pain. As I walk back to my car, I hear a familiar voice calling my name from behind.

"Erin?"

I turn round and see Nick, covered in sweat and breathing heavily. He removes his headphones and smiles. He looks different. He's wearing black shorts with a grey long-sleeved top and his hair is swept back, slick with sweat. He rubs a hand through his stubble.

"Hi."

"Are you leaving?"

I consider lying and saying I've just arrived, a quiet hope telling me he'll offer to walk with me. I stop myself, the dream from the night before still fresh in my mind. *It won't lead anywhere good.*

"Yes, I need to go and take some more painkillers." I hold my side, rubbing it lightly.

"I have some in the car," he offers. "And a flask of tea, actually."

"You take a flask of tea when you go running?"

"Is that strange?" he asks in mock seriousness.

"A little."

A silence settles, Nick not wanting to suggest anything further, and me not trusting myself to speak. He gets his car keys out.

"I'll grab my coat and the flask." He heads off towards his car, leaving me wondering whether I've agreed to stay. When he comes back, he's wearing a hoody and coat and has pulled on a pair of jogging bottoms. He's carrying a slim silver flask and an extra cup.

"You bring extra cups too?"

"Always be prepared!"

Before I know it, I've walked with him over to a bench a short distance from the car park. We sit down and he pours two cups of tea then retrieves a blister pack from his coat pocket.

"Paracetamol," he says, offering me the packet. I take it and pop two out, gulping them down with my tea. "Nothing better than a sugary cup of tea after a run."

I laugh. "How very English of you."

He grins then takes a long drink, draining his cup.

"How far have you run?" I ask.

"Ten miles."

"How long did it take?"

He glances at his watch. "Just over an hour."

"Impressive."

He looks at me and for a moment we make eye contact and I panic, unable to look away. He doesn't seem to notice and I'm thankful when he carries on talking.

"I wanted to apologise for the other night. I shouldn't have commented on your marriage, it's none of my business."

"No it's fine. In many ways, I ask myself that same question every single day."

"You don't have the answer?"

"I don't think I do. I know what people think, but it's not true."

"What do people think?"

I finish my tea and Nick reopens the flask and pours two more cups, emptying it.

"That I married him for the money."

"But you didn't?"

I shake my head. I'm reluctant to share more information, hesitant to admit that I met John when I had nobody and nothing in my life, that I felt rescued and got carried away in the comparative safety of belonging to someone. It felt like a transaction, almost – being nurtured turning seamlessly into dependency. I sit looking at the water, feeling the warmth of the tea in my hands. All at once, amidst the relative calm, a memory springs to mind: dinner with John at a castle in the countryside followed by a walk in the grounds, a little unsteady on my feet after a glass of champagne. One of the handful of times I've drunk, in the early days of a relationship that felt too young to cast doubt on our compatibility. We sat by the river in the fading summer sun and he took out a ring. Now, sitting with Nick, I feel the same sense of shame, for looking to a man to provide me with something – fulfilment; guidance; direction. It was never about the money.

"Sorry," Nick says, pulling me from my reverie. "Again, none of my business."

"It's okay, really. I'm just not used to talking."

"About your marriage?"

"About anything," I admit.

"I think it's all too easy to withdraw from a world that doesn't treat you very well."

I let his words settle and, as they do, they fill me with a comfort I probably don't deserve.

"I'd better be going," I say, checking my watch. I've left my phone in the car and I'm mindful that John may have tried calling, asking me to pick him up because Graham is in no fit state to drive. I stand and Nick follows.

"How are your ribs?" he asks.

"Sore, but getting there I think."

I get my keys out of my pocket and press the fob to unlock the car.

"I have your coat," I say. I open the back door and reach in and grab it. "Here."

"You didn't have to," he says, smiling. "I'd forgotten all about it."

I don't tell him I wanted it out of the house, away from John and the questions it would raise. I think fleetingly of the bracelet; the beginning of a trail I hadn't realised I'd started. I should have been more careful.

"Thanks for lending it to me."

"Sure, anytime. Take care of yourself."

"You too, Nick."

I get in my car and drive away, full of a warmth I tell myself is from the tea.

21

FIFTEEN YEARS AGO

At the end of the lesson I stay behind, slowly gathering my things and slipping into my burgundy school blazer. He's at the front of the classroom rubbing away the ink from the whiteboard, a diagram he'd drawn explaining the water cycle. He's wearing a new suit – navy with a light-blue shirt and silver tie. He'd taken the blazer off at the start of the lesson and hung it neatly on the back of his chair. I watch him now as he picks it up and carefully puts it back on, smoothing out the creases. When he hears the door close he glances up at me, his face breaking into a smile.

"Why didn't you say hello to me the other day?" I ask.

I've caught him off guard. He looks confused, as though our chance encounter has slipped his mind entirely.

"On Saturday," I clarify, "at the shop in town."

When he doesn't immediately respond I begin to doubt myself. Could I have imagined him seeing me?

"Were you following me?" he asks.

"What? No, of course not!"

He doesn't say anything, instead he carefully closes his desk drawer and locks it, placing the key in his pocket. In my head I'm screaming questions at him. *Why didn't you acknowledge me? Why didn't you at least smile? Why didn't you introduce me as your student?* But I don't push him because deep down I'm scared I already know the answer: I'm insignificant. I'm simply not worth the risk. But then he surprises me.

"I didn't trust myself."

I frown. "What do you mean?"

"I'm not a very good actor, I thought I'd give myself away. My wife–" he sighs heavily, "she's still very upset. She doesn't trust me. And my oldest daughter blames me."

"She knows you had an affair?"

"She definitely suspects," he says solemnly.

He walks towards me and perches on the edge of one of the tables, folding his arms across his chest. I stay standing.

"How old is she?"

"Thirteen."

There's a fleeting look of shame but he quickly recovers. "I couldn't risk her seeing us talking and getting suspicious. She'd tell her mum."

"I'm sure she wouldn't have thought anything of you saying hello to a student," I say, but I can already feel my argument losing momentum – it's my fault his wife is so suspicious. My stomach wrings with guilt knowing that his daughter blames him too.

"You know what you do to me." He grins, unfolding his arms and standing up. "It's hard enough to hide it at school."

"You could have just smiled. I spent the rest of the weekend worried I'd done something wrong."

He smiles and for a second he looks pleased, bordering on smug, as though this was the desired outcome.

"You looked amazing in that dress by the way – the blue-and-white stripy one. You should wear it for me some time."

He walks over to the classroom door and locks it, pulling down the blinds.

"We find ourselves alone, Miss Knight."

He slips his arms around my waist, pulling me into him and kissing me; softly at first and then with hunger, his fingers gripping the back of my head and becoming entangled in my hair.

"Here?" I whisper.

He shrugs. "Why not?"

"You had rules – not at school."

I'd thought the storeroom was a one-off, an allowance for our making up.

"That was when we could be a bit more flexible. Now I can't escape without my wife breathing down my neck."

He steps away from me, running his fingers along his jawline. I feel as though I'm losing him, that I've planted a seed of doubt and tainted the moment.

"I want to," I say. "I just didn't think you would, that's all."

"It's not ideal but I need to be with you, and it's here or nowhere."

I step towards him, closing the gap and hooking my hands around the back of his neck.

"Then here it is."

22

NOW

I arrive home to find Ray's car on the drive and him sat inside it, waiting, despite having a key to the house. He gets out as he sees me pull in.

"Hey Erin."

"Hi Ray, you could have let yourself in. It's freezing!"

"I kept the heater on, it's no bother. How you doing?"

"I'm okay, thanks."

"You're looking better, the bruising is healing up nicely."

I smile and unlock the front door.

Ray follows me in. "You haven't opened your card." He points to an unopened envelope on the side table.

"Sorry, I completely forgot." I realise this is a lie, perhaps as much to myself as it is to him. There is something about opening a card from my husband's dad and not my own that always feels particularly hurtful, despite this being the opposite of his intention.

"It'll wait," he says kindly, and I notice he's blushing slightly.

"I'll open it later. Promise!"

He goes into the kitchen and puts the kettle on while I hang up my coat.

"Have you been somewhere nice?" he asks.

"To the reservoir in Heatherton."

"Ah, lovely morning for it. I haven't been there in years." He makes us both a drink and we sit at the kitchen table chatting, effortlessly passing the time. After a while I hear a car pull up outside then the fumbling of keys in the lock. John walks in wearing last night's clothes; he looks terrible – red-faced and dishevelled. I wonder whether he's slept at all, or whether he's still drunk. He doesn't acknowledge me and I can tell Ray has noticed the friction, an awkwardness beginning to settle between the three of us.

Ray speaks first, purposely upbeat. "Hi, son. Good night I take it?"

"Yeah, where's Mum?"

I bite my lip.

"She's having lunch with some of her friends."

John opens the fridge and pulls out some orange juice, drinking it straight from the carton. "I need a shower," he says, leaving the room and closing the door.

Ray and I sit in shared embarrassment as we listen to John's footsteps pad up the stairs – I for the way my husband has treated his father, Ray for the way his son has treated his wife.

"He shouldn't treat you like that," I say, but the words could just as easily have come from Ray.

"He doesn't mean it, he looks tired."

"You're too forgiving."

"As are you, kid, as are you."

We sit on the cusp of a forbidden territory, an area we've never explored but been to the brink of many times before. Perhaps it's the accumulation of recent events, injecting me with a false sense of overcoming adversity, but I find myself pushing things I would usually let lie.

"Why does he treat you that way?"

Ray whispers, his eyes darting around. "Erin..."

"He doesn't treat Agnes that way. So why you?"

He looks down at his hands, avoiding my gaze. "Ray?"

He keeps his voice low, despite hearing that the shower has come on upstairs. "Look, it's not his fault. It's just..." He pauses briefly, searching for the words. "When he was young, Agnes and I separated." He must see the shock on my face and he quickly corrects himself. "Took a break, really. But it upset John, he couldn't handle it."

"Why does he blame you and not Agnes?"

He looks sheepish as he runs his hand through his hair, considering how much to tell me. "Well, John stayed with his mother and he believed – somehow – that I'd had an affair, ran off with another woman. He wouldn't see me or speak to me on the phone, nothing." He shakes his head as he remembers.

"But you hadn't?"

"No, of course not. I moved in with my brother for a few months, helped him with some work on a building site. Tell you the truth, I liked the work – real work, not like the things Agnes' dad had me doing."

"But you went back, for John?"

Ray nods.

"Why don't you just tell him the truth?"

"Too much time has passed now."

"Why didn't you tell him back then?"

"Agnes thought – *we* thought – that it would be easier for John to believe that than know the truth."

"Which is?"

He sighs heavily, his shoulders hunched under the weight of a secret that's probably older than I am. All of a sudden he looks smaller, broken – then I see it, the pieces coming together.

"Agnes was the one who had the affair, wasn't she?"

"It was a long time ago."

"I can't believe it," I say. "And she's let you take the brunt of John's anger for all this time?"

"It's not that simple."

"It sounds simple to me."

He shakes his head and I can see he is dealing with an internal struggle – battling things he hadn't counted on ever seeing the light of day.

"She ended up pregnant," he says, his voice barely above a whisper, "so it was a very difficult time for her."

I feel as though I need to physically move to dispel some of the shock, the disbelief almost tangible. I stand and pace the kitchen, trying to process what he has just revealed. I feel so intensely sorry for him, and so overwhelmingly angry at Agnes – the two conflicting emotions feel confusing, as though a silent storm is brewing.

"Erin, you can't tell John. You see that don't you?"

I nod. "What happened? With the baby?"

"I would have raised that baby as my own," he says firmly. "I didn't want her to have an abortion, but she felt she had no choice."

I sit back down again, opposite Ray. "Why?"

"The father, the man she had an affair with, he was a rising star in the world of politics. Nasty piece of work. He threatened her, for want of a better word. Said he'd make her life hell if she kept the baby."

"How old was John at the time?"

"Fourteen. We'd always wanted another baby, tried for years." Sadness clings to his words, a wound that has clearly never healed.

"I'm sorry, Ray."

He smiles, but it doesn't reach his eyes. "It was a long time ago, we've moved on now."

I feel an intense urge to reach out and grasp his hand, to

hold him and take on some of the weight he's been carrying, but before the urge materialises into action I hear the shower turn off upstairs and see Ray pulling away, withdrawing from his revelation.

"I mean it, kid, he must never find out."

"I promise, I won't say a word."

He gets up and tucks his chair back under the table. "I'd better be going."

I watch him as he puts on his coat and pulls the keys out of his pocket; he's in his early seventies but has always kept himself fit – a handsome man in his younger years, much taller and thinner than John, and with more hair. I've never had cause to doubt it before but now I find myself wondering whether Agnes had more than one affair, a marriage doomed from the start.

As he says goodbye, the bright November sun reflecting in his pale-blue eyes, I'm sure I see a single, solitary tear run down his cheek – but he turns before I can be certain.

I spend the rest of the day trying to subtly avoid John, his mood casting an oppressive shadow over the whole house. It's funny how a person's mood can consume everything around them, even poison your own state of mind, as though the darkness is somehow contagious; you don't need to be in the same room – sometimes not even the same house – when you know the very worst of someone has surfaced, you get sucked into the gloom. A black hole.

After a while I go into the spare room and scan the shelves upon shelves of books that line the back wall – my only input into the whole house. I choose an old classic I remember first reading at school – *The Collector*. I run a bath and lock the door, submerging myself into the water and another world – a world where a woman is held captive, at the mercy of a man who wants to possess her purely for her beauty.

I remember reading the book and being enthralled by its ability to spark a renewed appreciation for freedom; a realisation of the limitless potential of life that I had somehow taken for granted. It never occurred to me then that a prison may be one of your own making – one you will never escape.

23

NOW

John has left before I wake, an empty space in the bed next to me filling me with relief. There is a note on the kitchen table. *Should be home early tonight – sorry I was off yesterday, got a lot on at work.* I screw up the piece of paper and throw it in the bin, the only apology he is capable of making landing amongst the other rubbish. I put it out of my mind and make myself a coffee and some toast.

As I'm eating, I hear the drop of the morning post landing on the wooden floor; I finish my coffee then go to collect it. One of the packages is heavy, John's details printed neatly on the front. There is a letter from the bank, also addressed to John, and a couple of bills. I pile them up and put them on the kitchen table. At the bottom is a small white envelope with my name and address on the front, handwritten in capital letters.

I frown at it, wondering what it could be, lost in a series of possibilities that at first prevent me from opening it. I don't receive many letters, everything is in John's name, so seeing my name in black and white, a name someone else has taken the time to write, feels odd. I remember being eleven and receiving a letter from my local library – a reminder about an overdue book.

I felt so grown up, as though a wider world had opened up to me which had finally acknowledged my existence.

I don't feel the same excitement now, though, I feel anxious. I have a sudden urge to discard the letter along with John's apology, to ignore its existence entirely, such is the level of certainty I feel that I won't like its contents. I sit down at the table and open it, not realising at first that I have been holding my breath. The letter seems like an anticlimax, a contradiction to the hesitation I have felt – a pitiful note, A5 in size, folded haphazardly – unremarkable. I open the note to find just three words messily scrawled in black ink. *He was innocent.*

My heart seems to be suspended in time, life momentarily postponed. I can't pull my eyes away from the letters, at first disbelieving and then pleading, hoping against all logic that I have somehow misread what's in front of me – but of course, I haven't. It's right there in black and white, as clear as it is horrifying.

As the confusion begins to lift and a disturbing clarity settles, I run to the door and fling it open, my ribs protesting as I run out to the end of the drive. The illuminous orange of the postman's coat is visible up ahead, towards the arc of the road. The ground is cold and damp underneath my bare feet; it's rained overnight and the clouds above are threatening to deliver more.

I stand shivering in the cool morning breeze, wondering whether to chase after the postman, to ask questions about a letter that he won't be able to answer. As I accept the futility of the situation and turn back towards the house, I hear someone shout my name and see Pete, our neighbour from across the road, ambling towards me.

"Hi Pete," I say, suddenly aware that I'm still wearing my pyjamas. I fold my arms across my chest.

"Everything all right?"

"Yes, fine, thank you. I was just after the postman."

Pete stands looking at me and I realise he is expecting more information, not quite satisfied with my reply. "Mix-up with the mail, that's all."

"Ah." He raises his bushy grey eyebrows and looks over his shoulder in the direction of the postman.

"It'll wait," I say, hoping he doesn't try to shout him over.

"You sure?"

"Positive."

"Right, well, I was hoping to see John but since I've got you here." He looks me up and down. "Unless this isn't a convenient time?"

"No, no, it's fine," I lie.

He runs his fingers through his dishevelled beard, his eyes darting from side to side. He was a GP at the local surgery in town, well liked and respected. He retired a few years ago when his wife became ill. Soon after, she passed away. He's never settled into retirement, suspended somewhere between grief and boredom, the time he never had now a void he seems unable to fill. "I've seen a questionable-looking character around here lately, seems to have a particular interest in your house. Actually, to tell you the truth... in you."

"What... what do you...? I'm sorry, I'm not sure I follow."

"I don't want to scare you, that's why I was rather hoping I'd be able to speak to John first." He pauses, looking over his shoulder, lost in the burden of delivering unwanted news – a weight he hasn't felt for a while.

"It's fine, Pete, you can tell me."

"Well, I've seen a man loitering around here a few times now." He points vaguely in the direction of the corner of the driveway, where large shrubs and bushes line a six-foot wall. "I can't say for certain but... it looked like he was watching you."

"Watching me?"

"Yes, I mean, I could be mistaken but it cert–"

I interrupt. "When?"

"The first time was over a week ago, ten days perhaps? I don't remember the date unfortunately and he only stayed for a short while on that occasion. Then he was here again towards the end of last week, Thursday I think it was. It was raining heavily, I remember that because I couldn't see very well through the downpour. That time, he actually walked up to your house and I thought you must know him because I didn't notice him come back out. But then he was here again last night, and that's when I felt sure he was watching you."

"Last night? John was home last night, it could have been work-related, or one of his friends..." I'm clutching at straws.

Pete shuffles on the spot, checking over his shoulder once more. "Yes, perhaps, perhaps." He scratches his head, clearly holding something back.

"But?"

"But, well, I suspect that's not the case because I noticed when you appeared in the window up there," he gestures to the small window to the right of the house – the spare room where I keep my books – "you spent a while in there and the light was on, and the man, he moved out from behind the wall a bit and just stood looking up – staring at you, or at least that's how it appeared to me. Whereas John was in and out of the living room all evening and the man remained hidden behind the wall. Uninterested, you might say."

I wonder whether Pete has considered the irony of relaying our movements to us while reporting someone else for spying on us. But I know he's harmless – lonely and a little nosey, maybe – but his intentions are good, I'm sure.

He looks at me with concern; I can feel my heart hammering against my chest and I'm beginning to feel panicky and light-headed, the mask I am trying to put on for him is slipping.

"I'm sorry if I've alarmed you. I was going to call the police last night but by the time I felt sure I wasn't overreacting, he left."

"Did he have a car?"

"Not that I saw, he headed off on foot."

"Could you describe him?"

Pete pulls a face. "It was dark, Erin, and my sight isn't what it was."

"Anything?"

"Tallish, well-built but not fat." He gives a sympathetic shrug and I understand that this was an offering, his attempt at giving me something – anything. But really, it's nothing, or nothing useful at least. "Oh, and he stood smoking a cigarette, chain-smoking really. Filthy habit."

My heart sinks and I have a sudden flashback to the woods – the man grabbing me from behind; the heat of his body against mine; the weight of him; the smell of cigarette smoke mixed with rotting wood and damp earth. I physically shake myself, forcing myself into the present, to feel the cold wet ground beneath my feet and the icy morning breeze lifting the hem of my silk pyjama top.

I take a deep breath before replying. "Thanks for letting me know, Pete. I'll ramp up our security. Would you mind not mentioning this to John?"

Pete shifts awkwardly, caught off guard by a request he obviously hadn't anticipated. "You don't want him to know?"

"He has a lot on at work at the moment, I don't want to worry him. You understand, don't you?"

There's a momentary pause where it could go either way, and I hold my breath waiting for his response. Then he nods and I exhale, relieved at not having to deal with the additional complication. "Sure, we wouldn't want that, but you'll take care of your security?"

"Absolutely. Thanks, Pete." I watch him turn and walk back towards his empty house, forcing a smile on my face that doesn't really exist. It makes my cheeks ache in protest.

When he's out of sight I walk to the corner of the drive and check the area where Pete had indicated seeing someone smoking. On the ground lie three cigarette stubs, soaked by the rainfall. I stare at them for a moment, imagining the DNA evidence they could yield disintegrating; the saliva washing away into the drains. They can't help me. I turn round and go back inside.

Once I'm behind walls no one can penetrate, my body succumbs to the panic. My mind takes over, one chaotic half-thought hurtling after another, nothing making sense. *He was innocent.* It *has* to be referring to Danny. Who else could it mean? In my mind, I sieve through the years I have spent keeping a low profile since what happened, but there is nothing to focus on; just a series of bland and mundane memories. A life I have avoided living. The only thing that stands out is Danny.

My breathing becomes erratic at this conclusion and I feel as though I'm falling down an endless tunnel, infinite darkness suffocating me with no escape in sight. How could anyone know? I'm on all fours, shallow breaths implausibly loud and laborious.

I try to focus on a slight imperfection in one of the floorboards, a swirl that looks out of place so close up. *Anchor yourself, Erin. Help bring your focus out of your mind.* I try to slow my breathing, but it only seems to make it worse. I don't know how much time passes – it could be minutes or it could be hours – but I remain on the floor at the mercy of my mind until exhaustion sets in and my body is released from the grips of panic.

I am left feeling drained and vulnerable, a shadow of myself that I'm unable or unwilling to recognise. Eventually, I fall into a deep and welcome sleep, my breathing slowly returning to normal as I lie in a heap on the floor.

When I wake, it's like swimming against a tide relentlessly trying to pull you under. I can hear the rain outside and I become aware that I'm shivering, the cold aching in my bones and my ribs feeling worse now than they have for days.

As I get slowly to my feet, struggling against a fog of shame and frustration, I notice the defective floorboard I'd tried to focus on – the swirling pattern out of place against the grain of the wood, the colour a slightly different shade. Imperfect – damaged, maybe – but from a distance, you can hardly tell.

24

FIFTEEN YEARS AGO

His office is tidier. The progress has been gradual but the effort consistent, each time I visit another area has been cleared away, making room for our secrets. It's become our refuge. A place his wife can't penetrate – or doesn't feel the need to. The week has dragged, the only relief coming from stolen moments in his office or the store cupboard in his classroom. I've welcomed his sudden disregard for rules – encouraged them even. We've been left with no choice, unable to shake off his wife's suspicion.

"One day, we'll be together properly."

He's lying with his back on the floor, a blanket we keep hidden in his desk drawer now crumpled beneath him. I lift my head off his chest to look at him.

"But what about your wife and family? You said–"

"I know what I said," he says softly, "but things change."

"What's changed?"

"Everything." He's being deliberately vague but I don't give up.

"Really, what's changed?"

"Against my better judgement I seem to have fallen in love with you."

I don't say anything. Instead, I rest my head back down on his bare chest, feeling the warmth of his embrace. I want to suspend time – live forever in this moment that seems so impossibly perfect.

After a while he readjusts, moving to the side so I'm forced to prop my head up on my hand. I can tell he wants to say something but he's unsure, hesitating to get the words right in his head. Eventually, curiosity gets the better of him.

"What happened to your mum?"

I look away – not because it's painful but because I don't want to ruin the moment, to taint it with a story that feels too sad for the situation. I keep it simple.

"She died when I was young."

"I'm sorry," he says, and I can see in his eyes that he means it. "Kids should have their parents around. That's why I need to wait a little longer."

"So," I say, tracing my fingers down the centre of his chest, through the wiry hair that covers it. "You'll leave your wife one day?"

"One day, yes. I'll leave my wife and we won't have to hide anymore."

"When?" I feel impatient.

"When the kids are older. And when you're older. Then we'll leave this place and start a new life together."

"Move away?" The thought hadn't occurred to me before but now that I think about it, it seems obvious: we couldn't be together here.

"If you want to be with me properly, then yes."

"Well, we'd better start thinking where we'll go."

He squeezes me momentarily, his grip solid. "Anywhere. As long as we're together."

I kiss him, aware that our time for today is running out. "I love you too."

He laughs. "Better late than never."

25

NOW

It had been a long time since I'd last had a panic attack – years, in fact. The world I exist in is small but risk averse; I have become proficient at avoiding triggers, dodging precarious situations and evading meaningful relationships. I go to the same places and see the same people, study their behaviours and propensities, learn who I should keep away from. I had forgotten how tired they leave you, devoid of everything but emptiness intermingled with spontaneous unwanted emotions; guilt, humiliation, sadness, shame... none of which are easy to overcome.

It's an uphill battle in the cold light of day, but as the night draws in and the darkness echoes my own feelings, it becomes almost impossible to fight. I sink into hopelessness, falling in and out of short bursts of shallow, restless sleep. I'm tossing and turning when John arrives home. I hear the door shut then his footsteps on the stairs, followed by his voice.

"Erin, you home?"

I try to gather myself, ready to call back to him, but before I can muster up enough energy the door opens and he steps into the room. He looks exhausted; red-eyed and pale. His tie is undone and the top button of his shirt is open, revealing his pale-white chest and a tuft of hair.

"What you doing?" he asks. "It's not even seven." He makes a show of checking his watch to emphasise his confusion.

"I was tired, thought I'd get an early night."

He sits down heavily on the bed and I feel the mattress give under his weight. He keeps his back to me, his elbows resting on his knees, and puts his head in his hands. He sighs. "I'm sorry."

I sit up – unsure at first if I've heard him correctly – and rest against the headboard, feeling the familiar pain in my side. I consider how to reply but before I can decide he speaks again.

"I'm sorry for the dinner party and for being a grumpy shit yesterday. I know it's no excuse but work's been so stressful lately, more stressful than I've let on. But that's not your fault." He turns to look at me, twisting his body and pulling his knee up onto the bed. "I know things haven't been good lately, Erin. Our marriage, it's... well, it was never traditional, was it?" I smile thinly, unsure what point he's trying to make. "I know it's never been love for you, and that's okay, I didn't need it to be about that–"

I interrupt. "John, I–"

"Please, let me finish. I knew you weren't in love with me when I proposed to you, or when we married, but I always hoped that one day you would grow to love me. When I left this morning, I saw you asleep in bed and I thought, *You're an idiot, John. You have a beautiful wife who's always been faithful to you when she could have any guy in the world.* I tried to remember when I stopped trying; stopped believing I deserved your love; stopped thinking it was possible." He shrugs. "I couldn't remember. It must have happened so gradually that I didn't even notice."

I sit watching him, silenced by his words, trying to remember the last time we had a conversation like this. Over the years, his words have become empty, devoid of feeling or sincerity. Occasionally, he lets a little bit of himself shine through and I remember why I married him – why I felt safe with him.

"My point is, I'm sorry I stopped trying. Life got in the way, but I'll try to make it up to you."

He swings himself round on the bed so he's sat next to me against the headboard. He reaches out and takes my hand in his. I squeeze it gently, letting my head rest on his shoulder, lost in a moment of quiet mundanity.

For a second, I consider telling him the truth about everything, wanting to unburden myself from the complexity of keeping so many secrets, telling so many half-truths, but something stops me. Maybe it's experience telling me I could wake up to an empty bed and a cold heart; maybe it's the fear of it all being more than a coincidence, the attack and the letter connected to events that occurred fifteen years ago.

A fleeting image of Nick is the last thing I see before exhaustion overwhelms me once more.

The birds wake me. Their soft, relentless chirping rousing me from a light sleep. I keep my eyes closed, lost in their happy little world. A memory springs to mind: I'm sat on my dad's knee. The wind is blowing through the grassland, dandelion seeds flying weightlessly through the air – a storm is on its way. Clusters of clouds crowd the sky, a patchwork of greys, hostile and intimidating. Crows circle overhead, a series of loud caws piercing through the howls of the wind. I'm worried about them. 'Poor crows. They'll get blown away.' Dad pulls me close, his grip strong around my waist. 'They'll be okay. Their feet are special – when they relax, they grip. They'll find somewhere safe and they won't let go.'

The door opens, pulling me from my reverie. John walks in carrying two mugs. I sit up, propping myself up on the pillows. The muscles in my back and shoulders ache from the tension of yesterday's panic attack, my head is pounding and my neck is stiff. I roll my chin along my chest while John puts my coffee on the bedside table.

"Morning," he says, getting back into bed.

I check the time. "Morning, aren't you going to be late for work?"

"No meetings until eleven, so we can spend the morning together if you like?"

I pick up my mug and take a long drink of the coffee. It's too strong and he's forgotten the sugar – he's made it how he likes it, and I wish it didn't annoy me as much as it did.

"What did you have in mind?" I ask.

"Breakfast? Or we could just have a morning at home together?" He brushes my hair behind my ear, his eyes burrowing into me, searching for reciprocation.

"I'm starving, let's get some breakfast." I see a brief look of disappointment flit across his face but he recovers quickly and smiles.

"Sure, I'll get showered."

I stay in bed until I hear the water running, safe in the knowledge that he's occupied. Then I slip on my dressing gown and go downstairs, a short sharp pain protesting with every step. I'm looking for the letter. I vaguely recall slipping it under a pile of papers yesterday, burying it under the mail deemed too important to throw away but too insignificant to file.

I go into the kitchen and check the shelves above the worktops, tiptoeing to see. Amongst a selection of herbs and spices is a growing pile of paper. I pick it up and leaf through it, relieved to find the letter I'm looking for somewhere near the bottom. I shove it into my dressing gown pocket, my mind darting around the house, considering where to hide it. I could just throw it away. I *should* throw it away. Then why do I feel the need to hang onto it?

I go back upstairs and into the spare room, scanning the books on the shelf in front of me. I select a copy of *The Wasp Factory*, turning the old creased book I've read many times before over in my hand, deciding whether to hide the letter that could open a door to my secrets inside it. It almost feels too big to disguise, too impossible to tuck away and expect to go unnoticed. Feeling as though I have no other choice, I flick through the book and let it fall open somewhere near the middle. To a book fraught with the struggle for control, I relinquish mine, sliding the letter inside and tucking it neatly back on the shelf.

26

NOW

We drive to a hotel nestled between Kestwell and Heatherton – a luxury haven in the countryside where John plays golf. The restaurant is on the top floor overlooking the grounds and John asks for a table near the balcony. It's a large room but it's less than half full, the faint murmuring of conversations imperceptible as we walk to our table at the far side.

The waiter knows John by name and treats him with a respect I wonder if he's earned or whether his money has demanded. The waiter hands us a menu and John orders coffee for us both while we decide what to eat. I feel sick, a sense of impending doom still hanging over me from yesterday, the letter and Pete's words swirling in my mind. I'm struggling under the weight of it all.

"Remember when I brought you here just before we got married?" John sits looking at me, his elbows propped on the table and his chin resting on his fingertips. He's made an effort – crisp white shirt and charcoal suit with a light-blue tie – but I can't decide whether it's for me or his work. Maybe both.

I nod. "They had to ask us to leave," I say, lost in the memory.

We were getting married the following month – a long engagement drawn out by our cumulative lack of any sense of urgency or need to be anything more than what we were. We ate steak and John ordered champagne. He was excited about the wedding and it took a lot of effort to try to meet his enthusiasm. It felt like a big responsibility – his expectations. We spoke long into the night, John beginning to slur his words and rub his eyes. I was relieved when the waiter told us they needed to close. John fell asleep in the car and shouted at me when I woke him.

"It was a good night," he says, smiling.

The waiter arrives with our drinks and takes our order with a slight bow that makes me cringe. I'll never be comfortable in these types of places.

While we wait for our food we swap pleasantries that feel too forced to be genuine, too mechanical to be real. I'm acutely aware that the conversation feels like a chore – one that requires considerable effort – and I wonder whether John feels the same. I find it hard to concentrate, my mind drifting relentlessly back to the letter, then to my conversation with Pete. *I felt sure he was watching you. He stood smoking a cigarette.* My stomach churns. I tell myself I'm trying to piece parts of a jigsaw together that don't belong. When our food arrives I pick at it, too nauseous to eat, then push it to the side of my plate. John glances over but doesn't say anything, then when he's finished with his he checks his watch.

"We'd better get going," he says, raising his hand to get the attention of the waiter who seems to have lingered nearby all morning. After John's paid we leave in a sudden rush I hadn't expected and I struggle to keep up as he walks hastily back downstairs and out to the car.

"I've got to go to the office first, you all right getting home from town?"

"Sure, no problem."

We drive back into Kestwell in a silence I'm unable to read. I begin to analyse our conversations, trying to work out whether he's mad at me, but my mind is faltering under the pressure of being pulled into what feels like a million different directions. I relent, letting an exhausted silence replace the noise in my head, the only sound now coming from the intermittent squeak of the wipers. The rain has almost cleared, the sun breaking through the clouds and highlighting the still damp ground. The walk home will give me a chance to clear my head.

He drops me off outside Oakwood Park, pulling into a lay-by in front of the big iron gates. I look through them and into the park. The central walkway lies ahead, a steady stream of people walking up and down, going about their day without any idea where it could lead. It looks different somehow – less welcoming, more precarious.

"I'll be working late tonight but I'll see you when I get back." His hand squeezes my thigh gently and he turns to look at me. "I had a nice time."

I wonder for a moment whether I've imagined his hostility towards the end of breakfast, his sudden haste in getting to the car, the ominous silence on the drive back.

"Me too," I lie. I open the car door and pull away from him. "See you tonight."

He drives away leaving me standing at the gates questioning myself. I'm reminded of when we first moved here from the city centre, a small piece of the world suddenly free to be explored away from the hustle and bustle, where too many variables and too little space had left me feeling confined to our two-bed apartment.

We'd parked in town and walked down the high street, turning left at the end towards the church. There was a fine sprinkling of powdery snow on the ground; it looked picture perfect but I felt unable to appreciate it fully, an irking feeling that something was simmering away, out of my control. We'd been for an early dinner at Rosa Italia's then called at the shop for a bottle of wine – a toast to the new house, John had called it.

We walked to the park gates and down to the memorial, over the beams of light shooting up into the darkening skies. He'd uncorked the wine and sat on a bench, patting the empty space next to him. *Sit.* I sat and watched him drink every drop, freezing, wondering why – why here?

When he'd finished, he tossed the empty bottle into a flower bed and walked away, leaving me to fall in line. The following day I visited the park alone. I picked up the empty bottle and put it in the bin next to the flower bed. In a small and seemingly insignificant way, I took back some control.

I turn and look through the gates, challenging myself to stand through the discomfort I feel. I realise I'm scanning the face of every man I see, looking into their eyes for some glint of recognition and hoping I don't find it. After a while I turn and walk towards town, past the church and down the narrow cobbled street towards Nick's. I don't slow down, glancing only briefly as I walk past. The lights are on and there's movement inside but I'm gone too quickly to register faces.

I soon come to Mimi's, the smell of coffee lingering faintly outside. It's quiet; the lull between breakfast and lunch creating space not usually available. I go inside. There's no queue and Mimi is busying herself cleaning the cake display at the front of the room. She looks up and smiles as I enter.

"Erin, come in, come in. How are you?" She ushers me over to the counter then slips behind it.

"I'm good thanks. How are you?"

"Good, darling, good. What can I get for you?"

"Just a coffee please."

"No friend today, honey?"

I smile. "Not today."

"You're feeling better?"

"Yes, much better thank you."

"I have work coming up over Christmas, lots of parties. What do you say? You're my best waitress."

"Thanks, Mimi, but I think I'll have to pass this year. I appreciate the offer though."

She smiles warmly then turns to the coffee machine behind her. "Okay, okay, but let me know if you change your mind."

"I will."

While I wait, I try to remember the last time I waitressed for her. It must have been a couple of years ago for her son's wedding. She had asked me as a favour and I couldn't decline, though I probably should have. Our arrangement had started off small, helping her at the café during busy periods or covering when a member of staff was off sick. Then I found myself agreeing to a few catering jobs, helping to prepare food to drop off at events. Before long, I was waitressing for parties and weddings.

That's when it became too unpredictable – there were too many factors I couldn't control. I'm hit by a wave of nostalgia at the memories; I had a lot of good times working for Mimi. In the end, I let John believe I stopped working for her because he wanted me to – it never sat right with him, having a wife waiting on people – but it couldn't be further from the truth.

Mimi hands me my latte and I take a seat on one of the tall chairs by the window, watching the world go by outside. A man walks past with a little girl on his shoulders, her curly hair sticking out beneath a pink hat. I remember being on my dad's shoulders and feeling invincible as he gripped my legs, the wind no match for his strength. I look away, telling myself it's not healthy to live in memories, but at the back of my mind I can't help but think: they're all I have.

My phone vibrates in my pocket – a message from John.

Did you get home ok?

It's been barely half an hour since he dropped me off, he must have just arrived at the office. I try to see the positives in the effort he's making, rather than letting it push me further and further away. I hit reply.

Just in town. Have a good day at work.

I put my phone back in my pocket and take a sip of my drink. Out of the window, I notice a familiar face in the crowd – Ian. I feel myself physically try to shrink, shoulders slouching and head down, reducing any possibility of being spotted. He's with another man, taller and broader than he is, and younger too. Mid-twenties, maybe. He's dark-haired and clean-shaven, wearing jeans and a dark-blue coat. They're not in a hurry, walking leisurely while deep in conversation. I watch them as they disappear down the cobbled street, eventually lost in the crowds.

My phone vibrates in my pocket again and I take it out with a sigh, expecting to see another message from John – but it isn't him, it's a message from a number I don't recognise.

Just seen you walk past the studio. How you feeling? Nick.

I feel momentarily spooked, unable to work out how he could have my number. I look around instinctively, eyes darting, heart rate quickening – suspicious that it's all a trick. Then I remember I called him the night I saw someone outside the house, that's how he got my number. The memory of that night makes me shudder now that I have the added weight of Pete's words to cement what I saw. I think about deleting the message, distancing myself from this man I barely know, but for reasons I'm not yet ready to admit, I can't. I hit reply.

I was on my way to Mimi's. Still sore but okay.

I press send then watch as the little dots indicate he's typing a response.

Fancy some company?

My stomach knots as I read the words. This would be a premeditated meeting, pushing the boundaries of what I could explain to John, but even as I try to go through that in my head, even as I try to talk myself out of it, I'm writing a reply.

Sure, Mimi's or yours?

The dots appear and then disappear several times and I begin to think he's changed his mind. Then the response comes through and I put my phone in my pocket, finish my drink and leave, waving goodbye to Mimi on the way out.

Mine.

27

NOW

A few minutes later I arrive at Nick's. I wonder whether I should have waited a little longer and seemed less eager, I could have had another drink at Mimi's or had a browse around the shops, but it's too late now – I'm here. The lights are on in his studio but I can't see anyone inside. I look over my shoulder to check there are no familiar faces walking by, then, when I feel confident the coast is clear, I knock tentatively.

I'm suddenly unsure of myself: did he mean now? Could he still be working? Did I misinterpret the whole thing? Seconds later the door at the back of the room opens and he walks towards me smiling. He looks different – smarter than usual. It's the first time I've seen him wearing a shirt – dark grey, tucked into black trousers. His hair is neater too, brushed back slightly to reveal more of his face. He opens the door and stands to the side to let me in. He doesn't say anything so neither do I, stepping inside with a confidence I don't really feel. He shuts the door and locks it.

"Hi," he says.

"Hi." I follow him out of the studio and up the stairs, neither of us speaking again until we're in his flat. Bear comes running over, panting and leaning against my legs.

"He remembers you," Nick says. I stand stroking Bear, aware of Nick's eyes on me as he leans his shoulder against the wall, watching. "You look nice."

I look down at myself as though I have suddenly forgotten what I'm wearing – jeans and a silk black blouse, a semi-effort for a brunch date with my husband. My long camel coat suddenly feels too much in the warmth of Nick's flat.

"Thanks," I say. "Nice to see you made the effort too."

"Ha yes, well, I was actually about to change but you were quicker than I thought you'd be."

I shrug. "I'd finished my drink."

On a small wooden table by the door there's a trophy or award of some kind, a pillar of crystal with a black base. There's an inscription on it. He notices me looking at it and picks it up.

"An award," he says, looking at it as though he hasn't seen it before. "For a photo I took years ago." He puts it back down and gestures to a print hanging above the table, mounted in a thick oak frame. It's a photo of a full moon; it looks as though it has been taken from a lying down position, the camera pointing upwards and capturing a border of trees that appear to surround it, their bare limbs almost touching the silvery white outline.

"Wow," I say. "That's incredible."

He shrugs, looking a little embarrassed. "I don't really photograph things like that anymore."

"Why not?"

"Work took over I suppose. Now it's all product photography or the odd house or commercial building."

"Don't you miss it?"

He thinks about it for a second. "I suppose I do."

We're still stood awkwardly, caught between arriving and

staying, and he seems to suddenly notice, standing up straight and stepping away from the wall.

"Sit down, make yourself comfortable. Do you want a drink?"

"Sure." I shrug off my coat and sit down on the sofa. Bear follows, lying down at my feet. "Just some water please."

He brings us both a glass and places them on the coffee table, sitting down on a chair beside the sofa.

"Been anywhere nice?"

"Just out and about. Have you had a busy morning?" I try to steer the conversation away from any possible mention of John, trying to keep the two worlds entirely separate. I hope Nick doesn't notice my evasiveness.

"Yes, busy but productive. I signed a new contract this morning I'm really excited about."

"That's great news."

He sits back in his chair. He looks relaxed and I try to feign the same calmness he exudes, sitting back and turning towards him slightly, my elbow resting on the back of the sofa. It doesn't come naturally to me. I have a propensity to move, my body never able to keep up with the thoughts racing through my mind. There's something about him, an easy-going nature – it's infectious.

"I'm usually quite good at reading people," he says. "But I can't help feeling a bit lost with you."

I shift awkwardly on the sofa, taken aback by the sudden change in conversation. "I'm not sure what you mean."

"I'd like to get to know you, but I don't know whether you want that too or whether you're just being polite." He scratches his beard. "You don't owe me anything, you know?"

The thought is so absurd I have to suppress a laugh.

"That's not the case at all. I mean, I do feel like I owe you – you probably saved my life – but that's not why I'm here."

"Then why are you here?"

I think about it for a moment but I'm unable to come up with a coherent reply.

"I suppose I can't really answer that. I don't know why I'm here – I shouldn't be."

He leans forward, forearms resting on his knees, hands clasped together. "As long as you're here because you want to be, that's good enough for me."

I nod. "I'm here because I want to be."

We sit and share a moment of quiet, a moment that lies somewhere between awkward and exciting – not uncomfortable, but different. A mountain of possibilities between us. Somewhere, buried in a deep corner of my mind, a memory is trying to surface: fifteen years ago. I have felt like this before.

28

FIFTEEN YEARS AGO

It's Wednesday – my favourite day of the week. Geography is the last lesson, providing the perfect opportunity to be alone with Danny afterwards. Half-term is looming, a glimmer of hope that I'm desperately clinging onto – the anticipation that he'll be able to sneak a day away from his wife; real, quality time together without the pressure of family or school. The rest of the class filters out.

I watch Lauren and Holly as they leave the class together, arm in arm, deep in conversation. They don't offer to wait anymore. I pack my things away slowly, hoping that no one else stays behind. To my relief, they don't. The last student leaves and we both watch as the door closes behind him.

"Hey you," he says. He turns and opens the door to the store cupboard. I follow, slipping inside behind him and closing the door.

"Will I see you over the holidays?" I ask.

"I could probably get away with one morning." He's kissing my neck, his mind elsewhere.

I gently push him away, trying to make eye contact. "Just one?"

He sighs. "I know, baby, but she would be too suspicious if I tried to get away for more than that. I'll need to pretend I'm coming here."

"Can't you say you have a lot of marking to do? I just want you to myself for the whole day." I play with his tie, tugging him gently towards me.

"No, she won't buy that." There's a finality in his tone, a foregone conclusion I realise I won't be able to argue with. "I hardly ever come into work over half-term."

I poke my bottom lip out but he doesn't comment, just pulls me in close and continues kissing my neck, trying to unbutton my shirt.

"What about one night? Couldn't you sneak out?"

He stops abruptly and steps backwards with his hands on his hips. He's getting frustrated with me.

"No. We share a bed, you know. You do realise that, don't you?"

My stomach turns at the thought. I nod, tired of feeling as though I am competing for a love that will never be mine.

"Baby, come on, we don't have long."

"But I'll see you, won't I? Over half-term?"

"Yes, you'll see me. One morning, I'll let you know when."

"Promise?"

He sighs heavily. "I promise."

I succumb to his advances, kissing him back and savouring the time we have together, trying to ignore the depressing surroundings. He opens my shirt, not bothering to take it off entirely, and just as he's feeling for my bra we hear a noise – the door to the classroom opening then the soft click as it latches closed. We both stop, standing completely still, listening.

I look at him, trying to convey a question – who could it be? He shakes his head and puts a finger to his lips. I swallow hard and the sound seems to echo around the room, rebounding off the boxes. He slowly and carefully buttons up his trousers and straightens his tie.

"Mr Miller?" A woman's voice – unfamiliar.

He takes a box off the shelf behind him and gestures for me to stay against the wall. He opens the door narrowly and slips out.

"Ah, Mrs Watkins, how can I help you?"

Mrs Watkins. I try to wrack my brain to think who she is. I can't place the name at first but then it comes to me – one of the new history teachers. Holly had told me about her; she was the only teacher in the school who had a seating plan and Holly had ended up at the front with someone she didn't know. She'd moaned about her endlessly.

"I thought I heard voices?"

"Sorry, old habit, talking to myself." There's a pause before he continues. "I was rehearsing my states while I got some boxes out of storage."

"Your states?"

"Yes, the states of America, in alphabetical order. Alabama, Alaska, Arizona, Arkansas, California, Colorado, Con–"

She interrupts. "Oh, *those* states."

"Yes, got to keep the mind sharp."

"Right, yes, I suppose you do."

There's a brief pause, a moment of silence where I can almost feel the awkwardness.

"Working late tonight?"

"Not particularly. I've taken over the room across the corridor while some repairs are being done to mine."

"Ah, I see, I'll keep the volume down then."

"Thank you," she says.

"Anything else?"

"No, I'll get back to my marking."

"Enjoy!"

I hear the classroom door close and inhale sharply, feeling a sudden need for air. The storeroom door opens and Danny enters, pale and dishevelled. His tie is still askew despite him trying to straighten it, and his top button is undone.

"Shit," he whispers. "Shit, shit, shit."

29

NOW

I spend most of the afternoon at Nick's, huddled on the sofa with Bear occasionally resting against my legs. We talk about things that don't really matter – safe territory subjects that feel comfortable: books, music, food, films. Every time the conversation takes a turn towards something personal, I gently steer it back.

As the light begins to fade outside he cooks for us, Chicken Alfredo pasta which he prepares while I sit watching him, propped up on a chair at the kitchen island. His place is almost unbearably neat, bordering on impersonal, and I wonder whether it's the photographer in him, the need for neatness and aversion to clutter. We eat slowly, sat at his kitchen table with the conversation flowing effortlessly.

Afterwards, I tell him I should go but I make no effort to actually leave, the words floating away into insignificance.

"I had a nice time," he says.

I smile. "Me too."

It's as though I have slipped into a parallel world, one where life is easy, free from the worries that I've grown used to dragging around. I feel weightless, everything pushed from my mind: the attack, the man watching me, the letter, my marriage, things I thought I'd left in the past.

Nick sits back in his chair and folds his arms across his chest, his shirt pulling taut against muscle as he does. I catch myself slipping into the pitfalls of longing, a yearning ignited within – a position I promised I would never put myself in again. It suddenly dawns on me just how dangerous the situation could be, the hazards of thinking with your feelings. It gives me an unexpected sense of urgency – I need to leave.

I push my chair out, stand up and look around for my coat. He's hung it up by the door. "I'd better go," I say, clumsily slipping out from behind the table. I head over to the door, grab my coat and drape it over my arm, not wanting to stall my momentum with the slow process of getting it on. I grab my bag and he stands watching me.

"Okay." He looks confused by my abrupt need to put some distance between us. "I can drive you home."

"No, no, it's okay, I'll walk."

He smiles thinly and nods. "Okay. I'll come down and let you out then."

He follows me silently down the stairs, through the door to his studio. It's cold inside, the previous warmth lost through inactivity. I stop and put my bag on the sofa where I'd sat just over a week ago, wounded and scared. I wonder whether much has changed since. He moves towards me, helping me as I slip on my coat.

"Thank you."

"You're welcome," he says. There's no hostility in his voice, no annoyance or frustration. I wish there was. I wish he was able to push me away the way that I need him to. But he doesn't, he just looks at me and smiles. "You take care."

I walk back towards the church, taking the long way home so I have to pass the park again. I need to allow myself to feel the fear; I can't let the attack taint the places I've come to think of as mine. The park and the woods have been part of my life since we moved here almost seven years ago. It was just after Christmas, bright lights still covering the houses on the crescent as we pulled up with the keys. Ours looked bare in comparison, dark and unwelcoming.

We'd had the whole house renovated despite it being just five years old, leaving it sat empty for almost a year. Looking back now, perhaps we'd both tried to delay the move, stall the unavoidable seriousness of settling in one place. New kitchen, new bathrooms, new carpets and tiles. Everywhere painted white and grey. *Minimalist,* the interior designer had called it. It felt more cold than minimalist to me. It still felt empty.

The last of the light has long since faded, the street lights leading the way along the road and past the church. When we first moved here the church would come alive at night, the stained glass windows glowing in the beams of the floodlights. Now it sits in darkness due to the bats which roost there. 'They need the dark to hunt.' I can hear my dad's voice telling me about the need to preserve their numbers, halt their decline.

As a child, our local church had experienced the same problem, the floodlights interfering with their night-time hunting. Dad had become very involved with the issue. 'They're the only mammals capable of true and sustained flight. They're fascinating creatures. It's an offence to disturb them.' We'd been handed a flyer about it a few years ago while walking through town. John had laughed and called them pests that spread disease. I'd turned away embarrassed and – not for the first time – thankful he'd never met my dad.

I cross the road to the park. The gates are open and welcoming but what lies beyond fills me with dread. I've ran through the park countless times in the dark and never thought twice about it before. The forest is different, there is an occasional unease about it and that – along with the lack of lighting – has always prevented me from exploring it in the depths of darkness, but I've never had the same apprehension with the park. The familiarity felt comfortable.

I stand outside the open gates. I can see right to the end of the central walkway, to the war memorial standing on top of a raised platform, poppies still adorning the steps around it. The ground lighting is shooting up like beams, highlighting the faces of those walking past. There's a family heading towards me, two young boys just ahead of their mum and dad, riding their scooters towards the gates. Their parents shout at them to stop and on the third warning, they listen. They wait just before the gates and I watch them as they argue about who won. I turn and walk away, up the winding hill towards home.

My side aches as I arrive home and the beginning of a headache is forming, pulsating behind my right eye. I go straight into the kitchen to find the painkillers, swallowing two with a glass of water. As I put the glass back next to the sink I hear a knock at the door, short and sharp. I check my watch: almost six. My first thought is John – has he forgotten his keys? – but I quickly dismiss the idea, it's too early.

I sidestep over to the kitchen window and push aside the blinds slightly, looking to see whether there are any additional cars on the drive, but I already know I would have heard an engine – it's a quiet street. The security light is on but, as I suspected, there are no strange cars and nothing to account for the noise.

I let the blinds fall back into place and walk slowly into the hall. I listen intently, holding my breath, but there's nothing; no voices, no footsteps, no second knock. I move closer to the door until I'm brushing up against it. I rest my ear lightly to the wood, my hand resting on the thudding of my heart.

I don't know how long I stay there – I'm in a state of limbo, my ability to decide what to do caught up in the panic. My jaw throbs by the time I move away, the clenching and grinding of teeth leaving a lasting ache. My mouth's dry and my headache has worsened, the pain now spreading to my shoulders and neck. I step back, take a few deep breaths and unlock the door. I don't know what I'm expecting to find, the scale of my imagination is so vast and varied that I have considered just about every possibility.

At first, there is nothing but the night. The security lights have relented, the driveway is just as I left it. Across the road, I notice Pete's lights are on but his curtains are drawn and it occurs to me that it could have been him visiting quite innocently to check I have addressed the security – which of course I haven't. I make a mental note to do it tomorrow.

As I'm about to close the door I notice a small white envelope on the floor outside. There is a rock sat on top of it, stopping the wind from carrying it away. I take another look around, suddenly distrusting of my previous assessment that I'm alone. Evidence doesn't lie. This time I walk to the end of the drive, barefoot and struggling against the pain and growing disorientation of a migraine. Everywhere is quiet, the only noise coming from the distant sounds of an occasional car passing beyond the crescent.

I head back inside, picking up the envelope as I go.

30

NOW

I sit at the table, one hand holding a cold compress to my head while the other clutches the envelope. I will the pain to go away so I can regain some focus, trying to see through the blurred vision and ignore the growing spike of nausea. It's another small white envelope with my name and address on the front, handwritten in capital letters, the same as last time.

This time, though, there is no stamp – this one was hand delivered. The person who bought it risked knocking, risked me going straight to the door and seeing them there. The thought disturbs me, the brazen unnecessariness of it. Was he making a point? Or just trying to scare me? The envelope has been sealed with one long strip of sticky tape. I pick at its edge, toying with it before feeling ready for its contents.

I try to remember the sessions I went to, the ones my dad had asked me to try. The therapist with the bright colours – the red lipstick, the rainbow jumpers and butterfly jewellery. It was too much – too try-hard. It made me want to look away, repulsed by her outward display of positivity. Her room was decorated with the same garish taste; bright yellow walls; a large, cheap-looking tapestry depicting a sun rising over a meadow; plastic sunflowers in a vase in the window; blue-and-yellow-striped curtains.

Her voice matched the surroundings, artificially positive, a calmness that sometimes made her difficult to hear. 'Picture your happy place, somewhere you feel relaxed. Somewhere you feel safe and calm. When you feel an attack coming on, close your eyes and imagine being in your happy place. Think about how calm it is, how relaxed it makes you feel. What can you smell? What can you hear? What can you feel?'

I try to use it now, conjuring images of the beach in my mind; the lush green chalk cliffs looking out over the sea littered with fishing boats; the lighthouse we would walk to, up the cliff-face steps; the waves crashing around the pier; the wind coming in off the North Sea; the smell of saltiness mixed with the fresh crab wafting from the restaurant on the pier. All of it seems to pale in comparison to the sound of the waves, their ability to simultaneously intimidate and motivate.

'Look, Dad! Look how big the waves are tonight!' There's a show on at the pavilion and the pier is teeming with people all dressed up, smiles on their faces, anticipation in their eyes. The atmosphere is electric. He puts his arm around my shoulder as I hold onto the side of the pier, looking out over the ocean as the sun begins its journey to meet it. 'You know, Erin, as big as those waves are, there are bigger ones under the surface.' I turn round, looking at him questioningly, wondering whether he's teasing me. 'It's true,' he says. 'Internal waves are always bigger than those on the surface.'

As the painkillers begin to take effect, numbing the sharpness of the pain enough to be able to concentrate, I pull away the tape and carefully open the envelope. Inside is one single sheet of folded white paper. I open it, my heart feeling worryingly fragile, emotionally scarred from the past few days. It's the same messy writing as the first note, but this time it's bigger, taking up the entirety of the paper: *You have blood on your hands.*

John arrives home with a bunch of lilies under his arm and a carrier bag full of takeout. He's smiling at his efforts, believing he has done enough to compel me to fall into his arms. It has the opposite effect, it feels strange and out of character, too far removed from the man I'm used to. The smell of curry fills the kitchen as he begins unloading the little plastic containers.

"I took a punt on Indian, I know it's your favourite."

I want to correct him – *it's your favourite, not mine* – but I don't have the energy for a discussion. I pick at a chicken korma, my appetite non-existent. I can't focus on what he's saying, the letter relentlessly flowing through my head. *You have blood on your hands.* I keep imagining it tucked safely into *The Wasp Factory* along with the first letter, two pieces of paper echoing my darkest moments and forcing me to relive them.

"Erin, what's up?"

I look at him, compelling myself to focus. "Sorry, I'm just tired. I haven't been sleeping very well."

"I noticed," he says, as though my restless nights have been an inconvenience for him too. "I was just saying, it would be nice to try to get away on a winter break, don't you think?"

I force a smile. "Yes, it would."

"Don't be too enthusiastic."

"Sorry, it sounds nice, really."

"I'll see if I can get a week off after Christmas."

It's a prospect I could do without, a week on our own together somewhere new. I feel shaky, trapped by secrets, lies and plans I would rather not have. I think back to the last time we went away together – a weekend spa break in Edinburgh last year. I hadn't wanted to go but I didn't have the benefit of excuses. John's business had provided marketing services for a chain of spa hotels and the weekend break had been a thank you gift. We'd had a couples massage and brunch in the gardens; the perfect foundation for romance.

That evening the CEO, Devon, had joined us for dinner and had repeatedly thanked John for doing such a brilliant job with promoting his business. I liked him, he knew all the staff by name and thanked them when they brought our meals – something I had noticed by that point that John never did. Later in the evening Devon's wife, Sophia, had joined us. She was heavily pregnant, uncomfortably swollen ankles squeezed into strappy heels, but she was glowing. I'd watched Devon smile at her as she cradled her belly, as they finished each other's stories and held hands tenderly at the table.

Was that how it was meant to be? Until that point, I hadn't realised I had a total lack of happy couples in my life. My dad had always been alone, family was sparse and relatively unknown, and my own relationships left a lot to be desired.

Sophia was kind and personable, she had an infectious laugh and interesting stories; I found myself wishing I was more like her, more able to slip into situations and make the best of them. Instead, I have always found myself looking in, listening with nothing to add; I daren't reveal anything about my past and I have nothing of interest from my present. I'm always the spare part, laughing and smiling in all the right places.

Just after eleven, Sophia apologised mid-yawn.

"So sorry but my bed is calling."

Devon smiled. "Sleeping for two now."

He stood and helped her put on her coat, tucking the chairs into the table and shaking John's hand. As they were saying goodbye, some last words of business that couldn't wait, Sophia positioned herself with her back to them, catching my eye.

"Honey, I've been there, and it's not worth it."

"Sorry, I'm not sure what you mean."

"Money. It doesn't buy you happiness – I know that's easy for me to say now, but I met Devon when his first hotel was going under. He didn't have a penny to his name, but it didn't matter. Find someone who adores you, we all deserve that."

I stood, bewildered, trying to formulate a response but failing.

She kissed me lightly on the cheek. "It will just get worse." She smiled sympathetically, a certain wisdom in her eyes that spoke of experiences she would rather not share.

I wanted to defend myself – our relationship – but I remained speechless. She didn't know me and yet, with hindsight, she was disturbingly right.

"I'm going to go up," I say, scraping the food into the bin. I walk over to him and kiss him lightly on the cheek. "Goodnight."

He continues to shovel food into his mouth, hardly taking a break to chew. Through a mouth full of curry and rice he manages to grunt: "Night."

I toss and turn, unable to sleep, trying to break free from the thoughts escalating in my mind. When John comes up to bed an hour later I lie as still as possible, adjusting my breathing to pretend I'm in a deep sleep. He soon begins to snore, the rise and fall of his chest moving the covers I'm lying under.

Just after 3am I get up, careful not to wake him. I feel as though I'm spiralling, no longer able to abide by my internal set of rules that have allowed me to hold a marriage together for all this time. I need to think. I go into the spare room and turn on the lamp in the corner. I run my forefinger along the rows of books, unable to settle on anything too heavy and slowing as I skim past *The Wasp Factory*.

Eventually, my finger finds *95 Poems* by E.E. Cummings and I slide it out of its slot. I sit on the chair in the corner and pull a blanket over me. I flick through the pages – back to front – and land on *Maggie and Milly and Molly and May*. I read, wrapped up in my blanket, under the dim light of the lamp, entranced by the lyrical depiction of the power of the sea.

I suddenly realise what I need to do. The ocean is calling me.

31

FIFTEEN YEARS AGO

I'm sat on his chair, tucked in behind his desk. My shirt is on but undone, a thin layer of sweat clinging to my chest. He's pulling on his trousers, fumbling with his belt. The late afternoon sun is flooding in through a gap in the blinds, partially highlighting his face as he does up his tie; his strong cheekbones and the flecks of grey hair at his temples. He checks his watch.

"Baby, you should go."

I pout playfully. "But I don't want to, I want to stay here with you."

"You've been here every night this week. People will start getting suspicious."

I know he's right. Since Mrs Watkins' interruption we've steered clear of the store cupboard, hiding away in his office instead, locking out the world. He's been more cautious – bordering on paranoid – checking the halls before I leave. I've been careful but there are only two ways in or out of school – the front entrance or the back.

I've alternated throughout the week, avoiding others where possible and keeping my hood up and eyes down. There are after-school activities, revision classes and sports clubs, plenty of things to explain my extended stay at school – as long as I don't leave too late.

"No one's seen me leave."

"That you know of." He buttons up his shirtsleeves while slipping on his shoes.

"I'm careful. Besides, I'm not the only student here late."

"No, but you're the only student here late every night this week."

"What can I say? I'm eager to learn." I grin at him and he can't help but laugh.

He puts his hands on his desk and bends down to kiss me. "I do love it when my students enjoy my classes."

"Oh really, and do a lot of students take your after-school classes?"

He laughs again, brushing my hair off my face. "Just you, baby!" He grabs hold of the chair and spins me around. I grip onto the armrests, giggling and telling him to stop. I love it when he's playful, it's contagious. He stops the chair suddenly and kisses me hard. "Now go, or I'll be forced to punish you!"

I stand up and let my shirt slip off my shoulders. "Please, sir, don't!" I back away from him, towards the other side of the desk. "You'll have to catch me first!"

He plays along, running after me and trying to grab at my arms. Eventually I let him, and together we sink back onto the floor, caught in a moment of pure joy.

The after-school clubs have all finished, the cars in the car park reduced to just a few – the teachers want to get home early on a Friday. I slip past the windows at the front of the school, past the double-doored entrance to the reception area, and turn right up the long wide path to leave the school. I quicken my pace as much as possible, as fast as I can go without actually running. My hood's up, partially obstructing my view. I hear a voice coming from somewhere behind – a woman's.

"Miss Knight. Miss Knight! Erin!" The voice grows louder, so loud I can no longer pretend I haven't heard. I turn round, trying to look as casual as possible. "I thought I saw you pass, what are you still doing here?"

She's walking towards me, her long red hair blowing behind her. She's wearing a floral dress and tights with heeled boots. I've seen her at school but I can't think who she is. She must read the look of confusion on my face. "I'm Mrs Watkins," she says. "You probably don't know me, you don't take history do you?"

I do know her but shake my head, my stomach in knots. Mrs Watkins, the history teacher who walked into the classroom when Danny and I were in the store cupboard. I search my brain, trying to think how she could possibly know my name.

"I've noticed you've been staying behind after school quite a lot so I just queried with the ladies at reception who you were." She gestures behind her in the vague direction of the school entrance. "Have you been at a club?"

I don't know what to say. I hadn't anticipated anyone asking me where I've been except my dad, and I would be able to tell him anything – book club, netball, cheerleading – he wouldn't question it. I'm suddenly scared that she will check up on me, investigate whatever I decide to tell her.

"Erin, is everything okay?"

"I was smoking," I blurt out.

She looks surprised. It's not what she was expecting.

"Smoking?"

"Yes. I was smoking behind the back of school before I went home. My dad would kill me if he found out."

"So whereabouts have you been smoking, exactly?"

"Behind the bike sheds." I begin to gain confidence in my lie.

"Every day this week?"

I nod. "Yes, I think I'm addicted."

"Right." She sounds sceptical so I jump in, trying to add credibility.

"Please don't tell anyone. I'm going to quit, I promise."

"Erin, smoking on school property carries some hefty consequences. Not to mention, I should call your parents."

"Parent," I say, adding emphasis to the singular. "I don't have a mum, it's just me and my dad. He'd be so mad if he found out. Please don't tell him. Please?"

She sighs, running her hand through her hair. She's thinking about what to say, suddenly unsure of herself. I've played on her conscience by mentioning my mum, or lack of.

"You're going to quit?"

"Yes, definitely." I'm nodding enthusiastically.

"I'll be checking, I want to see you leaving at 3.30 every day."

I consider for a moment whether she has the motivation or the ability to check or enforce that, but I decide I have no choice but to believe her – at least for the time being.

"Okay, 3.30. Thanks, Miss."

She smiles thinly. "If there's anything else, anything you need to talk about, you can come and see me." She turns and walks away, back towards reception.

As I leave the school, coming out onto the main road, I wonder whether it's a coincidence that she's seen me leaving school every day this week, or whether she's been watching me.

32

NOW

I decide to drive to the south-east coast, an urge to be near the sea no longer able to be suppressed. I need to clear my head. The drive feels longer than I remember, despite the A2 moving quickly, but I don't stop, the urgency I feel overshadowing the pain I'm in. My ribs ache, crying out for a more comfortable position, and I arch my back and try to stretch as I accelerate towards the coast.

Two and a half hours later I arrive at Minnis Bay, the sprawling sands visible just past the coastal path, opening up onto views of the estuary. I park the car and open the door, breathing in the salty air, content to just sit and listen to the waves for a while. In the distance, forming neat rows parallel to the horizon, countless turbines make up the offshore wind farm. It's a clear day, the endless blue of the sky a reflection of the water.

There's a steady flow of people passing on the coastal path; walkers, cyclists, runners. I feel a pang of envy towards the latter. I get out of the car and stretch carefully, reaching up into the air until the sharp stab of pain warns me to stop. The sea is on its way out. An image pops into my head of a place on the other side of the ocean as high tide arrives – the give and take of Mother Nature.

I lock the car and follow the sea wall until I reach an opening down to the beach where I sit and take off my trainers and socks. As I trudge towards the water, shoes and socks gripped tightly in my hand, I glance up to my left; if I walked one hundred and fifty miles or so north I would arrive back at my childhood home, on the beaches I know so well. I wonder whether my dad still walks the coastal path, still sits on the sand watching the fishing boats come and go. I wonder whether he's there right now, mirroring my barefoot walk on the damp sand.

I try to conjure up an image of him fifteen years older, the same checked shirts and jeans, the same kind eyes. Every time I attempt to picture him a little greyer, a few more lines around the eyes, I'm brought back to the same man I last saw over the kitchen table. He's frozen in time, in memories etched into my mind, resolutely vivid and unaffected by the passing of years.

There's a chill to the air and I stop halfway down the beach to zip up my coat. The sand is cold underfoot but it's welcoming, it reminds me of being a child, running barefoot along the shore collecting shells in my little red bucket, showing the extra special ones to my dad who sits watching me with a contented smile, offering words of encouragement.

The beach is covered with wading birds foraging for food left behind by the tides, their long curved beaks dipping in and out of the shoreline. I stand watching them; they're within feet of me, undeterred by my presence. A man walks by with his dog, a black-and-white springer spaniel with boundless energy. The man throws a ball into the sea and the dog jumps over the frothing waves and into the water to retrieve it. The man doesn't wait, he continues walking, safe in the knowledge that his loyal dog will follow.

Further down the beach, another man is playing with his daughter. They're chasing the waves then running away from them in turn. She screams as they catch her, lapping at her wellies. Her dad pulls her away, returning her to the safety of the sand, but she immediately runs back, determined to outrun them this time. Their laughter carries across the sea.

A memory surfaces: we're on the headland in Norfolk, the sheer drop to the coast just a few metres ahead. It's summer, but we're on high land close to the ocean; the stillness of the ground has no place up here. The wind catches the hem of my dress and lifts my hair, obscuring my view. I try to tuck it behind my ears but I only have one hand free – my dad grips the other, tighter than usual. There's been a sighting of a whale this morning. 'It's rare for whales to enter such shallow waters.' We stand watching the ocean for a long time. I'm tired – it's been an early start and a long walk up the grassy headland.

After what seems like hours, we see it. 'There! Over there! See?' He passes me the binoculars and I see it. 'Yes! I see it, Dad, I see it!' We're caught up in the moment, thrilled about what we have seen, temporarily ignoring what it may mean for the whale. Throughout the morning, others join us. Some local, some from out of town.

There are reporters down on the beach talking to some official-looking people. 'They're from Marine Life Rescue,' Dad tells me. 'They're worried he's getting too close to shore.' We miss dinner, lost in the magnificence of the whale as he gets slowly closer and closer to the beach. 'No, go back, go back.' Dad's worried and as I look around I realise he's not alone – concern is etched on the faces of everyone watching.

As the day progresses, the coastguard arrives and things begin to look bleak for the whale. A disquiet settles. Hushed conversations grow louder with an increased sense of urgency, the clifftop heaving with people who have been drawn out by the chance to see a tragedy. I resent them. We came to see the whale, the chance to spot such a glorious creature. They came for the heartbreak. It strikes me that we should leave, refuse to be part of it, but we're already hooked in, invested unreservedly in the outcome of the whale.

Eventually, he washes up on the beach to gasps and faint mumbles of horror from the bystanders. 'Will he be okay?' I ask.

'No, I don't think he will be. It's sad but once whales beach they don't tend to survive.' Dad looks forlorn and I step forward and hug him, wanting to make him feel better.

'Why did he do it?' I ask. He kneels down so that he's at my level, looking into my eyes.

'The truth is, no one knows for sure.' I'm not used to him being unable to provide me with answers and it takes me aback for a moment, shocked by this sudden grey area of information.

'But what do you think, Dad?'

He looks out to sea, thinking for a moment before answering. 'Did you know that whales evolved from land mammals?' I shake my head. 'It's true. They once walked on four legs. Maybe he was in trouble and his instincts told him to head to land. Maybe it was like going home.'

I don't say anything but in my mind I think: *Silly whale. You've evolved for a reason, you shouldn't have gone back.*

I'm sat on the beach when the tide begins sweeping back inland. I've been lost in the slow voyage of a ship in the distance, my toes buried in the sand. I hadn't noticed it getting dark until I saw its navigation lights, a glimmer between the windmills on the horizon. The seagulls are my only companions now, flitting in and out of the waves, grey and unforgiving in the fading light. The other beachgoers who had endured the cool winds of the day have thought better of the cruel, harsh winds that come with dusk. They've left me to brave it alone.

I sit shivering, the cold unrelenting. I check my watch: just past five. The sun is sinking, consumed by the vastness of the ocean, leaving nothing but a warm orange glow spilling thinly across the horizon. The loud shrieks of the gulls remind me of home, the days spent on the beach with my dad; the long walks looking for birds; the campfires on warm summer nights; picnics while crabbing under the pier. Gulls are everywhere now, adapting to urban living, no longer seabirds confined to the coast, yet there is something about their cries with the backdrop of the crashing waves that makes it distinctly nostalgic.

I move up the beach, away from the waves as they stretch further and further inland. I try to think about the letters and what I should do about them – or whether I should do anything at all – and when I fail to come up with a solution I try to clear my head and think of nothing. Faces keep springing into my mind, my imagination forcing me to look into the eyes of the man I had once loved so unquestionably.

I'm exhausted, tired of carrying secrets that have tainted half of my life, secrets that were formed in childhood when I should have been focused on other things. I should have sought refuge in nature, in the tranquillity of the environment on my doorstep. I curse my younger self for my naivety, the innocence and inexperience of childhood costing me greatly. I can't take the letters to the police, it would all unravel, the aftermath burning at my feet. I feel powerless.

After a while I reluctantly get up and leave, snaking my way up the beach towards the car park. I don't stop to put my shoes back on, instead I paddle barefoot across the coastal path and into the car park, the sand clinging to my feet. I open the car door and sit sideways on the seat, brushing the remnants of the beach off one foot at a time, careful not to overstretch my side.

I put my shoes and socks back on and start the engine, taking in one last deep breath full of the salty air. It's an inexplicable connection I have to the sea, a bond built on childhood memories and the ultimate mystery of the ocean, its ability to create peace and wonder, demand harmony and respect. It will show us its surface but hide mountains in its depths. An enigma. One of the hardest things about leaving Dad – leaving my home – was the acceptance that it also meant leaving the sea, moving to the city but unable to adapt to urban life as easily as the gulls.

33

FIFTEEN YEARS AGO

I t's the last day of term, an uncharacteristically bright day for October. It's as though the summer has decided to stay, refusing to give way to darker days. I've skipped lunch again, choosing instead to spend the hour with Danny. Since being interrogated by Mrs Watkins I have been more careful, making the most of the lunch hour instead of staying after school.

I haven't told him about what happened and I can't tell whether it's because I want to protect him or myself – this way I feel safe from his rejection; his tendency to withdraw affection whenever he feels vulnerable and exposed. He says he has a lot more to lose than I do – his family, his job, his reputation – but all I can think is that losing him seems enormous enough to me. He is everything.

His office smells of coffee and I can taste it on his lips when we kiss, a sharp bitterness now lingering in my mouth. He looks tired and he seems distracted, his eyes wandering, lost in thought. It's nearly the end of my lunch break and I've got to make it across to the other side of school before the bell. I kiss him, trying to pull him away from his thoughts and back towards me.

"I have to go," I say. I'm sat on his knee, nestled in the chair behind his desk. His arms are around my waist, holding me close. I play with his tie, tucking it back neatly under his collar. "Do you know which day we can meet yet?"

He straightens up in the chair, shifting my weight with ease. He's so strong. He clears his throat. "I'll text you."

"Promise?"

"I promise," he says, but he avoids making eye contact, watching as he tenderly strokes my arm instead. He lets go of his hold on me, ready to release me back into the deep voids of the school.

I don't have time to stay and talk, to gently ask him questions until I get an answer that makes me feel reassured. I kiss him goodbye and rush out of the classroom, tossing my bag over my shoulder and hurrying down the corridor, breaking into a jog as I take the stairs. I leave the south block and head across the quad, passing a few late stragglers as I push through the double doors into the north block. The bell rings as I'm climbing the stairs and I quicken my pace, eager to get to class before my absence is noted.

The classroom is already full but I manage to slip in unobserved amidst the pre-register noise, navigating through the rows of desks to find my seat. At the far side of the room, by the window overlooking the quad, I sit down next to Holly and take my books out of my bag. She doesn't acknowledge me at first, she's busy chatting to Lauren on the row in front. As Mrs Tate clears her throat and calls for quiet, she neatens her books in front of her then turns to me.

"Where have you been?" Her tone carries a hint of accusation but I choose to ignore it. It all seems trivial to me now – the friendships I've spent years forming – they're reduced to insignificance in comparison to my relationship with Danny. Nothing else matters.

"Erin?"

"Nowhere, I just had some stuff to do."

She rolls her eyes and turns away. The lesson is unsettled, everyone feeling the excitement that comes on the brink of breaking up. Halfway through, Mrs Tate seems to give in, telling us to discuss our revision timetables in small groups. Chairs are pushed out immediately, everyone moving around the classroom, reforming small groups crowded around desks.

Holly is talking quietly to Lauren who's turned her chair around from the desk in front in order to face her. I don't interrupt, I'm too busy planning in my head how I can make my time with Danny over half-term special. I consider places we can meet and – getting a little carried away – I wonder whether a day trip might be possible, somewhere no one knows us, where we can just pretend to be a normal couple. Maybe the beach – not the local one, but further south. Somewhere in Suffolk, maybe; South Beach or Aldeburgh. I imagine walking barefoot across the sand towards the sea, the transcendent beauty of it mesmerising us, allowing us to stand still and appreciate each other in a way we are unable to at school.

I know deep down he'll say no, too afraid of being spotted in some freak coincidence that sees us there at the same time as another teacher or pupil, or a member of his family. Instead, we'll be forced to meet in the forest by the old abandoned house again. Although even that place, as strange and eerie as it is, might not be completely abandoned on an autumn day in the midst of the school holidays. The graffiti and the empty bottles of vodka must have come from somewhere.

After a few minutes, the conversations in the classroom seem to come to a sudden halt, a quietness descending which pulls me from my thoughts. Everyone is moving towards the window – those already there are standing, pressing their foreheads against the glass to get a better look. I stand on tiptoes, bending to one side to see around Holly. Out on the quad, two police officers are walking towards the south block escorted by the headmaster, Mr Anderson.

Someone behind me shouts, "What's happening, Miss?"

I turn to see Mrs Tate looking flustered, her pale cheeks streaked with red. "Come away from the window, I'm sure it's nothing."

No one listens and she doesn't repeat her instruction. Instead, she joins us at the window, looking out over the quad as the birds scatter to make way for the three men. The police officers swing open the doors to the south block without hesitation, Mr Anderson in their wake. The doors close shut behind them and they disappear from view.

"What the hell...?" Lauren looks from me to Holly. "You reckon it's a student or a teacher?"

"Student, probably." I sit, feigning disinterest. I'm light-headed and there's an uneasy feeling in my stomach that's rising up into my chest. I flip through the maths book in front of me but can't make out the words; tears are distorting them, reducing them to a blur.

Holly notices and sits down next to me. "You all right?"

"Yeah, I'm fine."

"You think they're here for Mr Miller, don't you?"

My heart sinks. Lauren has pulled a chair over to the table. "It's okay," she says. "We know."

34

NOW

I pull into a service station on the way home. The traffic has been relentless and I curse myself for heading home in rush hour. The stop-start of the journey has eaten away at some of the calm imposed by the beach, chipping away at my renewed composure. I take some deep breaths and swing into a parking space near the entrance. Before I get out of the car I check my phone and find two messages. The first is from John.

Where are you? I got home early.

He'd sent it just before six – only fifteen minutes ago. I hit reply.

Parked up and had a walk. Be home in an hour or so.

I'm an hour away, at least, so I decide to grab a coffee and a muffin from the kiosk at the front rather than go inside. I take them back to the car and eat quickly, suddenly aware of how hungry I am. Before I leave, I pick up my phone and check the other message – it's from Nick. The sight of his name on my phone catches my breath. I've toyed with deleting his number, erasing all traces of him from my phone in case John were to look through it, but the chance of that happening seems so remote that I've left him in there, nestled between Mimi and Ray in my sparse list of contacts. I open the message.

I'm heading to the reservoir with Bear – fancy joining us?

I look at the timestamp – 2.05. I press reply.

Sorry, hadn't seen your message. Hope you enjoyed your walk.

I press send. John isn't a jealous person – probably because he's known me long enough to understand my usual lack of social life and my tendency to enjoy being alone – but just in case he ever felt inclined to check, I delete the message. As soon as I do, a new one pops up in its place.

We'll be there again in the morning.

I delete the message, turn on the engine and head home.

I arrive home just after 7.30. Clouds have gathered above and a few drops of rain have started to fall. John opens the front door for me as I'm getting out of the car, a thin smile on his face. I can't tell whether he's pleased to see me or not.

"Hi," I say as he moves aside to let me in.

He locks the door behind me. "Nice walk?"

"Yes, thanks. I needed some fresh air."

"Where did you go?"

"The reservoir." I don't know why I lie, but I knew before I drove to the beach this morning that I wouldn't tell him about it. I feel the need to protect it, to keep it hidden, but I can't explain why – even to myself.

"What have you been there for?"

"Why not? It's nice."

He shrugs. "You don't usually venture that far. Getting bored of the park after all these years?"

I swallow hard. "It's not the same when I can't run. I just wanted to go somewhere different."

"We could go somewhere different together this weekend if you like?"

"What about work?"

He shakes his head. "No work this weekend."

"Okay," I say, because I can't think how I could possibly say no.

"Good, I'll have a think about where we can go."

I smile. "I'm going to go and shower."

Mindful of the grains of sand that may still be clinging to my feet, I leave my shoes on, go straight upstairs and into the bathroom, putting the shower on full blast while I undress. I tip my shoes upside down and shake them over the sink, then do the same with my socks. Sand scatters, sticking to the damp sides of the basin. I turn on the taps and watch as it washes away.

I step into the shower, the heat of the water easing the aches and pains which have accumulated during the long drive. The bruising on my side is still there, a patchwork of colour changing from blues and purples to browns and yellows. My face has cleared up much quicker, yellow bruising remaining around the cut on my head but all else fading to nothing, as though it were never there at all. I tip my head back, letting the jets of water pummel my face.

As I begin to relax, letting the stress of the journey melt

away, I hear the bathroom door creaking slowly open. My heart jumps and I haul back the shower door, images of the man in black creeping into the room suspended in my imagination – but it's just John. I put my hand on my heart, feeling it thrashing against my chest.

"You made me jump!" I say. I notice I've turned away from him, feeling exposed and self-conscious.

"Sorry, but I thought you might like some company."

The relief is short-lived. I don't reply, turning away from him so I don't have to watch him undress or feel repulsed by the look of longing in his eyes. I let the water run over the top of my head and down my face, flooding my senses with anything other than what's about to happen.

I feel him get in the shower, his cold hands holding my arms as he begins to kiss my shoulders. I feel sick, the coffee I drank on the drive home threatening to force its way back out. I'm powerless, I realise. I can't say no but I don't want to say yes, so I say nothing at all. I tilt my head into the flow of the water and go to my happy place. As his hands roam, hungry and impatient, I close my eyes. The thing with water is its raw power – it can erode even the strongest rocks with time, relentlessly chipping away until it consumes everything in its path.

35

FIFTEEN YEARS AGO

The pain is paralysing. The sense of helplessness unbearable. There is nothing I can do. I lie in bed refusing to speak to anyone – a stream of people wanting to help but inadvertently doing the opposite. Why can't they understand we're in love? I say nothing, barely opening my eyes to see them leave.

Everything seems so pointless, as though my future was in Danny's hands and I'm no longer able to access it; there's just a wall in front of me and I can't break it down to let in the light. My bed has become my refuge, my room as cluttered as my head; school work dumped on a desk full of half-empty glasses, clothes I no longer wear scattered across the floor. 'Chasing Cars' by Snow Patrol plays softly from my CD player, the orange glow from my lava lamp the only trace of light.

Dad sits perched on the edge of my bed, his back to me and his head in his hands, doing his best to be simultaneously near and far. It doesn't matter; he won't be able to reach me regardless of space. A deep crevasse has opened between us, the aftermath of an earthquake so strong it has shaken everything he believed to be true. I can tell he wants to help me, to guide me through my heartache, but he's also repulsed by it. He can't look at me without seeing him.

When he talks, it's barely more than a whisper. "He's older than me." He's pinching the bridge of his nose, squeezing his eyes shut as though to dispel an image forced on him by his imagination. I don't say anything, not wanting to get into a discussion about his age as though it were of any significance.

"Forty bloody four, Erin, for Christ's sake. What were you thinking?" Again I say nothing, preferring the silence in which I have grown to find comfort. Words have hurt me so much lately. "I want to be here for you but I need to understand. Please, help me understand." He doesn't shout, but there's a growing intensity to his voice that draws me into the moment.

"I love him, Dad," I breathe through muffled sobs.

He still doesn't look at me. He rubs his fingertips against his eyes then over his stubble. "Love? You think this is love?"

"I know it is!" I shout through the tears, rubbing my face on my sleeve.

He shakes his head, still unable or unwilling to look at me. "How did I miss this?"

I want to reach out to him. I want to tell him it's not his fault. I'm caught in limbo, balancing my desire to protect Danny with my longing to comfort Dad, to offer him the reassurance he needs.

"I'm sorry," I say, settling for a truth somewhere in the middle.

He sighs. I'm picking at a thread on my pillowcase, suddenly feeling like a little girl again.

When I look up I notice he's crying. A quiet, restrained cry, tears falling freely down his cheeks, a slight shuddering of his shoulders, but no sound. A man of restraint, never one for grand displays of emotion. I sit watching him, not wanting to acknowledge the ways in which I have broken his usually solid exterior; the ways I have implicated him in something he does not deserve; the ways this will undoubtedly leave scars on us both, deep and lasting.

Eventually, I shuffle over to him, kneeling behind him on the bed. I wrap my arms around his shoulders and hold him, my cheek settling into the curve of his neck, and for one small moment in time everything else fades to insignificance.

36

NOW

I wake early, the emptiness of the bed a welcome sight. I pull the covers over my head, hiding from the world. I'm exhausted, emotionally fatigued and physically drained. I'm out of sync, out of routine. The lack of exercise has upset my usual predictability. I'm not eating enough and I'm sleeping too much, lethargy testing my resolve. I toss and turn, pain creeping up my side; John had quickly forgotten about my injury last night, lost in the grip of desire. I get up, slip into my robe and head downstairs.

I make some coffee and toast and sit in the chair by the window, watching the world go by outside. There isn't much to see; from our house can see Pete's place directly opposite and part of the houses on either side of his. To the right, I see Zara loading the twins into her Mercedes, neatly dressed in their dark-green uniforms. After she's fastened them both in, she runs back into the house and returns a minute later carrying their lunch bags. I watch as she drives away. She'll be back after dropping them off at school, then she'll spend the day going out to Pilates classes, walking her miniature sausage dog or meeting her friends for coffee. I've seen her in Mimi's on several occasions, but she never speaks.

When I've finished my toast, I find my phone and check my messages – nothing. I try to recall the wording of Nick's message yesterday. *We'll be there again in the morning.* There was no mention of a time. I check my watch – 7.45. I go upstairs and shower, feeling safe in the knowledge that John is at work. I must remember to lock the bathroom door in the future.

I put on my running kit: leggings, sports bra and a long-sleeved black top. I dry my hair then brush it back into a ponytail. I dig out my running shoes, grab my coat then head for the door. I know I won't be able to run but I'm enjoying the feeling of preparing, the routine of it. I know where I'm going, but I don't acknowledge it. Not yet anyway.

There's a layer of ice on my windscreen, it reflects the glow of the security light as I spray de-icer sparingly over the front and back of the car. I sit waiting for it to work, the hum of the engine and the heaters filling the car. I check the dashboard – just one degree above freezing.

Eventually, I pull out of the drive just as Pete is leaving his house. He holds up his hand in a suspended wave and heads towards me. I step on my brake and open the passenger side window. He walks over, a look of concern on his face.

"Morning, glad I caught you. Any luck with the security?"

Shit. With everything that's happened I haven't got round to calling anyone. I don't even know who I need to call.

"No, not yet. I will though, I promise."

He sucks in air through his teeth. "It's just the man I told you about, he was here again day before last. He knocked and dropped something at your door."

"Yes, I received a letter." I instantly regret telling him.

"Oh? Nothing sinister I hope."

"Not really, no. Did you get a better look at him?"

"Unfortunately not, he was fast. Caught me by surprise actually."

"Fast?"

"Yes, he seemed to drop the letter then sprint away. He ran off towards the main road."

"Right," I say. I feel a strange sort of relief – he's not as brave as he would have me think, running away so as not to get caught.

"I really think John would want to know about this."

I take a deep breath in, trying to buy myself some time to think of any further reason for John not to know.

"Pete, it's not a good time for him right now. He's really stressed with work and – I'll be honest with you – it's putting our marriage under a lot of strain. I don't know if we could survive the stress of all this as well." I play to his good nature, his kindness and compassion. "Please, could we just keep this between us and I promise I will sort the security issue out later today?"

He puts his hands on the window frame and leans forward so he's practically in the car.

"I don't want to cause any trouble, Erin, but there are other people living here to think about. What if this man's dangerous?"

"He's not," I say, using all my effort to sound certain.

He arches an eyebrow, confused. "You know who this man is?"

My heart rate quickens at the realisation that I'm digging myself a hole, a huge void which I'm about to start filling with lies. "No, not exactly."

"Erin, if you're in some sort of trouble, you need to speak to the police."

"No, no, it's not like that. Just someone from a long time ago... I think."

He looks around, checking no one is passing, then looks back into the car conspiratorially. "An ex-boyfriend?"

I take his suggestion, nodding. "I don't know for certain but it's looking that way."

He licks his bottom lip and stands, relinquishing his grip on the car. I stay sat with my foot on the brake, waiting for his decision.

Eventually, after what feels like minutes but is probably seconds, he bends back into the car, his kind eyes filled with worry and apprehension.

"I implore you to report this. You know Terry?" Pete gestures to one of the houses further up the crescent. "He's a detective. You could speak to him. I don't think it's his area but I'm sure he'd be happy to advise you."

I shake my head.

He continues. "If you won't, then at least get some decent security, better surveillance that might deter him."

"I will, I will."

He sighs heavily. "I have a daughter, you know? Heather. She lives in Australia."

"No, I didn't know that." I had always assumed they'd never had children.

"She's about your age. If I knew something like this was happening to her." He shakes his head as though ridding himself of such an awful idea. "It doesn't sit right with me, but neither does interfering in other people's lives, especially when it's going to cause problems of a different kind."

"Thanks, Pete, I really appreciate it."

"I'll be keeping a close watch." It's not a question or an offer but a condition of our understanding.

I nod.

"And you'll ring some security companies today?"

"Absolutely."

He smiles thinly, an agreement reached, although I can see in his eyes that it is not one he's happy with.

"Take care then." He stands back from the car, allowing me to leave.

"See you, Pete." I drive off, closing the window and gripping the steering wheel until my knuckles ache.

~

I drive past the town centre, sleepy and still, store owners beginning to prepare for the day while the cobbled streets lie quiet. The traffic flows, the usual commuters heading out of the suburbs and into the city.

Once I'm past Kestwell I drive down the winding country roads and the unmarked lanes until I see the sign for Heatherton. I turn right, avoiding the town centre, and drive down a narrow lane until the car park comes into view, the reservoir looming behind it.

As I pull into the car park I look around, searching for Nick's car. I see it parked in the far corner next to a line of thick shrubs, but he's not inside. I turn the engine off and get out, grabbing my coat from the back seat. The surface of the reservoir has frozen around the edges, thick sheets of ice suspended on the water, the middle now a refuge for the ducks and swans who all congregate there.

The car park is quiet, just five cars including mine. I stand at the entrance and look around the edges of the reservoir, the paths that trace the outline of the water, trying to pinpoint Nick and Bear. A runner passes, a middle-aged woman wearing a London Marathon T-shirt. I watch as she runs away from me, feeling a pang of jealousy towards a woman I don't know.

I can see people in the distance; a couple with a dog, another runner and – at the other side of the reservoir, tiny against the horizon – a man. I can't make out his details but as I continue to watch I see a familiar flash of white – Bear. I turn and walk anti-clockwise, towards him. The wind blows freely through the open space, the noise catching on the water and whipping through the undergrowth. My hair has come loose and I fight a losing battle tucking it behind my ears.

As we get closer to each other I'm aware of a quiet nervousness simmering in my stomach, a feeling which both excites and disappoints. After six years of marriage, co-existing with a man who borders on being a stranger, I thought I'd developed a resistance to emotions. My own rules have dictated my life and the people in it, the limits on my interactions and relationships, but now I find that my capacity to feel is greater than I'd foreseen.

An urge to turn away materialises from nowhere, sudden and imposing, a need to be alone, somewhere familiar – this all feels wrong. Why did I come here? Driven by basic desires I thought I'd learned to ignore. But it's too late, he's too close.

37

NOW

Nick waves, Bear at his heels. "You came," Nick says, smiling.

"I did."

I turn and walk with him, falling in line beside him.

"How are you?" he asks.

The image of the letters forces itself into my mind, unwanted and alarming all over again. I try to push the thought of them away, refusing to acknowledge their hold on me.

"I'm okay," I lie.

"Ribs feeling any better?"

I grimace. "Still aching, and I had a long drive yesterday which didn't help."

"Where did you go?" he asks casually.

I consider for a moment the implications of telling him the truth, deciding that there probably aren't any. "To the beach. A little bay in Birchington-on-Sea."

He grins. "It's a bit cold for the beach isn't it?"

"I see, you're one of those."

He looks puzzled. "One of what?"

"You only go to the beach for the sun."

He shrugs, smiling. "I guess so. I don't think I've ever been to the beach in winter."

I raise my eyebrows. "You're missing out. The coast's deserted in the winter. It's peaceful. Not to mention the wildlife."

"The wildlife?"

"Yes, seals, pink-footed geese, snow buntings..."

He's still grinning at me, too polite to laugh but too amused to keep a straight face.

"My dad was a conservationist so I grew up learning about nature and the environment." I'm speaking without thinking, divulging things about myself that I haven't told anyone in years. I tell myself to be more careful.

"Has he retired?"

I look at him, confused.

"Your dad – you said he was a conservationist? What does he do now?"

I think about his question, and about the million others it raises.

"I don't know," I answer truthfully. "I haven't seen him in a long time."

"Oh. I'm sorry."

"Don't be."

We walk on in temporary silence, an awkward impasse, both letting the quiet account for a conversation unfinished.

Nick clears his throat. "So did you enjoy your day at the beach?"

"I did. I hadn't been for so long, I just needed to be near the sea."

"Did you grow up on the coast?"

I nod. "I'd go there every day."

"You miss it." A statement, not a question.

Bear has fallen behind, sniffing at something in the

undergrowth. Nick calls his name and he catches up, nuzzling at my hand as I walk.

"Sorry I left suddenly the other day," I say, looking ahead to the turn in the path. An elderly man is walking towards us, a thick scarf partially hiding his face and a scruffy brown dog at his side. When it sees Bear, it runs up to him in greeting. We walk on, exchanging brief pleasantries with the man as we pass.

"It's okay," Nick says, picking up where I'd left. "I'm sure you had your reasons."

"It was still rude. Did I even thank you for cooking?"

"No, you just ran off. I seem to have that effect on women."

I can't help but laugh. "Is that right?"

"You tell me," he says, a seriousness in his voice. "Why'd you leave?"

I run my hand through my windswept hair, brushing it off my face only for it to be blown back again by the wind. Ahead, in some overgrown shrubbery, a couple of sparrows sit swaying in the breeze.

"Do you ever wonder why sleeping birds never fall out of trees?"

His eyes narrow, perplexed by my sudden change of conversation. "I can't say I have. But since you mention it, why don't sleeping birds ever fall out of trees?"

"They have special feet; when their muscles relax, they grip. It's an involuntary reflex. It keeps them safe."

"Interesting," he says, but I can't tell if he means it.

We arrive back at the entrance to the car park and come to a stop.

"Another lap?"

"Sure."

We start walking again, clockwise, past a jetty where an elderly woman now stands feeding the ducks with a little boy, his rosy cheeks matching his red coat. The seagulls are getting most of the bread, the ducks trapped in their circle of refuge, barricaded by the ice, except a few brave mallards who have taken to walking across the slippery surface. The caws of the gulls rise and fall in the excitement as they catch the bread mid-flight. The little boy laughs, throwing the pieces higher and higher. I notice Nick smiling at them, watching the little boy in his bubble of joy. When we're past the jetty, he turns back to me.

"You didn't answer my question."

"Hmm?"

"Why did you leave?"

"I guess it was an involuntary reflex. Whenever I feel out of my depth, it seems easier to leave than confront it."

"I know it's not an ideal situation, but a really horrible thing happened to you. If you can't tell your husband about it then I'm happy to be that person you can talk to – whether you do or not is up to you. The point is, you can."

I want to tell him everything in that moment. I want to tell him about the naïve fifteen-year-old drowning under the weight of secrets too heavy for a child; about the community that turned against her; about the man in black watching me, leaving me letters; about my fear of reporting it to the police; the fear of revealing everything to stop something which is already in motion.

"What is it?" he asks.

I realise I've been staring into the distance, lost in colliding worlds and conflicting emotions. I shrug. "Nothing, really. Just thinking about how I ended up here."

"That's a big question."

I sigh. "It is, isn't it?"

We step to one side to make room for a group of four runners, all wearing matching orange T-shirts with 'Heatherton Road Runners' printed on the front. My arm touches Nick and I'm close enough that I can smell him – a musky aftershave, not overpowering – he smells nice and I find myself lingering, breathing him in. I catch myself and step away, restoring the space between us as we begin walking again, side by side.

"I was married once," he says. "A few years ago now."

I'm not expecting him to tell me something so personal and it catches me off guard. I had suspected he'd been married – there's still a trace of a wedding band on his ring finger. There's no trace of a woman in his flat though, no womanly touches, photos or possessions that I've seen. I would have guessed he'd been divorced for a few years. Still, I hadn't expected him telling me.

"What happened?" I ask, trying hard to play down my intrigue.

"She died." He speaks softly but frankly. I look at him as he watches Bear walking ahead, his eyes fixed on him so he doesn't have to look at me. There's a sadness in him, deflated under the enormity of the information he's just divulged. I feel sorry for him, that our conversation has led him to this painful memory.

"I'm so sorry, Nick."

He doesn't say anything, and I understand that in that moment, there is nothing else to be said.

"I've been getting letters," I say, changing the subject. "I think they're from the man who attacked me, but I'm not sure." I realise it's been a trade-off – his pain for my own. Confessions being exchanged like currency.

"What sort of letters?"

"Not very nice ones."

"Saying?"

I don't know how far I'm willing to go, how much I'm willing to divulge. Telling him the content of the letters will only leave me open to further questions, more revelations.

"Erin? What do the letters say?"

"He's just trying to intimidate me, that's all. Nothing specific."

Nick stops walking, turning to face me head-on. I mirror his stance but struggle to meet his gaze, the seriousness of his eyes making me feel like a child.

"Have you gone to the police?"

I shake my head.

"What makes you think it's the same person who attacked you?"

"I've seen him at my house. The day you came over..." Nick starts to speak, to protest this line of reasoning, but I interrupt: "I know you didn't see him, but he could have gone over the back onto the allotments." I shrug. "I know what I saw."

He scratches his chin then turns to start walking again. I follow. He doesn't say anything for a while and before I know it we're halfway around the reservoir. I look across the water to the car park and can see it's busier than when I first arrived. A young couple walk towards us, hand in hand, and we fall into single file to pass.

When I'm beside him again, he finally speaks. "So, say it is the same person who attacked you. He's now sending you intimidating letters, coming to your house. Surely you see that things have escalated? You need to report this, Erin."

I think about it for a minute, wondering how much to tell him. I feel oddly comfortable with him in a way I haven't felt before, and I can feel I'm having to hold myself back from revealing everything, from purging myself of my sins.

"I know it won't make any sense to you so I don't expect you to understand, but I can't go to the police."

"You're right, I don't understand. So help me out, help me understand."

I take a deep breath, knowing that whatever I say I will pick apart later, reliving the entire conversation a thousand times in my head until I can't take any more.

"When I was fifteen I had a relationship with someone who got into a lot of trouble. The police were involved and things got really bad. For everyone."

He frowns, his forehead creasing. "Why did he get in trouble?"

"He was an adult."

"Oh," he says flatly. "How old?"

"Does it matter?"

"I think a fifteen-year-old having a relationship with an eighteen-year-old is a lot different to a fifteen- and thirty-year-old."

I wish he hadn't given arbitrary ages, knowing now that if I tell him it will seem even worse.

He must see the look on my face. He raises his eyebrows. "Older?"

I nod. "Forty-four."

He exhales exaggeratedly. "Forty-four?"

"Yes. I know now how wrong it was but at the time I couldn't see it."

"You were a kid. Just a kid."

"I know, but I didn't feel it."

"So, what happened?"

"It just got really bad, for a lot of people. It would have been better left alone."

"And your dad? Is that why you don't speak anymore?"

"Indirectly, yes."

"It must have been hard for him."

No one used to ask my dad how he was, even when at times it seemed as though he was struggling the most. It used to frustrate me, all the questions directed at me when he clearly needed help as well.

"Yes," I say, "it was awful for him. He was so angry and upset, but there was nothing he could do. And every time he tried to help me I pulled further and further away."

"Have you never thought about contacting him?"

"Every day," I say without hesitation. "I'm reminded of him constantly – in nature, the environment, the weather. Not a day goes by where I don't think about him."

"Then what's stopping you?"

"It's complicated. I left *for* him. Going back now would just be wrong."

"I can't imagine he feels the same."

"No, he doesn't. But people don't always know what's best for them."

We arrive back at the entrance to the car park which is almost full despite the cold. We slow down and come to a halt by the bench where we'd sat before.

"I brought a flask," he says, smiling.

"I wouldn't expect anything less!"

He goes to his car while I sit and wait, watching as people pass by in different directions. Across the pond, about a quarter of the way round, I notice someone stood at the edge of the reservoir. I sit watching them, the tall dark figure dressed all in black, but it takes me a minute to realise he's also watching me.

"Here we are." Nick's reappeared, holding a flask with a spare mug. He sees the look on my face and follows my gaze across the water, to where the man in black is stood watching. A second later, he turns and walks away. "Is that him?"

"I think so. Is there another way out that way?"

He nods, frowning. "A few back routes." He puts the flask down on the bench and turns towards him and I can see what he's thinking.

"Don't," I say. "You wouldn't be able to catch up with him now anyway."

"You didn't notice him while we were walking?"

I shake my head. "No." I feel flushed, suddenly hot and panicky. "Maybe I should go."

"He knows where you live. That's my point about going to the–"

I interrupt. "I won't change my mind," I say bluntly. "I'm ringing a security company later to see what they can do." I'm still watching the man as he disappears behind some trees in the distance.

Nick sits down heavily next to me. A second later, his hand is on mine, squeezing it softly – strong yet gentle. Despite the logical part of my brain screaming at me to leave, I don't; I sit and enjoy the warmth of Nick's hand, my eyes fixed across the water, my heart barely able to be contained.

38

FIFTEEN YEARS AGO

I can't eat. I can't sleep. I'm lost in a devastating cycle of memories, the longing worse than any pain I've ever experienced. It feels so endlessly unfair that what we had has come to an end through no fault of our own. I'm desperate to know who reported him, who decided that it was their responsibility – I need someone to blame, a place to direct my anger and hate. An image of Mrs Watkins pops into my head – her concern, the suspicion in her eyes – could she really have reported him without any evidence?

Dad and I are sat at the kitchen table pretending to eat lunch together, though neither of us have touched our sandwiches. Dad looks tired, shadows under his eyes which aren't usually there. I play with my lemonade, circling the top of the glass with my fingertips to distract myself from what I have done to him.

"You need to eat," he says.

"So do you."

We've reached a stalemate, both of us knowing what's best for each other but not for ourselves. He sits back in his chair, his shoulders slumped.

"You need to think about what you're going to do here, Erin. You need to think about whether you really want to stay silent."

"I'm not telling them anything they can use against him."

"They've already got enough evidence, you see that don't you? They found everything they need on your phone. I'm not trying to be cruel but I need you to understand that, to come to terms with it. He's going to prison with or without your cooperation."

"He hasn't done anything wrong."

"You're fifteen, Erin. He's forty-four and a teacher, a position of trust. And he's married with his own children. It's morally wrong, and it's wrong in the eyes of the law."

"But not in mine."

Dad sighs heavily and removes his glasses, wiping them on the hem of his shirt. I begin to cry, my face contorting with the effort of trying to hold it back.

"It'll get easier," he says softly. I look at him through the tears brimming in my eyes, afraid to admit that I need reassurance, to be told that this pain won't last forever. He meets my eyes and I see it again – the absence of something that's usually there. Pride maybe, or respect. It would break my heart further if that were possible. "You'll pick yourself up and you'll be stronger for it."

"Will I?" I ask, and it's a genuine question, one that I need him to answer. Will I ever feel happy again? Will I ever feel confident and capable?

"Yes, you will. We don't have a monopoly on love and loss, Erin. These emotions span far and wide across the animal kingdom too. Why? Because pain is useful. We learn from it."

He sits up and picks up his sandwich, taking a bite. I wipe my tears on my sleeve and do the same, chewing through the nausea and forcing myself to swallow. He smiles and I try to reciprocate, appreciating the effort he's making despite his own pain.

"I'm sorry, Dad."

"I don't need you to be sorry, I need you to promise me you'll learn from it, that it won't all be worthless. Can you do that?"

"Yes. I promise."

After we've finished I head up to my room, my mind still on the promise I've made to Dad: I promise to learn from the pain, I promise it won't all be worthless. I need something good to come from this, I need to know that one day we'll be together.

Nick and I part ways at the car park, but only after I've promised to call the security company as soon as I get home: a promise I've made to two separate people in the space of a few hours. I drive back towards Kestwell, following Nick's Rav4 as we wind slowly round the country lanes and ascend into town. He switches on his indicator to turn left and I raise a hand to say goodbye. He does the same, a one-handed wave visible as he drives away.

Once I'm home I trawl through paperwork, from guarantees for TVs and fridge-freezers, to MOT certificates and life insurance documents. It's endless; a mountain of formalities, all things which I usually leave to John. Eventually, I come across details for Sandstone's Home Security Group Ltd. I look over the paperwork, finding a phone number and a customer reference. I dial the number which is quickly answered by a man who introduces himself as Ed.

He's friendly and is obviously in no rush; after answering a few security questions he delves right into the policy we have and my options for upgrading – police-monitored systems, extensive CCTV cameras, panic buttons, and wireless alarms.

When he's finished reeling off their list of services, he tells me I can have it all linked up to my phone or tablet so I can monitor the property twenty-four hours a day. The prospect feels daunting and I begin to wonder how I'm going to explain the sudden upgrade to John. In the end, I decide the promise I made to Nick and Pete outweighs my reservations and I make an appointment for Tuesday at 2.30, my conscience feeling a little lighter.

I fall asleep at some point in the afternoon and wake up to find it dark outside. There are no lights on in the house and it feels empty and eerie, the shift from sleep to reality an abrupt transition. I turn on the lamp next to the sofa and flick on the TV, leaving it on the news channel John must have been watching last night, a droning reporter satisfying company for background noise. The house feels cold. The dull ache in my side feels worse for sleeping hunched over and my head is groggy with sleep. My phone beeps softly from the kitchen table and it occurs to me that I probably shouldn't leave it lying around anymore, the chance of getting a text from Nick feeling exciting but unnerving. I wonder how people who have full-on affairs – perhaps even multiple – cope with the risk and the stress it must cause. I decide to keep it in my bag from now on. I look at the display – it's Nick.

Did you sort the security?

I press reply.

Yes, appointment on Tuesday to install more CCTV, lighting and a panic button.

I watch as he types.

Good. Hopefully see you soon.

I lock the phone and put it in my bag, zipped inside a pocket. I feel a pang of disappointment – no date or time suggested, just 'soon'. The feeling makes me remember lying in bed at night waiting to see Danny the following day, to just catch a glimpse of him at school or pass him in the halls, knowing the secret we shared, the meeting we had arranged. The anticipation used to keep me awake at night, imagining conversations we'd have or things we'd do.

I cringe at the thought now. My first love – my *only* love. The first time it happened – the shift from professional to personal – was so subtle I didn't even realise it was happening until he'd gone. I was at an athletics club run by Mr Bentley, the PE teacher. Halfway through I ran inside to use the toilet, using the entrance to the south block. Danny was just coming down the stairs, a long black coat draped over his arm and a brown leather briefcase in his hand, ready to go home for the day to his wife and children. He was my geography teacher, familiar enough to say hello to but nothing more. He had an air of confidence about him that bordered on intimidating, and he held himself well and dressed smart, always in suits and tailored coats. I didn't know how old he was. I would have guessed about the same age as Dad – late thirties – their hair beginning to grey. Danny stopped when he reached the bottom of the steps.

"Miss Knight, what are you doing here?" He checked his watch and I felt as though I'd been caught doing something I shouldn't be. I stopped in front of him.

"I'm at athletics club, sir." I was in my PE kit, black shorts and a white T-shirt displaying the school emblem. It was a warm afternoon, one of those cloudless spring days that promised summer was on its way.

"Ah, what are you doing today?"

"Long jump, trying to beat my record."

"Those long legs will come in handy for that." He looked me up and down and something passed between us, fleeting but unquestionable. I felt my skin prickle, his gaze lingering for a moment too long to be comfortable. "Right, I'd better be going. Have fun." He walked out the double doors leaving me with the beginning of an idea, a spark that would soon turn into a raging fire, wild and uncontrollable.

～

John arrives home just after nine and I've rehearsed a story, a reason why we need to increase our security.

"Hi," I say. "Did you have a good day at work?"

He smiles, pleased with the effort he believes I'm making, unaware it's a façade. "Not bad. What did you get up to?"

"Not a lot, I went out for a walk this morning then came home and did some reading. Actually, I noticed a couple of men hanging around outside. They looked a bit suspicious, I think we ought to get some additional security. What do you think?"

"Are you sure they weren't working? Simon and Yvonne are having some work done next door."

I shake my head. "No, definitely not. They were loitering."

He laughs. "Loitering? Christ, Erin, this is a nice neighbourhood, not like the dives you used to live in."

It seems so unnecessarily cruel, a comment made with intent to hurt. I turn and walk away, leaving him standing alone in his superiority.

"Erin, sorry, I didn't mean..." He follows me. "Sorry, that was unfair. If it makes you feel safer then of course we can ramp up the security."

"You do realise living in a nice neighbourhood doesn't give

you a free pass, don't you? Rich people can be victims of crime too."

"I know, I said I'm sorry, okay?" He sighs heavily and runs his hand through his thinning hair. "It's been a long day."

I'm not sure what else to say. I stand looking at him, dishevelled after a hard day at work, feeling conflicting emotions; on the one hand mad at him for his hurtful comments, on the other hand, relieved to have been given the go-ahead about the security.

As I turn and go up to bed, letting him kiss me briefly on the cheek, I think fleetingly of Pete and a promise fulfilled, then of Nick, his face lingering in my mind as I drift off to sleep.

40

NOW

Red sunlight strews across the still-dark sky, the sun teasing its imminent arrival. I sit wrapped in a blanket, cradling a mug of coffee and looking out of the window. There's something captivating about twilight, bordering on magical – the night is over but the day has yet to begin – a void in time unaccounted for. It feels full of possibilities. Unspoiled.

John left early for work, the slam of the door being shut with a little too much force waking me from a dream I can't recall. Outside, the crescent is quiet, houses sit in darkness, cars still parked neatly on driveways. The birds are singing, though I can't see them. An invisible beauty, their chorus the perfect backdrop. I close my eyes, my hands wrapped around the mug of tepid coffee, and try to enjoy the peace. It doesn't last – a car engine starting next door hurls me into the present, where thoughts of the man in black and the intimidating letters come crashing back.

I get up, leaving the sun to break the horizon unobserved, and toss my coffee into the sink. My mouth feels dry and my throat tight; I know I've been sleeping tense, my body poised and ready for fight or flight. The increased state of anxiety is taking its toll on me physically. I grip the sink and take some deep breaths, slowing my thoughts and my natural tendency to constantly move.

I feel as though I'm on the verge of a panic attack – at the tipping point between holding on and letting go. I focus on the mug I have placed in the sink, taking in every colour, every different shade and scratch, the contours and the smooth curve of the handle. I focus on the tiny details, the mundane particulars, flooding my mind with useless information that cannot harm me.

When I first started having the attacks, before I'd even acknowledged that what I was experiencing was anxiety, I thought I was dying; heart palpitations, dizziness, vomiting. I couldn't breathe. I was certain in that moment that I was going to die. It wasn't until it began happening more frequently that I realised I wasn't having a heart attack, and that a panic attack – although utterly terrifying – couldn't kill me. That knowledge didn't help in the middle of the night though, when I would be catapulted from sleep with numb limbs and a wildly beating heart, a sense of impending doom at the forefront of my sleepy mind. I dreaded the loss of control, worried about the spontaneous nature of them, and all that worry and dread only served to fuel further episodes.

I let go of the sink, composing myself and allowing the light-headedness to pass before I turn and head upstairs to shower. I need to get out of the house, escape the place that should make me feel safe. It feels bigger than ever, full of hiding places and entry points I'd never considered before, a sense of danger lurking around every corner. The crux of the problem is: I have no idea what to do to make any of this any better.

∼

When I'm showered and dressed I go outside and begin walking into town, taking my phone out of my bag to check for messages – nothing. I had half expected a message from John and half hoped for a message from Nick. The sun has crept above the horizon – the beginning of a new day. The clouds block its path from time to time, the wind carrying them along and intermittently casting shadows on the world.

I arrive in town a little before nine and find that the Christmas spirit has arrived on the cobbled streets overnight, the other shop owners catching up with the eager few who'd struck out early. Lights adorn the shop windows, Christmas trees stand amongst festive displays, and *'Merry Christmas'* hangs in multicoloured lights from the town hall. I shake my head; it's not even December yet. I pass the library which is still sat in darkness and walk further down the street and into Mimi's. She's kept her decorations minimal – a small, white pre-lit Christmas tree on the counter and some fairy lights hung around the window. The breakfast crowd are sat huddled around the tables cradling mugs of coffee and bacon sandwiches. The smell wafts through the air and makes my stomach rumble.

"Morning, Erin. How are you?" Mimi chirps, handing some change to the man in front.

"Morning, I'm good thank you, how are you?"

"Good, darling, good. You look much better."

I smile. "Thank you."

"What can I get for you?"

"I'll have a coffee and a toasted teacake, please."

She presses some buttons on the till and I pay, noticing a queue forming behind me. "I'll bring it over, honey," she says.

I take one of the remaining seats at a small round table by the back of the room. A few minutes later, Mimi comes walking over with a tray, dodging in and out of the other customers. She puts the tray down on the table and I notice a small white envelope resting against my coffee. On the front, my name is scrawled in capital letters. My stomach sinks.

"This came for you." She picks the envelope up off of the tray and grins, oblivious.

Questions race through my mind, too thick and fast to pick them apart. Eventually, I manage to take the envelope from her. "Who from?"

"I don't know, it was here when I opened up this morning. Could it be from your *friend*?" She puts a particular emphasis on the word friend and raises her eyebrows, as though we share a secret she's eager to explore. I don't respond. She must be able to see the panic on my face because her expression changes, suddenly concerned. "What's wrong?"

"Just... it's... nothing, nothing's wrong." I'm staring at the envelope, trying to slow my thoughts, to think logically.

Mimi hovers next to me. "You don't think it's from your friend?" I don't know how to answer. "Why don't you open the letter and see?"

"I will," I say, putting it into my bag.

She lowers her voice and bends closer. "You must talk to me if you're in trouble."

"No trouble, just a bit confused."

She lingers by the table, concerned but resigned to being kept in the dark. "Okay, but like I said before, our door is always open to you."

"I know, thanks, Mimi."

She walks back to the counter to serve a middle-aged man in a suit, a brown briefcase in one hand and his mobile in the other. He orders while still holding the phone to his ear, between shouting commands at the unfortunate person on the other end. Mimi smiles politely, forever gracious.

I sip my coffee and take a few bites of my food, the hunger

from moments ago gone, replaced with the familiar nausea, the twisting and turning of my insides. I can see the street from where I sit, snippets of the life outside going by. The morning rush has arrived, the cobbled streets full of people in a hurry. Among the crowd I spot a familiar face – though I can't place where I know him from. He's in his twenties, tall and dark-haired. He walks alone, sipping on a takeaway coffee.

As I watch him walk past, twisting on my chair and craning my neck, it comes to me – it's the young man I saw Ian with a few days ago. My mind drifts briefly to Trish and Ian, their relationship and his supposed affair, the conversation we had at the party, but it's only a brief reprieve from my own life. I take a last sip of my coffee before getting up to leave. As I grab my bag I realise it feels heavier somehow – the letter inside an almost unbearable weight.

41

NOW

I leave Mimi's under a new cloud of dread. It's as though the man's invading every part of my life, every place where I've grown to feel familiar and safe. I look up and down the street, in all the shop windows, scanning the faces in the crowds. I don't know what I'm looking for, it's not a logical thought process but an intrinsic need to scan my surroundings, to check the places I had once wandered so freely.

As I turn right towards the library – one of my last remaining places of solace – I feel a hand brush my elbow, grasping for my attention. It makes me jump.

Lucy, Graham's wife, stands smiling, pulling her long red coat closed against the cold. "Erin, hi! What are you doing here?"

I want to walk away, to pretend I haven't seen or heard her, but her hand still lingers at my arm, holding me in her grip.

"Hi, I was just leaving actually…"

I can't stop and chat, I can't pretend as though everything is normal with the thought of the letter and what it may hold churning in my mind, stopping all other coherent thoughts.

"Where are you off to?" she asks.

"Home. I've been running a few errands."

"Same," she says, holding up her shopping bags as evidence. "I'm supposed to be meeting Graham actually but he must be running late."

She laughs uneasily and I can't work out whether it's due to the awkward conversation or the mention of Graham.

"Well, I'd better be going." I move away from her, a forced smile frozen on my face.

"Of course, of course. We should organise a girls' night out some time, it would be fun!"

She speaks with so much enthusiasm that it's hard to respond, to match her spirit no matter how forced. I wonder what she's trying to make up for or whether she genuinely wants to organise a night out. I can't help thinking it's just an easy way for her to piss off her husband, and I can't blame her.

"Sure," I say. "Speak soon."

I walk away towards the library but as I get into my stride I notice someone watching me, his back against the wall – he isn't trying to hide, he's just standing there, watching, his red hair standing out against the black of his suit. I refuse to be intimidated by him. As I pass I smile brightly.

"Hi, Graham."

He smirks, walking in the opposite direction towards his wife.

I come to the library and enter through the double doors at the front, heavy and stiff on their hinges, and through the second set of doors which lead into the maze of books in which I immerse myself. The coldness seems to accentuate the darkness, the high windows intermingled with the stained glass ones, not letting in nearly enough light for such a large building. The librarian smiles as I come into her view, but she doesn't speak – another reason I like it here; words are not wasted.

My eyes scan the spines of the books as I browse – the new

and the old, the ones I have visited countless times and the ones I have yet to encounter. I end up with a copy of *Moby Dick,* carrying it with me to the back of the room where I'm pleased to find it empty, the three large armchairs in the corner all deserted. I opt for the one directly under a patchwork of light filtering in through the stained glass window, slipping my trainers off and tucking my legs underneath me.

I flick through the book, reading about Ahab's pursuit for revenge; I wonder if the man sending the letters feels the same way. The thought sends a chill down my spine and I find myself looking around the library, checking I haven't been followed.

I open my bag and take out the envelope, looking over the familiar handwriting on the front; no address, just my name written in capitals. I take a deep breath, readying myself for something I know I don't want to see but nonetheless feel compelled to read. I open it and slowly remove the contents – a single A5 piece of paper. On it, written messily in black ink: *You killed them all.*

I swallow hard, shoving the paper back into the envelope and zipping both inside my bag, out of sight but not out of mind. I feel unable to think clearly. What if the two events are entirely unconnected; the attack and the letters? Have I been reading this all wrong? I put my head in my hands and rub my eyes. I've never believed in coincidences. I get out my phone and send a text to Nick, overriding my better judgement.

Are you free?

I sit back and wait for a reply. I don't have to wait long.

I can be in ten?

I press reply.

I'll come to you.

I return *Moby Dick* to its place on the shelves and leave.

~

Ten minutes later I'm at Nick's. He's sat at a desk typing away on a computer. He doesn't see me at first, engrossed in whatever he's doing, and I suddenly feel guilty for disturbing him. I watch as he works, occasionally moving the mouse around and then returning to his typing. He's dressed smartly again, a light-blue shirt tucked into a pair of black trousers, and he's trimmed his beard back so his jawline seems more defined. He looks younger. I knock lightly and he turns and smiles, waving me in. He stays seated and a moment later the printer whirrs to life.

"Sorry," he says. "I just needed to get this printed off then I'm free." He collects some paper from the printer and inserts it into a folder. "You okay?"

"I got another letter," I blurt out. I need to tell him before I decide it's a bad idea, another thing to keep to myself, hidden amongst the other doubts and fears.

"What does it say?"

I sit down on the sofa and he turns on his chair to look at me.

"He knows things about me."

"What do you mean?"

"I just wish this wasn't happening."

"Erin, what do you mean he knows things about you? What things?"

"He knows what happened when I was younger."

"The man who got into trouble?"

I nod and Nick runs his fingers through his stubble, thinking.

"Could it be him? Could he be sending the letters?"

"No." I shake my head. "It's not him."

"How do you know?"

"Because he's dead."

"Jesus. Okay, what about his family? Anyone else who might hold a grudge?"

I try to think but I can't. Tears begin to fall, fear taking hold as the magnitude of the situation is finally spoken out loud. Without saying anything he moves his chair closer so our knees are almost touching. He takes my hand in his and holds it. Our eyes meet and I have to fight the urge to move closer.

I want to kiss him, to become lost in him, to temporarily feel something other than terrified. The power of lust; its ability to remove everything else from your mind – all sense and logic, all foresight and reason – and render you at the mercy of the moment.

I stand, letting go of his hand. "I shouldn't be here. I'm sorry for disturbing you."

He pushes back on his chair, making space for me to leave. "You know, it's not always easier to leave. It might feel it at the time but in the long run..." He throws his arms out to the side, deflated.

"I'm sorry," I say.

"Don't be sorry, just don't run off every time we get close." He stands up and steps towards me, edging nearer. "I know you're married, I'm not asking for more than you can give. But don't you want to see if this is real? I feel something I haven't felt in a really long time."

So do I. I feel it with a force I haven't felt in fifteen years. A force that's wild and exciting but so terrifying that at times it feels paralysing. I don't know how to respond, how to tell him how I feel without revealing the things that will put an end to it all.

At a loss for words that will never come I reach out and take his hand. He responds, pulling me into him and holding me close, his arms a barrier between us and the world. My cheek rests against his chest and I become lost in the steady beat of his heart.

42

FIFTEEN YEARS AGO

I spend a week going through the motions with Dad, trying desperately to show him I've put myself back together, repaired the shattered pieces so well you can hardly see the cracks. After a few days, I begin to notice he's happier, content in the face of my obvious recovery. At times I feel bad, knowing full well that I'm manipulating him, intent on only one thing: I want him to feel comfortable enough to return to work, or at least leave me alone for long enough that I can go. The house has become a prison, a fortress with my own personal protector. I can't take it much longer.

At the end of the week I cook for us – a roast dinner with all the trimmings. It's barely edible but he eats it happily, appreciating the effort that's gone into it. When we're finished, I broach the subject casually while tidying away the plates, scraping the remnants into the bin.

"You know, Dad, I've been thinking: maybe you should consider going back to work?"

He stops what he's doing and watches me closely. "What makes you say that?"

"Well, I know how much you love your job. And I don't need

you here anymore, I'm getting the school work sent every week and I'm ahead with it all."

"I don't know, Erin, I think it's too soon."

"Dad, I want things to go back to normal. Or at least as normal as they can be. I'm trying to move forward." He sighs heavily. "I need this, Dad."

He looks down at the floor, avoiding my gaze. I can see he's thinking it through so I don't push him. I set about washing the pots, busying myself while he considers my proposal. Eventually, he grabs a tea towel and begins drying the plates that I've stacked on the draining board.

"Okay," he says simply.

"Okay?"

"Okay. We'll give it a go. I'll go back tomorrow, just for half a day. Then we'll take it from there."

"Thanks, Dad."

He leaves early, checking on me before he goes. I pretend to be asleep and that seems to satisfy him. He closes the door softly and I hear him creep down the stairs and out the front door, locking it behind him. I wait until I hear the sound of his engine before I get up. I'm already dressed – I was up before the sun, eager to start the day. I brush my hair and clean my teeth then head downstairs. There's a note on the kitchen table. *I'll be home for lunch. Dad.* I grab my coat, unlock the door and leave, hoping to get ahead of the morning rush.

The sun is rising, glorious shades of golden yellows, oranges and reds streaming from the horizon. It's a cold morning, winter is well and truly on its way, autumn almost a memory – one I'd rather forget. I ache for the summer, to relive the long warm nights with secret meetings in the forest. My eyes prickle at the memory.

I cut through the outskirts of the woodland, avoiding town and the early morning crowds, the familiar faces and judgemental whispers. It takes me just over half an hour. I'm careful – checking around corners and along the streets and lanes until I'm sure I won't bump into anyone.

When I get to his street, I wait on the corner. I can see his house – number twenty-three – stood back from the road, two cars parked on the driveway in front. I watch for a while, waiting, unsure what I'm hoping or expecting to see. A neighbouring family leaves in a flurry – first the mum hurrying three children into a car, then the dad five minutes later who leaves on a pushbike. I wait until they're all out of sight then I quickly cross over and slip down the side of the neighbouring property – the ones I have just watched leave.

I walk all the way to the end of the path so that I can peer over the fence and onto Danny's garden. I can see the chair where he sat when I came to see him. I can picture him now, the look on his face as I walked towards him, my skin prickling in anticipation, his eyes alive with expectation. I close my eyes and let my mind drift back to that night, to a moment in time that makes my chest ache with a longing that feels like a disease.

A noise to my left pulls me from the safety of my thoughts to the vulnerability of reality, making me jump. A door slamming. As I look around I see someone hurrying along the pavement, stopping as they come to the entrance to the property where I'm standing. A woman.

"It's you, isn't it?"

She walks down the path until she's standing a few steps away from me. Our eyes meet and I know instantly who she is. I've only seen pictures before, ones on Danny's desk, but it's unmistakeably her – Melissa, his wife.

"How dare you come here!" She keeps her voice low, barely above a whisper, yet it carries so much hate.

"I... I'm sorry, I just wanted..."

"Wanted what? Haven't you caused enough damage?"

I don't say anything. I feel like a child next to her. She looks like she's dressed for work, a fitted black pencil skirt with a dark-blue blouse tucked in. Her hair's redder than it looks in the photos, a deep auburn colour, and it hangs loose and wavy over her shoulders. She looks tired and drawn, her eyes red against her pale skin. As I look at her, wondering what I could possibly say, I notice a tear run down her cheek.

"You've taken everything from me," she says, her voice breaking. And in that moment I have never felt smaller, a sudden realisation that this woman is not just a name or a picture, she is a real person with emotions, with feelings and a full beating heart – one I have helped to break.

"I'm sorry." I try to hold back the tears that are trying to force their way out. "I'm so, so sorry."

She doesn't say anything at first and the silence stretches out for so long that I begin to wonder whether she is going to say anything else at all, or whether she is waiting for me to leave. Eventually, she dabs at her eyes with the back of her hand and I can see that she's been trying to compose herself, to hold back emotions I do not deserve to see.

"You're just a child," she says. "It's not your fault."

I can't tell whether she is trying to be cruel. "I'm just as much to blame as..."

She holds up her hand to me. "Don't. Don't say his name." She bites her lip. She's shivering, standing in the crisp morning breeze without a coat. "Do you want to come in?"

"Your house?" I ask, confounded by her invitation.

"Yes. Don't worry, he's not here. He's staying with his folks and the children are with my sister. I needed some time alone."

"Are you sure?" I don't know whether I'm asking her or myself. I've replayed all of the possible scenarios in my head a hundred times – it's all I've thought about all week – but this situation is beyond anything I could have expected, one I don't feel prepared for.

She nods and turns to walk back to the house. I follow – up one path and down another. She lets us in through the front door into a small but tidy living room with cream walls and beige carpets. I didn't come in here last time.

"Sit," she says, gesturing to an armchair. She sits opposite on the sofa and pulls her skirt down to cover her knees.

I do as she says. "I'm sorry I came," I say, and I realise I am. It's such an invasion of privacy, how could I not see that before? Why had I expected that he would still be here?

"Why did you come?"

"I wanted to tell him that it wasn't me. I didn't report him."

"I know that," she says calmly.

"You do?"

She nods. "Yes. I was the one who reported my husband."

My heart races. "How did you know?"

"My husband has had many affairs." She pauses for effect and it works, the revelation landing like a blow to my stomach. "But he has never slept with one of his students before. I could let so much pass for the sake of our children but this." She gestures to me as though I am a prop in a story. She looks repulsed. "I couldn't let him get away with it."

"How did you find out?" I need to know.

"He's not a clever man, and you are just a child." She doesn't elaborate and I know better than to push her further. I shouldn't expect anything from her. "Tell me something," she says. "Who pursued who?"

I feel an urge to leave, her questions embarrassing me and

causing me to question everything. "I should go," I say, getting up.

"Please don't, I think you owe me an answer."

I sit back down again, unable to argue. I do owe her. I owe her more than I could possibly give by answering her.

"Both, I guess. It was both of us."

"Oh come on, one of you must have made the first move."

"Me," I say, hoping to put an end to this line of questioning. "I made the first move."

She raises her eyebrows. "It's very noble of you to try to protect him, but you should know this: never has a man been less worthy of your loyalty."

She gets up and walks over to a bookcase in the corner of the room. It's mainly books but there's a shelf near the top that's full of pictures, all neatly framed. She picks one up and hands it to me. It's a photo of them on their wedding day. She looks beautiful – unchanged by time, her auburn hair pulled back off her face, a veil trailing to the floor. He looks younger, still handsome but different. He's smiling at her as she beams at the camera, her hand resting on his chest. I stare at it for a moment, not wanting to look but unable to stop myself. Then she takes it back, looking at it with a pained expression so raw that it catches my breath.

"Fifteen years ago," she says. "Fifteen years of marriage to a man I don't know." She sits back on the sofa, placing the photo face down on the armrest beside her. "You aren't the first, and you won't be the last." I look at my hands clenched in my lap, avoiding having to look at her; at the consequence of my actions. She carries on. "I know what you're going through, I know all the ways you're trying to justify it in your head, telling yourself he's not a paedophile."

I recoil at the word. How could she call him that? I stand to leave, moving towards the door. "I have to go, my dad will be wondering where I am."

"Of course." She gets up and opens the door. As she does, she stands closer than she had before and I can smell the distinct odour of alcohol – a spirit of some kind. Whisky, maybe. There's also an undertone of something else – sweat, I think. Closer to her, I can make out the make-up that's been there for days, the hair that's begun to knot. I wonder how long it's been since she showered. "Forget about him, Erin, I have."

I hear the door close behind me, then the desperate sobs of a broken woman clearly audible from inside. I walk home, trying to forget the only man I've ever loved while all the while remembering him. How easy it was to fall in love, and how impossible it seems to forget.

43

NOW

I pull away, embarrassed. "I'm sorry."

Nick steps towards me, closing the gap I've tried to create. I wish he wouldn't, I wish he would tell me to leave because I don't feel strong enough to let go, to make the choices I promised myself I'd make. He reaches out and brushes my hair away from my face, his eyes burrowing into me in a way that makes me feel so uncomfortably vulnerable.

I feel like he can see inside me, as though he is reaching into my mind and plucking through the chaos with his eyes. I'm scared he won't like what he sees. I look down at my hands but he gently puts his finger under my chin and lifts my face up to meet his.

"Stop apologising," he says softly. He smiles and his eyes light up with it. I can't help but smile back.

"I have a meeting after lunch but I'm free until then. Come on, I'll make you a drink." He takes hold of my hand and leads me to the back of the room, holding the door open for me. I head up the stairs, Nick following. When we reach the top, he opens the door and Bear comes over to greet us, his tail wagging. "Hey, boy," Nick says, fussing him. "Look who's come to see us."

We go inside and I stroke Bear while Nick goes straight over to the kitchen and grabs a couple of mugs out of the cupboard.

"Coffee?" he asks.

"Please."

I hear the coffee machine come to life as I take a seat at the kitchen island.

"Have you always lived here alone?" I surprise myself, I'm not usually one to pry.

He carries on busying himself in the kitchen. "Yeah, can you tell?"

I look around at the sparsely decorated flat, the classy but minimal furnishings. "You're very tidy."

He sits down opposite, handing me a mug full of coffee. "I like to be organised. What about you, have you always lived in Kestwell with your husband?"

The mention of John makes me cringe. "Yes, I've never lived on my own, actually."

"Never?"

I shake my head. "Never."

"So where did you live between leaving home and meeting John?"

I shrug. "Various places, lodging or flat sharing."

"It must have been hard, leaving home and going it alone."

"It was." I think back to those first few weeks. The loneliness was suffocating, almost unbearable.

"You're very resilient," he says.

"I don't know about that."

"You've been through a lot, and you're still so young."

"Not *that* young." I smile.

He raises his eyebrows – a question in his eyes. *How old are you?*

"Would you believe it was my thirtieth birthday on the day we met?"

His face drops, his eyes suddenly sad. "It was your birthday on the day you were attacked?"

I nod.

"That's really awful. I'm sorry."

"It's not your fault. Besides, it's not like I had any plans."

"You weren't going to celebrate?"

"No, I just wanted it to pass by without a fuss."

I laugh at the irony, but it's hollow. I can see on his face that he wants to say more than he feels able to. He goes to speak but hesitates, taking a drink from his mug instead.

"What?" I ask.

"Didn't your husband want to make it special for you?"

I look away, feeling my cheeks burn. The sun is streaming in through the open curtains, bathing us in a soft golden glow. I look at Nick, his silhouette clear against the backdrop of the sun; his broad shoulders and strong arms. I feel as though I might lose myself in the chaos of having two conversations at once; one with Nick and the internal one, warning myself not to let it go too far. I try to focus. He shifts in his chair.

"Sorry," he says. "I didn't mean to make you feel uncomfortable."

"No, it's okay. He was away and some things are just easier to ignore when you're on your own."

Something flickers across his face and I can see he feels sorry for me, though he's trying not to show it. It makes me want to physically withdraw, to create space between us for his pity to fall so that it doesn't reach me.

"You don't have to feel sorry for me," I say softly. "This is nothing new."

"I don't feel sorry for you, I just..." He trails off, searching for the right words. "You deserve better."

I have a nice life, I think. I have a home and financial security. I have resources. It's more than I deserve. Yet, somehow, faced with the prospect of Nick it all feels like nothing, as though I've been avoiding the one thing that makes it all worthwhile.

"What happened," I ask tentatively, wanting to change the conversation entirely, "with your wife?"

He immediately looks away, as though looking at me in the wake of my question is too painful. I wonder if I've made a mistake, expected too much, but I wait out the silence, knowing I can't take it back.

"She wasn't well for a long time."

"How long ago did she pass away?"

"Almost three years."

"I'm sorry," I say. And I mean it. I wish I could ease the pain he feels.

"It's strange; I knew she wasn't well and it wasn't exactly unexpected but..." He trails off again.

"Nothing can prepare you for grief."

He nods. "No, it can't."

"How long were you married?"

"Almost nine years."

"You must have met when you were very young."

I'm surprised by my own curiosity, the level of intrigue I feel. It's overriding the voice in my head telling me not to pry.

"Yeah, I guess we *were* young." He doesn't expand. He seems lost in a memory and I leave him to come back to the present on his own, watching as the corners of his mouth lift into a half-smile. "Do you want another?" he says, breaking away from his memory and lifting his mug.

"No, thank you. I'd better let you get back to work."

He checks his watch. "Let me take you home."

"No, it's fine, I enjoy the walk."

"I don't like the idea of you walking home alone. It's not safe."

"It's midday and I'll be sticking to the main roads. I'll be fine, honestly."

He thinks it over for a moment, clearly not wanting to overstep the boundaries we are still establishing. "Will you text me and let me know you get home okay?"

I smile. "Sure."

"Fancy a walk tomorrow?"

John's plan surfaces – *We could go somewhere different together this weekend if you like?* I shudder at the thought of spending the day with him, pretending to each other and the world that we're a happily married couple.

"Tomorrow might be tricky," I say.

"Course, it's the weekend. Say no more." He speaks without any resentment which only makes it harder.

"If I can make it work, I'll let you know."

He smiles, a glimmer of hope in his eyes.

We walk back downstairs and into his studio. The cobbled streets beyond the windows are alive with the lunchtime rush – I feel exposed, as though we're on display. Nick seems to notice and heads straight for the door.

"I'll let you get off," he says. "Just let me know you get home okay."

"I will."

As I slip out the door his hand briefly connects with mine – one tight squeeze before he retreats back into his studio. I walk slowly back through town, the sun high and bright in the sky. And all the way home I think about him: the kindness in his eyes, the strength in his arms, the sound of his heart beating. The way he is slowly becoming my undoing.

44

FIFTEEN YEARS AGO

I walk back through town, too angry to care about the stares and the whispers. A couple of women pushing prams walk towards me, their hushed conversation growing deliberately louder as I pass them. *A respected teacher... with a family...* I look away, repulsed at the thought of two strangers judging me, basing their opinions on tabloid stories and local gossip, and putting things together that don't belong.

I go over and over my conversation with Melissa, trying to understand how she could have known. I know it must have been the bracelet. I grimace at the realisation that my own stupidity planted the seed of doubt, set her on a path of suspicion that led her, somehow, to me. I still can't work out how. I go over and over the same questions in my mind, answers never materialising, only more questions.

Outside Marks and Spencer's I see Aiden Rogers from school, bunking off with a couple of faces I don't recognise. "Look," he shouts, "it's that slag that shagged Mr Miller then dobbed him in to the pigs." I walk faster, aware of the attention his shouts have garnered.

"Slow down, I just want to talk." He's caught up with me,

walking at my side and blowing the smoke from his cigarette into my path. "Just thought I'd offer my services now Miller's out the picture." I carry on walking, ignoring him and silently pleading with a god I don't believe in to make him go away. "Too young am I? Hello? I'm talking to you."

"I'm not interested," I snap.

"Suit yourself, slag." He stops walking, though he doesn't return to his friends. Instead, he stands shouting insults at me, so loud I can hear him for what seems like miles, his voice reverberating between the stares of everyone I pass.

I get in the house and collapse into a fit of tears that never seem to end, an outpouring of emotions I'm unable to contain. I feel as though I'm trapped in a life I'm not prepared for, facing consequences that seem too harsh. Over and over again I think, *all I did was fall in love.*

Dad arrives home earlier than I'd expected and finds me red-eyed, in a pathetic heap on the living-room floor, cuddling a cushion covered in my tears. He swallows hard and I see it flit across his face: the realisation that it was a mistake to leave me.

"What happened, Erin?" He sits down beside me, his back against the sofa, and puts his arm around my shoulders. "You left the house, didn't you?"

"Everyone hates me," I cry.

"No," he says flatly. "No they don't." He kisses my head repeatedly, buying time to think about what he should say. But there's nothing he can say; I am not the victim in this, I'm the promiscuous teenager who led a respected family man astray. "You need to speak to the police, Erin. You need to tell them the truth." He strokes my hair, just like he did when I was little. "You were with him the night you told me you were at that party, weren't you?"

I sit up, looking at him. "Yes. I was at his house." I feel

something shift between us; the acknowledgement that I've reached my limit on lies, the truth now beginning to seep out.

He grimaces, repulsed by the idea. "Please, talk to the police. Tell them everything."

Tears begin to fall again. "He'll never forgive me."

"Don't you dare protect him, he hasn't given you the same courtesy."

"He was scared, that's all. He would never deliberately hurt me."

Dad sighs heavily then grabs my hand, holding it in his. "He said you pursued him. That you made a nuisance of yourself at school. He said he asked you to stay away from him."

"I know what he told them, Dad. I know. It's not true. He would never have told them those things if he had any other choice."

"You know, Erin, you can never judge a man by how he acts at his best. You have to see him at his worst; at his weakest. You have to watch him try to overcome adversity, then you'll see him for who he really is."

45

NOW

I arrive home and let myself sink into the sofa, emotionally drained. I close my eyes hoping for the exhaustion to slip seamlessly into sleep but it never comes, always slightly out of reach. I keep seeing images of the man – his pale, milky eyes beneath the balaclava, the faceless figure watching me from outside. I go to the windows – first the lounge and then the kitchen – and check the road outside, craning my neck to try to see beyond the driveway. It's all quiet.

Across the road, Pete's house sits in silence. I check the door and check it again – it's locked but somehow that no longer gives me the assurance it once did, a simple lock now seeming quite trivial. I've left my mobile in my bag in the hallway and I hear it beep softly as I pass. I pull it out and check the display – a message from Nick.

Did you get home okay?

I realise I forgot to let him know, not used to people waiting for me to check in.

Yes, home now. Thanks for the coffee.

Seconds later I get a reply.

Anytime. Let me know about tomorrow.

I think about it for a while, wondering whether there's any way I could put John off spending time together this weekend. He usually works on Saturdays and is happy to spend Sundays playing golf or recovering from the night before – an arrangement we've silently agreed upon over the years. We used to spend Sundays together in the early days – lunch in town or lazy days at home – but it seems like a distant memory now. I wonder if that's what he's trying to get back. I can't think of anything I could say or any reason I could give that would be believable and reasonable. I don't want to offend him, I can't afford to create bigger problems right now. I need to keep everything else in my life as calm as possible.

A memory comes to me, unwanted yet vivid: I'm waiting to go in the sea. Dad's sitting in his rickety blue-and-white-striped deckchair, a newspaper in his hand and a beige bucket hat perched on top of his head. 'You must respect the water, Erin. No more than knee-deep, okay?' I nod. I have a new bucket, it's orange and shaped like a castle.

I paddle in, excited to use it, to catch the waves and whatever is in them. I scoop up the froth and examine it for shells and fish but there is nothing but sandy water. I empty it back into the waves and scoop up another bucketful. This time, I find a cockle shell inside, a flawless fan shape. I pick it out and turn to face my dad, waving it at him from the sea, but he isn't looking. He's talking to Mr Brooks, the fisherman who lives around the corner. I shout to them but they don't hear me over the sounds of the beach; it's busy today, busier than I've seen it in a long time – the sun has enticed people from out of town.

I turn away from them, stepping further into the sea. The waves seem to have calmed, a flat mirror-like surface stretching all the way to the horizon. *Another few steps won't hurt,* I think. I walk further in, unafraid and invincible. The water is up to my waist and I turn round expecting to see my dad dashing towards me, demanding I get out. But he isn't, he's still lost in conversation with Mr Brooks.

I turn back to the sea, to the eerily calm waters that, just moments ago, had been chopping at my knees. Then it all happens so fast: my feet are swept out from under me and I plummet beneath the surface, taking in a mouthful of salty water as I hit the seabed. I can feel myself being pulled, an invisible force moving my weightless body, suspended somewhere between floating and sinking.

I kick upwards and gulp at the air. 'Help! Help! Dad! Help!' I am being pulled out to sea by unseen tides at my feet, rough and wild. I kick at the floor but it's disappeared, the seabed vanishing from under my feet. I try to swim, I know I *can* swim, but the force is just too much, I can't fight against it – I am at the mercy of the sea.

The beach is drifting further and further away. My eyes are sore from the sea water and I feel nauseous from the amount I have swallowed. I have given in to panic; early attempts to keep calm now lost in the rough waters that have claimed me. I take a desperate gulp of air before I am dragged under once more, propelled downwards and yet further out to sea. I close my eyes and surrender.

A hand grabs first at my shoulder then my wrist, pulling me until I break the surface. I'm gasping for breath, greedy, desperate gasps. My dad's pulling me, but not towards the beach. I don't question it, I kick the water to ease the burden of my weight. He turns to me and shouts: 'We need to get out of the rip tide.' He never lets go, pulling me parallel to the shoreline. Moments later, I feel a shift in the sea, an easing under the surface. Calm being restored.

We swim back towards shore – Dad's hand firmly wrapped around my arm – until his feet find the seabed where he picks me up and carries me until we are back on land. I cry into his chest for a long time, shivering in the midday sun, then he wraps me in a towel and kneels down in front of me, his breathing laboured.

His eyes are watering but I can't tell whether it's from the sea or the emotion. I hope it's the former. His hair sticks to his forehead and his checked shirt clings to him. 'That was a rip tide, Erin. You can't swim your way out of a rip tide. You have to swim parallel to the beach, if you can, until you come out of it. If you can't, you float. But you never panic. Erin, tell me, what do you do in a rip tide?' I repeat it back to him, through sobs and shaky breaths, his hands never once letting me go. 'It looks calm on the surface but the current is hiding underneath. Calm on the surface does *not* mean calm underneath. You must remember that, Erin. You must remember that always.'

That night I fall asleep on his chest dreaming about my orange bucket drifting over the ocean towards exotic lands. At some point in the night I am woken by unfamiliar sounds. Dad's dreaming, indecipherable words full of urgency. I go to wake him, my hand gently on his chest, when he shouts out: 'I can't save you! I can't save you! I can't save you!'

The next day, bright and early, we return to the beach. No deckchair this time. No conversations with the jolly old fisherman. Half-smiles and tentative steps towards the sea. But we do it – we swim in the waves until our arms ache and our bellies growl with hunger. 'We respect the sea, Erin, but we don't fear it.'

~

John arrives home late. I hear an engine ticking over outside, distant conversation standing out amongst an otherwise quiet evening. I turn out the light and go to the window. On the pavement beyond the driveway a taxi idles, the lights illuminating the road ahead. John is fumbling around in his pockets, talking to the faceless driver hidden among the shadows. I watch, waiting for him to pay and let the taxi drive away, but he doesn't. He staggers towards the front door and rings the bell, over and over again. I unlock the door.

"Babe, I need cash," he slurs.

I don't say anything. I grab my bag from the hallway and take out my purse, handing him a twenty-pound note.

"Keep going," he says.

I pass him another ten which he snatches from my hand. He stumbles back towards the taxi and tosses the money inside, slamming the door behind him. As the taxi drives away I notice a light come on across the road, in the window above the kitchen – Pete's bedroom, most likely. I take a deep breath then pad out onto the driveway to escort John back inside. He slings his arm around my shoulders and I grimace under his weight, my ribs protesting.

"Watch your step," I say, guiding him inside.

I shut the door and lock it, noticing the light across the street is still on.

"Good night?" I ask.

"Just went out for a few beers with the lads."

He stands at the bottom of the stairs balancing against the bannister. "Let's go to bed." His eyes are glazing over and he can't stop moving, swaying against the bannister he's clinging onto.

"Where's your wallet?"

"You just want my money."

"John, have you lost your wallet? Do you need to cancel your credit cards?"

He shrugs. "Fuck 'em."

I decide to leave it – if he doesn't care, why should I?

"Go on up to bed, I'll bring you some water."

"You're no fun anymore. Why aren't you fun anymore?"

I think about his question and how to respond. He seems to be waiting for an answer, genuinely curious. I wonder if he means because I don't drink myself into the states he gets in, but that's nothing new – apart from the odd glass of champagne when we started dating, I've never drunk, always too afraid to relinquish control. I think about asking him why he isn't kind anymore, why he doesn't make me feel safe and loved, but I know there is no point – it isn't really him talking, it's the alcohol encouraging him to pick a fight, to ignite something he can mistake for passion.

"Go to bed, John."

I begin to walk past him, into the kitchen to fetch him some water, but he grabs my wrist on the way past, pulling me back. It startles me. "Ouch. What are you doing?"

"You know what my friends say about you?" he asks, but he doesn't wait for a reply. "They say you're a stuck-up little bitch. That you're only with me for my money." He laughs, maintaining his grip on my wrist. "Why don't you fuck me anymore, huh?"

His face is red, his pupils a pinprick against the green of his eyes.

I step backwards, trying to pull away from his grip, but he doesn't let go. "John, you're hurting me."

A silence stretches out with so much hanging in the balance, a potential for things that can't be undone. I look him in the eyes, daring him to cross the line. Then he drops my wrist and turns to go to bed.

I go into the kitchen and pour myself a glass of water. I'm shaking, the adrenaline pumping through my veins. I take some deep breaths, controlling my breathing and slowing my thoughts. Amidst the anger, relief begins to surface. I finally have my excuse.

46

FIFTEEN YEARS AGO

"There's been an accident."

Dad's face is pale, his eyes alive with a panic he's trying to suppress. He's leaning against the kitchen worktop, his hands holding onto the edge; I can't tell if this is a necessity. He looks suddenly very faint and I begin to worry.

"What's wrong, Dad?"

My mind flits between family members scattered around the country – Aunt Kath in Manchester, Grandma in Kent, Uncle Wayne in Lincoln – all of them distant in every sense of the word. It doesn't feel right, the reaction on his face doesn't match the possibilities I can think of.

Dad takes off his glasses and places them on the worktop, rubbing his eyes with his fingertips.

"Dad?"

"Mr Miller," he says. "He's dead."

47

NOW

I sleep on the sofa, dressed and ready to leave early. My wrist hurts, an angry red line circling where John's hand had been. Part of me is pleased; it adds credibility to my reason to abandon our plans. I read for a while, enjoying the comfort of familiar words, unable or unwilling to sleep.

It's not the first time John's drinking has been a problem but I'm keenly aware of the escalation in recent years. Six months ago, he didn't return home after work on a Friday. I'd gone to bed only to be woken at 6am by a window smashing and the alarm whirring to life. He'd lost his keys and tried to break in.

When I'd opened the door, he'd stumbled into the shattered glass and cut his arm. Bleeding, he looked me right in the eye and told me to clean it up. 'It's about time you did something to help out around here.' I'd walked out and got in the car, leaving him alone with the fallout of his bad decisions. I'd driven to the beach. It was May, a beautiful spring day. The sun had kept me company late into the evening. I hadn't wanted to leave but had nowhere else to go.

When I arrived home, he'd asked me where I'd been. I told him what had happened and he looked genuinely ashamed of himself. It made it harder to hold onto the anger, but the disappointment remained. He didn't drink for a month after that. I wonder whether he'll remember this time.

Shortly after 3am I reluctantly surrender to a restless sleep, my eyes no longer able to fight the invisible force compelling them to close. But it's short-lived and before long I am pulled from a nightmare I can't recall, my heart racing and a thin layer of sweat covering my body. I check the time, listening for any indication that John is awake, but it's only 5.30. I quietly get my coat and bag and rummage around for my keys on the sideboard. Jumble has accumulated, things we neither want to put away nor throw away – mail yet to be opened, flyers and advertisements, my headphones and John's work phone. Amongst the odds and ends I find Ray's card and slip it into my bag, then I grab my keys which I find under a pair of John's leather gloves.

The night has yet to be tainted by the sun, the black skies penetrated only by a tiny sliver of the moon which hangs high above the horizon. It doesn't look real, the contrast so vivid. The early birds are awake, their songs muffled by the dull howls of the wind. I get in the car and take out my phone.

I don't think he's going to answer at first, the ringing seems to go on for longer than I should have allowed, but eventually he picks up.

"Hello?" I hear Nick stifle a yawn.

"Sorry to wake you."

"Erin?"

"Yeah, sorry to call you so early."

"It's okay, my alarm's due to go off any minute."

"Really? Why so early?"

"I was going to go for a run. You okay?"

"I'm okay. It turns out I'm free today, if you still fancied a walk?"

He laughs. "I'd love to, but why are you up so early?"

"I thought we could go somewhere different."

"I'm intrigued."

"I'm in the car, I can come and pick you up?"

"Park round the back and I'll drive, you still need to rest."

I smile. "Okay, but it's a long drive."

"I'd better get ready then, hadn't I?"

Ten minutes later I'm pulling into the small car park behind the back of his studio. I grab my bag off the passenger seat and lock up. The studio is in darkness but I see a light on upstairs. I ring the bell, not expecting him to hear, then the window above me is pushed open and I see Nick leaning out, smiling.

"Give me five minutes?" he asks.

He's shirtless and his hair is wet, fresh from the shower.

"Sure, I'll wait in the car."

I walk back round the corner and sit and wait in the warmth of the car. I look in the mirror and run my fingers through my hair, trying to make myself look more presentable. As I do, I catch a glimpse of the brown envelope of Ray's card poking out of my open bag. I pull it out and open it. It's a simple, square card with *Happy Birthday* written in gold on the front. I open it and feel something fall out onto my lap. It's a rectangular piece of paper that I recognise instantly – it's a cheque. I frown, confused. Ray always sends a card, but he never buys me gifts or gives me money. I read the card first, looking for an explanation. *Happy Birthday, Erin. Thirty is still young. Love, Ray.* Puzzled, I pick up the cheque, turning it over and reading it with a lurch to my stomach. Written in capitals, then repeated in digits, is the amount – Two hundred thousand pounds.

I pull my phone out of my bag and search for his number,

checking over my shoulder to make sure Nick hasn't appeared. It's just past six and I wonder whether it's too early to call Ray, but I can't wait. Just as I think it's about to go to voicemail, he answers.

"Hello?" His voice is barely above a whisper and I can hear the muffled sounds of movement, a door closing softly. He's moving somewhere quiet, away from Agnes.

"Ray? Sorry to wake you but I've just opened my card."

"I was beginning to wonder when you'd call."

"What the hell, Ray? Two hundred thousand pounds? Why?" The questions are coming out without thinking, too many at once.

"I was left some money when my mum died. My brother and I sold the house and shared it between us."

"That doesn't answer my question. Why have you given it to *me*? I can't accept it."

"You're young enough to start again, should you wish. I don't want you to think you don't have options. That's how I ended up where I am."

I can hear the sound of a car in the background – he's stepped outside.

"I don't understand, Ray. I really don't. Are you telling me to leave John?"

"No," he blurts, "I'm not telling you to leave him." I hear him sigh. "I've spent the biggest part of my life married to a woman who makes me feel inferior at every opportunity. Have I lived a good life? Sure, I can't complain. I've had an easy life. Would I do things differently if I could turn back time?" There's a pause and I wonder whether it's a rhetorical question but then he speaks, sounding dejected. "Money can't buy happiness."

"But you've always defended John."

"He's my son," Ray says flatly.

"And Agnes – why didn't you leave her? Why didn't you start again once John was older, or after she'd had an affair?"

"I didn't know how to. I was in too deep. My home, my family, my job – it all depended on her."

"Not now. You could keep the money, start over."

"I'm too old for that, Erin. But you aren't."

"I don't know what to say."

"Then don't say anything. Just open a bank account in your name and deposit the cheque. Then it's there if you decide to use it."

I don't respond, looking at the cheque in my hand.

"I see a lot of myself in you," he says softly. "I know who you are. I know you must have been desperate. Scared. John must have seemed like a safe place to lay low."

My heart is racing. "What do you mean? What do you know?"

"Danny Miller. I know what happened. It wasn't your fault."

I have so many questions I want to ask but I can't seem to formulate them, to turn them into words.

"It's okay," he says, "I've known for years. Your secret's safe with me."

"How?"

I try to think of ways he could know – I wasn't in the newspapers, my identity only known locally due to the constraints of living in a small town quick to criticise and ostracise.

"Let's talk properly. Next week. I'll come and see you."

I hold the phone to my ear in a trembling hand, full of emotions I can't seem to process.

"Erin?"

"I'm here."

"Just keep the cheque safe and away from prying eyes. We'll speak properly next week."

"Okay. Okay. See you next week."

I let the phone drop into my lap, staring ahead at a brick wall, unable to break my stare. I feel as though I have just had information poured into my brain, chaotic and unorganised, and I can't move for fear that it will escape. I try to absorb it, to make sense of it, but in the process I'm startled by a knock at my window.

It's Nick. His smile turns to concern when he sees the look on my face. He opens the door slowly, as though he's afraid I'll fall out, too weak and vulnerable to hold my own weight.

"You okay?" he asks.

I sit looking at him, suddenly feeling very tired. I realise I'm still holding the cheque, the weight of what it stands for suddenly burning in my hands. I shove it inside my bag.

"Yes. Yes, I'm okay," I say, trying to pull myself together.

"You sure?"

I nod. "Sure."

I get out and he unlocks his car, walking to the driver's side. I get in and buckle my seatbelt.

"You're not bringing Bear?" I ask.

"I wasn't sure where we were going so I've asked a friend of mine to walk him." Nick starts the engine. "So, where are we going?"

"The beach," I say.

He smiles, reversing out onto the quiet cobbled streets.

"The beach it is."

48

NOW

I direct him to the south-east coast, to the same beach I'd walked along just days ago. The journey is smooth, the roads moving easily as the sun breaks free from the horizon. The winds continue, the howls protesting as we speed east towards the sea.

"So, what was all that about earlier?" he asks.

"What do you mean?"

"I saw you on the phone. You looked tense – I didn't want to interrupt."

"Oh. It was nothing really."

I want to forget about the phone call and cheque, about John and the letters – I want to put everything else temporarily out of my mind.

"And what about the bruising on your wrist? Is that nothing too?"

I turn to look at Nick, surprised and mortified that he has seen. I don't want to drag him into my marital problems. I look down at my wrist which is an angry red and pull my coat sleeve down, trying to cover it.

"Did *he* do it?" he asks.

"Did who do what?" I say, trying to act oblivious.

"Did your husband cause that bruise on your wrist?"

I put my head in my hands and take a deep breath in, unable to keep telling half-truths and lies. I don't want to lie anymore. I don't want to hide something from everyone.

"Yes, but it isn't what you think. He'd had too much to drink and grabbed my wrist, that's all."

"That's all? Has he hurt you before?"

"No," I lie, my mind drifting back to his birthday in October. I'd hit my head on the wall as he pushed past me. To this day, I'm still unsure whether he meant to do it.

"It's not right, it's not right at all. He doesn't deserve you."

Nick seems angry, gripping the steering wheel hard enough to turn his knuckles white. I want to forget about last night.

"You don't have to worry about me."

"But I do worry about you. Surely you see that?"

We come to a roundabout and he slows to a halt before easing out into the flow of traffic.

"I'm sorry," I say, and I realise it could apply to so many things. "I'm sorry I've complicated your life."

"You haven't."

"We both know that isn't true."

He glances at me. "You're going through a hard time, and I get the feeling I only know a small part of it."

"You and me both."

He raises his eyebrows then moves over to the fast lane to overtake a car towing a caravan. "How do you mean?"

"I don't know – the letters, the attack."

"You can't think of anyone who has motive?"

"A lot of people didn't like what happened – it was a small town and a lot of people thought it was my fault but..." I trail off.

"But you don't think they disliked you enough to do this?"

"I honestly don't."

I've thought about it a lot over the past few days, trying to access the darkest corners of my mind to reach memories from long ago. Faces surfaced that I hadn't thought about in years, but no one who harboured enough hate to track me down over a hundred miles away and attack me in the woods. No one who's still alive, anyway.

We arrive at Minnis Bay just after half past eight, the sprawling sands a welcome sight beyond the coastal path. I swallow down an urge to fling the door open and run barefoot towards the sea. It's choppier today, the waves rough and wild, gusts of wind pushing and pulling them towards the land. The tide is in, leaving only a narrow stretch of damp sand, the swash almost covering it entirely in the aftermath of the waves.

Nick sits watching the sea, his hands still resting on the steering wheel. "Let's go," he says.

We get out and cross the car park to the coastal path, quiet except for a couple of morning walkers.

"Do you want to get a coffee first?" I ask.

"Sure." He looks around. "Which way?"

I point ahead, along the path which leads to a seafront café I've visited a few times before. We walk quickly, the wind fresh and harsh against my cheeks.

"Is this where you came the other day?" he asks.

"Yes, it's the closest bay to Kestwell."

"Really? I've never been to this stretch of the coast, always further north."

I look in the direction of Norfolk, of Dad, wondering if that's where Nick means. I want to ask, but I stop myself. We reach the café and head inside, grabbing a table by the large windows overlooking the seafront. Seagulls cover the wall, waiting for an opportunity to dive down and grab any scraps of food left behind by the steady stream of customers.

"Shall we get some breakfast?" he asks.

I read from the menu above the counter and end up ordering the same as Nick – a bacon butty and a coffee. We sit opposite each other and wait for our food.

"So," I say, "what do you think to your winter beach experience so far?"

He laughs. "I'm enjoying the company."

He reaches out across the table to take my hand. I let him. He pushes back my sleeve and gently rubs the red line that encircles my wrist, a solemn look on his face.

"This isn't okay." There's something about how he says it that makes me feel as though he's talking more to himself than to me. "You need to leave him."

I pull my hand away, retreating to my side of the table. The waitress arrives with our coffees, placing them down heavily and causing them to spill.

"Whoops," she says, mopping it up with some napkins. "Your food will be out in just a sec."

When she's out of earshot Nick tries again, his voice hushed but firm. "Erin, you need to leave him."

"I can't," I say, but already I'm beginning to question whether that's true. I rest my hand on top of my bag on the seat beside me, the cheque stuffed safely inside. It isn't the chance of having my own money that's set the thought process in motion, it's what it represents: the acknowledgement from Ray that it is possible, the support from someone championing a future I had written off long ago.

"Why?" Nick asks.

"I... I..."

"I get it – it's not an easy decision. It's hard to make huge changes, to bet on yourself."

"It honestly never occurred to me that my marriage would ever come to an end."

It's the truth. When I married John I was happy to remain in a little bubble for the rest of my life, never imagining anything or anyone would feel worth disturbing the calm for.

"Things change," he says.

The waitress returns with our food and sets it down in front of us. "Can I get you anything else?"

"No thanks, I think we're good," Nick replies.

She wipes her hands on her apron and heads back behind the counter.

My phone vibrates softly from my bag. I pull it out and check the display – John. I let it ring out then place it on the table.

"Is that him?" Nick asks.

I nod. "Probably calling to see where I am. I left before he was awake this morning."

Nick takes a bite of his food and I do the same. My phone springs to life again, vibrating against the table – a message from John.

Where are you?

I look at Nick who raises his eyebrows. I switch my phone off and return it to my bag – John can spend the day alone with his guilt, asking himself whether he went too far this time.

After we've eaten we stroll back down the coastal path, stopping when we come to an opening. We take off our shoes and socks and walk leisurely down the beach towards the sea which has begun its retreat. I don't stop.

"You're not going in are you? It's freezing!"

"You have to get your feet wet at the beach."

I roll up my jeans and paddle into the waves so the water skims my ankles. He stands a few steps away, looking at me as though I've lost my mind.

"Come on!" I laugh.

Reluctantly, he rolls up his jeans and walks towards me, wincing as his feet meet the icy temperatures of the sea. I turn to face the horizon and he copies, his hand finding mine.

"It's a mystery," I say, more to myself than to Nick.

"What's that?"

"The sea. You never know what you're going to get."

He looks first at me then back out at the water as though he is trying to see what I see, searching for some hidden meaning in the vast expanse of blue.

"You belong here, don't you?" He turns in the water so he's facing me. "You're happy here – at peace."

"Yes," I say. "Yes, I suppose I am."

49

FIFTEEN YEARS AGO

The darkness is comforting. I could be anywhere, with anyone. I imagine he's with me sometimes, the memories of him so intense that I'm sure I can hear him. But I don't always allow myself this simple imaginary pleasure. Sometimes, I don't feel as though I deserve it, and instead I imagine the darkness as a presence, oppressive and cruel, filling every available space with the absence of all else.

Other times, when I really need to torture myself, I think about it. I think about that day and what happened. I imagine him plummeting into that lorry at seventy miles an hour, glass smashing and the bonnet crumpling into nothing. He becomes a faceless gruesome figure; unrecognisable. I imagine the screams of his wife, horrified as he steers the car into the path of the lorry, her sense of helplessness in the face of forty tonnes of steel hurtling towards them. I wonder whether she thought of me in that moment. I wonder whether he did.

Despite the horrors I make myself endure over and over again, I never allow myself to think about his children. There are some places your mind won't let you go for fear it might never come back.

50

NOW

Nick and I get back in the car with feet so cold we can barely feel them. He starts the engine and turns up the heaters. I'm laughing, really laughing, and it strikes me how long it's been since I felt the weightlessness of it, the freedom.

"See," he says, pulling on his socks, "no one else is going in the sea!"

He's looking ahead to the beach, watching as a handful of people trace the shoreline, never venturing into the water.

"They're missing out then, aren't they?"

"I bet they can still feel their feet."

He's smiling, twisting in his chair so that he's facing me.

"I had fun," he says.

"Me too."

The thick cloud remains as we drive towards home, one of those dreary grey days that seems to trap the night, never fully giving in to the day. As we get onto the A2 I take out my phone and turn it on. It springs to life with a series of beeps in quick succession.

Nick glances at me. "Someone's popular."

I read the messages, all from John.

Erin?

What happened last night?

Erin, where are you? I thought we were going to spend some time together today.

I had too much to drink last night, I'm sorry if I said something out of line.

Please call me when you get this, I can't get through to you.

I consider replying but decide against it – we're only an hour away. I switch it off and return it to my bag, out of sight.

"You're not going to reply?"

"No, I'll speak to him when I get home."

"You don't have to go home, you know."

"I do," I say matter-of-factly.

He doesn't say anything for a while, weaving in and out of the late afternoon traffic. The silence gives me time to think and my mind drifts back to the cheque in my bag and the revelation that Ray has known who I am for years. I'm trying to think whether there's anything I've told him that could account for him knowing, but just as I'm trying to relive countless conversations, Nick begins talking again.

"Does John know?"

"Know what?"

"About what happened when you were younger?"

"He knows what I had to tell him." I shrug. "Honestly, he's never asked me a lot of questions about it."

When we arrive back in Kestwell we find the local council have added miniature Christmas trees to the lamp posts that light up the cobbled streets. It looks picturesque.

"It's beginning to look like Christmas," Nick says, grinning.

He pulls into the car park behind his studio and pulls on the handbrake.

"How come you haven't decorated yet?"

"I haven't got round to it. I know, bah humbug."

"I haven't either."

"Will you?"

"I suppose so."

I grab my bag and get out of the car, fishing around for my keys.

"Thanks for today," he says. He walks around the front of the car and leans against the bonnet. "I don't always like this time of year. It's the anniversary of my wife's death."

He crosses his arms and looks away and for a moment I can't think of a single thing to say. He looks different when he talks about her and the change is so sudden that it surprises me, the happiness in his eyes gone in an instant. I want to ask her name, to know more about this woman who has had such an impact on his life, but I don't.

"I'm sorry, that can't be easy."

"No, but days like today make it easier."

I'm tempted to tell him that I understand – the anniversary of Danny's death looms large too – but I stop myself. With each year that passes it doesn't get any easier, only more familiar – less shocking. I'm still tormented by the memories, haunted by those that refuse to relinquish their power. I've come to think of them as my keeper, a constant unrelenting presence in my life that forces me to live within the confines of certain rules. But lately, those rules have been pushed and pulled in ways I have never allowed before.

I step towards Nick and place my hand on his shoulder. "I should go."

His mouth turns into a half-smile, his eyes still held by the memory of his loss.

"I'll see you soon," I say.

I unlock my car and climb inside, reversing out onto the road. As I drive away, Nick walks out to the edge of the pavement, his hand stretching out into a wave.

I pull up onto the driveway and sit in the car for a while, the engine off, enjoying the quiet. It's been a long day and I suddenly feel drained, the lack of sleep catching up with me. I close my eyes and take some deep breaths, allowing my mind to drift back to a conversation I had with Ray in the weeks preceding the wedding.

"Who's going to walk you down the aisle?"

"It's not that kind of wedding, Ray. I'll walk down the aisle by myself."

"Wouldn't your dad want to know? Wouldn't he want to be here?"

"That's not really up to him."

"You could live to regret it, kid."

Now that I think about it, with the benefit of hindsight, he's always been in my dad's corner – the quiet voice advocating for him.

The front door opens and John walks out towards the car in his slippers. He opens my door, his bloodshot eyes full of guilt.

"Aren't you going to come in?"

Silently, I get out of the car and grab my bag, heading into the house. I don't want to talk about last night, I don't want to have the conversation that he needs to have to rid himself of the guilt and the shame, but I know he's going to try.

"Where have you been?" he asks.

"Out."

"Yeah, I know that much. I've been trying to call you all day. I've texted you almost a dozen times." He pinches the bridge of his nose and squeezes his eyes shut, no doubt still suffering from the effects of last night's binge. "Look, I don't remember much about last night..."

I can't help but laugh. He pauses, looking wounded.

"It's the truth," he says. "But obviously I upset you so I'm sorry."

I take off my coat and hang it on the end of the bannister then slowly pull up the sleeve of my jumper. I show him my wrist.

His eyes widen, a momentary flicker of horror. "What happened?"

"You did this, John."

His eyes move between my wrist and my eyes, and I can't decide whether his confusion is genuine or a façade.

"You might not remember, but I do. And I won't forget."

I turn round and go upstairs, too tired to care. By the time I reach our bedroom my mind is already elsewhere, flitting between the letters, Ray, the attack and Nick. I take the cheque into the spare room and slip it into *The Wasp Factory* with the letters – the place where my secrets have begun to gather. Then I get undressed and fall into bed, no longer caring about the sand between my toes.

I'm pulled from my dreams suddenly and with a finality I can't fight, heart thrashing and sweat dripping freely down my chest.

The sheets are damp, sticking uncomfortably to my skin; I push them away. I was watching Melissa stride into the police station, screaming desperately from the other side of the road for her to stop, but she couldn't hear me despite the eerie silence that had descended all around us. I was frantic, calling out to her in unrecognisable cries until my voice broke under the strain.

Stop! You don't know what you're doing! You have no idea what's at stake! Stop! You will lose everything!

But still she walked on, setting things in motion she could not even imagine, purposeful steps towards her own death. When I saw her again she'd lost her head. I watched, horrified, as it rolled across the road and into the path of a lorry, eventually exploding under the weight of its wheels. I looked up into the cab of the lorry to find my own eyes staring back at me through the splattering of blood on the windscreen, the wipers doing nothing but mixing it with the rain that had begun to fall.

51

NOW

I didn't think I would be able to drift back to sleep, disturbed by a nightmare so vivid it lingered, a dark shadow refusing to be silenced, but at some point during the early hours I must have succumbed to the exhaustion. The sound of footsteps padding along the floor wakes me, followed by the *clang* of a mug being placed on my bedside table. I open my eyes wearily, squinting against the daylight flooding in through the open blinds.

"It's almost noon."

John sits carefully on the bed beside me as though he's unsure whether it's the right thing to do. His shame has led him to doubt himself, to question his core. It's happened before, after the bumped head. It bled – caught just on the edge of a framed photo hanging on the wall. His concern flooded out the next morning, the sight of blood on the crisp white pillowcase a stark reflection of what lies beneath his self-control. I don't think he meant to hurt me, I just don't think he cared enough to restrain himself, to ensure my safety.

"I've made you coffee. I thought we could go out for lunch?"

I can't think clearly, the lack of sleep causing my mind to

cloud. I slowly sit up, the dull ache in my ribs always worse in a morning. He's showered and dressed in a pair of jeans and a smart black jumper but his eyes give him away, red and tired. I wonder where he slept, or whether he slept at all.

"I'm tired." I pick up my coffee and take a sip – he's even remembered the sugar.

"You had another nightmare, you know?"

I look away.

"You were screaming. Do you remember it this time?"

I shake my head and he sighs heavily.

"Erin, I'm sorry. I had too much to drink, you know I would never mean to hurt you."

I sit cradling my mug, my back resting against the headboard, wondering what it is he wants from me. Forgiveness? Reassurance? Or does he simply want me to forget? I can't help but think of Nick; his consistency and stability. It's such a glaring contrast to John; his moods, his drinking, his selfishness.

"I know you're sorry, I know you had too much to drink, but that doesn't change what happened and it doesn't change the fact that it's not the first time."

He looks away, trying to escape the reminder of things he would rather forget.

"What can I do?"

"Nothing," I say, and I realise that it's probably the truest thing I've said to him in a long time. There's nothing he can do. "I need time to think."

He sighs again. "Of course. I'll get out your way."

I don't want to admit that I enjoy the shift in power, the sense of having the upper hand and being in control. It makes me want to drag it out, to keep us suspended in instability. He gets up to leave but just as he's closing the door he looks back.

"It's not how I saw my life either, you know. Everyone wants to feel loved; even me."

A short while later I hear the front door shut and a car engine spring to life. I look out of the window just in time to see him turning out of the driveway. Across the road Pete is cleaning his car, a jet washer blasting soapy water all over his Jaguar. He watches as John leaves, holding up one hand in a hesitant wave. I hope he isn't worrying, waking in the depths of the night by the weight of what he hasn't told John. I feel a wave of guilt; I never wanted the fallout of my choices to impact others.

I check my phone, half expecting to see a message from Nick, but there's nothing. I consider ringing Ray and asking him to come round today and explain how he knows things that he shouldn't, but I decide against it. Instead, I turn it off and zip it back inside my bag. I have an urge to be alone, to allow the chaos in my head to slow down.

I spend the rest of the day lazing around the house, in and out of a light sleep that only serves to make me feel more lethargic. I have no reason to leave the house and no incentive to find one, happy to enjoy the peace and quiet. Every now and again I find myself checking the doors, ensuring they're locked, and peering out of the windows through tiny gaps in the blinds, checking that no one is lurking beyond the driveway.

I go to bed before John arrives home and I begin to wonder if he's decided to stay out all night – maybe he's sleeping at the office or sought refuge at Graham and Lucy's – but just as I'm drifting off to sleep I hear keys in the front door, followed by careful footsteps on the stairs moments later. I hear the bedroom door creak quietly open, then, after a few seconds, close. He's treading carefully, giving me space. I can rest easy tonight.

I wake to a barrage of knocking at the door, loud and frantic, followed by the bell ringing over and over. My heart beats wildly against my chest, struggling to adjust between the comfort of sleep and the sudden panic of my reality. The bed is empty beside me and my first thought is that it's John banging at the door, drunk and lecherous, but then I remember him arriving home late last night. He must have already left for work. I get up and check the security monitor. There's a man at the door, short and slim, but I can only see the back of his head. I go to the top of the stairs, one hand poised on the bannister, holding my breath to listen for signs of who it could be. A few seconds later, there's a shout from the front door.

"Erin, I know you're home. Answer the door."

It's Ian's voice, followed by more knocking. I check my watch – it's not yet seven. I wonder what he could possibly want. I tie my robe and head downstairs. When I open the door I find Ian looking pale and dishevelled, his tie loose and his top buttons undone. He's stood with his phone in his hand, bloodshot eyes flitting between me and a message he seems halfway through sending.

"What did she say to you?"

I ignore his question. "Do you know what time it is?"

"What did Trish say to you? At the dinner party?"

I raise my eyebrows, still trying to work out what he's doing here. "Have you been drinking?"

He turns and walks a few steps away from me, exasperated, then he slips his phone into his trouser pocket and turns back to face me. "No, Erin, I haven't been drinking. And yes, I'm aware of the time and I'm sorry for disturbing you. I've been up all night looking for Trish." He speaks slowly, with an air of calm that obviously takes a lot of effort. "I think she's left me. Now please, tell me what you spoke about at the dinner party?"

I shrug, remembering my promise to her that I wouldn't say

anything.

"Nothing, just small talk. She's left you? Why?"

He throws his arms out in the air. "I don't know. I don't know."

I watch him as he paces around in the glow of the security light. He looks like a broken man.

"Did you do something stupid, Ian?"

He looks at me confused. "What do you mean?"

"I don't know. Did you have an affair? Could she have found out?"

"No, I didn't have a fucking affair. Why would I? I love her."

He scratches his head and for a moment he looks lost in thought, clearly considering something significant.

"What is it?" I ask.

"I suppose she could have thought I was cheating. I'd been going out a bit more. I wasn't always honest about where."

"Ah well, I'm sure you had your reasons," I say sarcastically. A part of me, cruel and spiteful, is enjoying seeing him in distress.

"I wasn't having an affair," he says flatly. "But I was meeting someone."

"Ian, either tell me or don't. I'm not playing your games."

There's a long pause. I stand watching him, the cold air blowing into the house.

"I found out recently, a few months ago, that I have a son. Not a kid or anything, he's twenty-two. But I didn't want to scare Trish off."

"You have a son?" I suddenly recall seeing him walking past Mimi's with a younger man.

He nods. "Yes, I have a son, Jamie. He found me a few months ago and we've been meeting up, getting to know each other. He'd actually get on really well with Trish."

"Then tell her."

"I'm going to. But I don't know where she is and she isn't answering my calls." He pauses and I see in his eyes that he's had an idea. One I'm not going to like.

"You could call her."

I sigh. I don't want to get dragged into other people's relationships, the very idea of it feels like interfering.

"Look, Erin, I know we don't see eye to eye. It's no secret that you can't stand me and I get it, I do. But I'm not the same arsehole you met years ago. I just want to find Trish and explain. I love her, I really do."

In spite of my better judgement, I begrudgingly step to one side and let him in. "Let's make this quick."

I reach Trish on the second attempt and hastily explain the situation, but not in its entirety – I ask her to give Ian a chance to explain. After the initial confusion, I promise her that she won't regret speaking to him and it seems to work – my willingness to vouch for a man I don't like adding validity to my request.

"She'll meet you at yours in an hour," I tell Ian.

He smiles, hope returning to his eyes. "Thanks, Erin. I mean it – thanks a lot for this."

I walk towards the door but before I open it he speaks again.

"Look, John's been a good friend to me over the years..."

I roll my eyes, expecting him to echo Graham's sentiment from the dinner party – *He takes good care of you, maybe you could show him the same courtesy.*

"But one good deed deserves another. You know the parcel I picked up?"

"Yes?"

"How often does John have parcels redirected here? Has that ever happened before?"

I shrug. The thought hadn't occurred to me but now I think about it I can't recall another time.

"He said they were important... sensitive."

Ian continues. "Oh they were sensitive all right. I knew something was going on, even before that. Then with the documents..."

"What are you trying to say?"

He looks uncomfortable, shifting on his feet. He takes a deep breath, clearly preparing to tell me something important.

"He's broke. It's been coming for a while. The business is going under."

"That's not possible," I say, though even as I say it I realise I haven't got a clue about the business and his finances.

"They're going to take the house. He's done his best to hide assets but there's not much left. And what he does have is in his name."

He raises his eyebrows and I realise he's trying to emphasise the importance of this – is he planning to leave me with nothing?

"But... but... He's been so busy," I say weakly.

"We all have – a lot of our big clients heard about the money problems and pulled out. We've been trying to get new contracts."

I feel like I'm missing pieces of a puzzle, none of it seems to make sense.

"I'm sorry, Erin."

"What do I do?" I ask, my shock allowing my barriers to fall enough to ask for advice from a man I have always avoided.

"I don't know, but look out for yourself. That's what John's doing."

Ian opens the door and heads towards his car.

"Good luck!" I shout after him.

He turns briefly, a sad smile on his face. "You too."

52

FIFTEEN YEARS AGO

"You like it?"

Dad stands next to an artificial Christmas tree, sporadically decorated with mismatched baubles and tinsel. I know he felt obliged to put it up, a gesture of normality. It took a lot of effort and I want to match his commitment but no matter how hard I try, I can't fake it. He holds out an old gold star to me – I remember balancing it on top when I was little.

"Do you want to do it?"

I shake my head. I'd moved from the comfort of my bed to the sofa, a blanket wrapped around my shoulders, but I know it isn't enough. He needs more.

"Sorry, Dad, I'm not in the mood for Christmas this year."

"Well, we can't cancel it. We just have to make the best of it this year."

He sits down next to me, fiddling with the star in his hands. He's lost weight, his cheekbones protruding under his glasses – the kind of sudden, unhealthy weight loss that makes you look ill. Yesterday, I'd wandered downstairs in the early hours for a drink and found him sat at the kitchen table, bloodshot eyes and a glass of whisky in his hands. I hate what I'm doing to him.

"You have to try. You have to pick yourself up and carry on until one day you realise you're not chained to what happened anymore. You'll set yourself free. You just need time."

I rest my head on his shoulder and he slips his arm around my back. I look at the tree, the multicoloured lights reflecting in the window overlooking the garden. Above, the crescent moon hangs suspended in an impossibly clear sky, pinprick stars littering the vast expanse of darkness. I want to turn out the lights on the tree and wipe all brightness from the sky. I want to fade back into the darkness, to hide in the hours of sleep that provide the only slight reprieve, all for the second I get when I wake where everything is unclear; was it all a dream? A second of uncertainty before the nightmare continues.

We sit together for a long time, our grief combining to provide some degree of comfort; mine for Danny, Dad's for me – for the happy easy life I'll no longer lead.

"How about a cup of tea?" he asks, breaking the silence.

I nod imperceptibly but he isn't really looking for an answer, he needs to feel as though he's taking care of me. I follow him into the kitchen, my blanket still draped over my shoulders. He flicks on the kettle and takes a couple of mugs off the draining board. As he places them down on the worktop, I hear a shout from outside followed by some muffled talking. Dad stops and turns, looking towards the window that overlooks the street outside.

"Go upstairs," he says flatly.

"What, why? Who is it?"

"I don't know. Go upstairs, Erin, now."

He leans towards the window, trying to get a better view of the group that's gathered. I can hear several voices, their shouts getting louder.

"Erin, I said go upstairs."

I turn to go but it's too late. The window explodes, glass

shattering with a piercing crash, pieces scattering in every direction. I feel them rain down, falling at my feet.

A voice shouts: "You're not welcome here, slag!"

Dad turns to look at me. He's bleeding, his face caught in the blast of broken glass. At his feet lies a brick. He looks at it, and then at me, endless patience in his eyes that I don't deserve. He's hurt because of me. I feel a shift somewhere in the depths of my mind; it's no longer about me and my pain, it's no longer about Danny or his family. I have to protect my dad, he's all I have left.

53

NOW

I decide to pack a suitcase while I think about what to do; it can't hurt and it gives me a sense of purpose. It feels as though everything is falling apart, no longer held together by routine and rules, familiarity and predictability. The only part that feels consistently stable is Nick.

Just after nine I hear a car pull up outside followed by a soft tapping on the door. I know before I open it that it's Ray.

"Hey, kid."

It's raining heavily, a greyness descending. He's stood in his raincoat, the hood pulled up against the drumming of the water.

"Come in," I say.

I head into the kitchen and take a seat at the table. He follows, slipping off his coat and smoothing it over the back of the chair. I watch him, waiting. He sits down opposite me and clasps his hands on top of the table in front of him; he's ready. There are no pleasantries today, no offers of drinks or chats about the weather – we both know why we're here.

"How do you know?" I ask.

"Do you remember when you first moved here? You gave me a key and I would come by from time to time. Sometimes you were here, other times you weren't. And once, someone else was here. Your dad."

I don't say anything, frozen yet pumped with adrenaline. I need to move and yet I can't.

"He's a good man, we got on well. He asked about you, of course, and I told him what I could. He was so happy to have tracked you down, but so scared you weren't ready. He asked me to keep an eye on you, to check in with him every once in a while. So I did and, truth be told, we became friends. I didn't go looking for information about you, but your dad trusted me enough to confide in me eventually."

"Is... is he...?" I trail off, not wanting to finish my question. A tear runs down my cheek and I wipe it away. It occurs to me that the cheque might not have come from Ray, but rather left to me by my dad. The thought is horrifying and I plead to a force greater than myself to not let it be true.

"Paul's fine." Ray smiles. "Still working but he teaches now, wildlife conservation."

I smile, fresh tears of relief falling freely. The thought of my dad teaching brings me such joy, his passion being passed on to others.

"Does he still have the house?"

Ray nods. "He never moved. He holds onto the belief you'll go home one day."

We sit passing the time without talking, content in each other's company while I let the information settle. Eventually, Ray breaks the silence.

"Is he right?"

The thought of going home fills me with such conflicting emotions that my mind has always refused to consider the idea, shutting it down at the first hurdle. It wouldn't be easy, but if I'm being honest with myself, neither is staying away.

"I don't know. It's not something I ever saw happening."

"Sometimes, the oldest and simplest advice is still the best: listen to your heart."

He gets up from the table and bends over to kiss me briskly on the top of my head.

"Thank you, Ray. For everything."

"I should really be the one thanking you. All my life I wanted a daughter. You've given me a few years of feeling like I have one."

The effort of trying to hold back the tears renders me speechless so I just sit and watch him leave, wondering if we've said a goodbye I hadn't been prepared for.

I pull my suitcase out to the car and lift it into the boot. The wet weather has relented, leaving the ground damp and the musky smell of rainfall in the air. I'm taken back to being a child, walking the clifftop coastal path from Overstrand to Cromer with Dad. I can see the lighthouse and the pier. I can hear the waves crashing, consuming the rain that has just fallen. 'Petrichor, Erin, it's the scent of rain in the air.' He inhales deeply, eyes closed. I copy him, taking in the sweet earthy smells.

I consider leaving a note or sending a text, letting John know I won't be back, but I decide that's more than he should expect and settle on posting my key when I've locked the door. As I get to the car I hesitate for a moment, turning my wedding band round on my finger, then I go back to the door and post that too.

Standing back from the house, I look up and try to take it in – the place I've called home for the past seven years – expecting to feel some degree of sadness at the thought of leaving, but I don't. I get in the car and turn round in the driveway, watching the house disappear in the rear-view mirror as I leave. I spot *The Wasp Factory* poking out the top of my bag, the letters and the cheque tucked neatly inside.

I glance over at Pete's house, half expecting to see him loitering around outside or making his way over towards the car as I leave, his hand up in the air trying to catch my attention. But he isn't there, the street is deserted. I say a silent goodbye as I drive away, a quiet acknowledgement of his good intents.

I drive down the winding road into town, the park coming into view on my left. I pull up into the lay-by outside, a sudden decision which surprises both me and the car behind, the man beeping his horn in protest at my careless driving. Not intending to do anything other than sit and look at the place that has provided me with a sense of belonging, sheltering me when at times I felt I had nowhere else to go, I keep the engine running at first.

But despite my intentions I find myself turning it off and getting out of the car. I head through the familiar gates and walk slowly down the tree-lined path, avoiding the puddles that have collected along the way. There's a black iron bench at the side of the memorial which overlooks the park and its entrance to the woodland. I sit, watching as a man exits the treeline with a couple of border collies. One of them drops a ball at his feet and the man bends to retrieve it, hauling it across the park. Both of the dogs give chase and the man follows. I instinctively scan him for any hint of recognition, but there's none.

I think back to that day – to the attack and meeting Nick – and wonder what my life would look like now if that day had never happened. Am I glad that it did? All the hours John has spent at work recently, the long days and trips away. Why didn't he tell me? I wonder whether things would be different if he'd just been honest.

A few weeks before we got married, John produced a prenuptial agreement that he wanted me to sign. There'd been no discussion about it and it was such a casual request – over breakfast one Sunday morning – that it seemed almost insignificant. Regardless, my dad's voice had popped into my head: 'Never sign anything without reading it first, you could be signing your life away.'

I'd asked for some time to read through it before signing, assuming John would understand, but he didn't. He became angry and questioned my motives. So I signed it, afraid of what he'd think of me if I didn't. It was only when I found a copy of it a couple of years later that I realised the extent of what I'd signed away. I look at the mark on my wrist, the red fading to nothing. If I'm really honest with myself – money or not, rich or poor – I would probably have stayed with him, never quite feeling strong enough to leave. What I can't deal with is another thing in my life falling apart. I can't stay and watch his demise.

I feel a drop of rain and look up to the sky; clouds are moving in from the south, heavy and grey. I stand to leave, taking another look towards the woodland, thick and dark in contrast to the park. Looking at it now, I don't know how I ever felt safe there. I walk back towards the gates, aware that I'm instinctively scanning the faces of everyone who walks past, but the man who attacked me isn't here.

I get back in the car just in time; the heavens open, the sudden onslaught of rain bringing a darkness that disguises the day. I start the engine and make a right turn towards Nick's, the rain lashing against the windscreen and hammering on the roof, drumming sounds filling the car with a dull thudding. The blinds are shut in the studio but as I drive into the car park I see his Rav4 is there. I pull up next to it.

Only now does it occur to me that it's Monday; he could be working or with clients. I sit listening to the rain, the countless thoughts in my head still unable to form one single cohesive thing to say to him. What have I come here for? Is it because I have nowhere else to go? Or is it to tell him I'm tired of losing everything in the constant battle between my head and my heart? I want to tell him I'm ready to bet on my heart for the first time in fifteen years.

54

FIFTEEN YEARS AGO

"We had several reports of a leatherback turtle today," Dad says.

I sit across from him, waiting for him to ask me to stay; knowing that I won't. He's made drinks neither of us wants and is delaying a conversation both of us needs.

"They don't usually wander into the North Sea, away from the Gulf Stream."

"That's exciting," I offer, not really in the mood for a tale from work.

"It's certainly significant." He clasps his hands together and leans forward in his chair, resting his elbows on the table. I can see the scars scattered down his forehead and cheek, the tiny white crevices where glass was once pulled from his face – a constant reminder of how I failed him. Even after all these months, they're still shocking. I look away.

"The thing is, no matter how many thousands of miles they travel, they will always return to the beach where they hatched."

I look away, towards the door where my suitcase waits.

"You'll come back when you're ready," he says. He stands up

and kisses me on the forehead. "You'll come home. And when you do, I'll be here. Waiting."

55

NOW

I walk round to the front window to try to catch a glimpse inside between the blinds. The rain has eased but the darkness remains, sporadic drops falling on the damp ground. Through a narrow opening near the far side, I can see his computer is on but he isn't there. I wonder if he's gone upstairs to get a drink. I try the front door and to my surprise it's open. I step inside, closing it behind me.

"Nick?" I call.

There's no reply, just the low hum of his computer. I decide to go upstairs, the idea of catching him by surprise suddenly appealing. I gently open the door at the back, a nervous excitement beginning to gather in my stomach. It's darker in the stairwell than in his studio, a single pane of glass in the back door casting a narrow beam of silvery white light over the steps.

As I get to the top I reach my hand out to knock but the door is pulled away from me, opened by a man I'm not expecting to see. I smile, automatically polite, before my eyes meet with his – the cold pale-blue eyes I have seen before, the overwhelming smell of cigarettes, his build, so large and intimidating it seems there is nothing else.

The recognition sits suspended between us for a moment, a second of indecision, his initial expression of surprise quickly twisting into a scowl. I think of Nick, then I shout for him – a strangled cry quickly muffled by the man's sweaty palm against my mouth, his other hand pushing me forcefully against the wall. He moves his mouth to my ear.

"Ssshh," he says. "Be quiet."

I look at him, taking in his face for the first time – the pale pockmarked skin, the shaved head and single gold stud in his left ear. The scar on his forehead, a small white line almost touching the top of his eyebrow. The discoloured teeth and crooked nose. My eyes dart around looking for Nick, worrying about him, concerned that his involvement with me has compromised his safety. Then I see him, hovering in the doorway just out of reach.

"Shit," he says.

The man glances over his shoulder towards Nick. "What's she doing here?"

His hand is heavy against my mouth, pushing the back of my head into the wall. His other hand is on my shoulder holding me firmly in place. My arms hang lifelessly by my side, too scared to fight back.

"I don't know," Nick says.

"You don't know? Fuckin' hell."

He spits as he talks and I close my eyes, desperately trying to process what's happening. Why is Nick talking to the man who attacked me? I want to shout and ask him, to demand an explanation.

"Calm down, Connor..."

"Don't tell me to calm down, she's seen my fuckin' face."

"Go," he says flatly. "Go now and I'll deal with this. She won't report you, will you?"

Nick looks at me for the first time, his eyes full of the secrets he's been keeping from me. He seems to expect an answer from me despite the huge hand over my mouth. I try to move my head, to signal my compliance.

"Are you out of your mind? She's seen my face, I can't just leave. I'm on fuckin' parole."

"She won't say anything, Connor."

"I'm not going back to prison because of this."

His hand is moving from my shoulder, inching closer and closer to my neck.

"Just let me explain everything to her–"

The man – Connor – interrupts. "You want to explain yourself to her? To the bitch that ruined your life?"

I look at Nick, disbelief so heavy that my knees buckle under the weight of it. He looks away, unwilling or unable to face me. I try to talk, muffled shouts against a solid hand, then when that fails I thrash and flail my arms, lashing out at the man who has me in his grip, wanting to reach for the man who I thought I could trust.

"Quiet," Connor spits, "fuckin' quiet or I swear to god I'll fuckin' kill you."

I look at him and I'm reminded of that day in the woods, the threat in his eyes so clear that it leaves no doubt as to what he's capable of. He breathes heavily, trying to still my struggling body which is lost in the grip of a terrifying panic.

"Stop struggling," he warns.

His fingertips find my neck and clasp around my throat. I hit out at him, grabbing at the arm that's holding me in place, but it's no use, his arm remains steadfastly solid; I'm no match for his size. I'm desperately trying to get air into my lungs but I'm struggling, his grip is getting tighter and his other hand is partially covering my nose too. Blood pulsates against my temples, a dull thudding growing louder and louder. I can feel my eyes bulging, darkness threatening to take me.

"Connor, stop!" I hear Nick shout, his words washing over me as I slip further away.

My legs falter, unable to support my weight, but Connor's grip around my neck remains strong, propping me up against the wall. I close my eyes and feel as though I'm underwater, caught in a rip tide – no longer in control. I can see the sun beaming down on me through the water. I can feel the internal waves pushing and pulling me further out to sea. I can hear the rushing of the water and the gulls up above. I relinquish control and let go.

56

FIFTEEN YEARS AGO

I head straight for the train station, lugging my suitcase behind me on rickety wheels, across unforgiving pavements in the heat of the mid-morning sun. I don't look back. As I round the corner, the suitcase struggling to manoeuvre the turn, I wipe away a solitary tear with the back of my hand. A couple of seagulls refuse to move out my way, too distracted by the discarded chips that lie scattered and squashed on the pavement. I pull the suitcase onto the road, leaving them to enjoy their meal.

As I navigate around crumbling potholes I hear voices coming from behind me; hushed but urgent, followed by the sound of muffled laughter. I keep walking, too afraid to look over my shoulder. I feel something hit my back – not heavy, but warm – then the sound of footsteps running away. I turn round in time to see the backs of their heads – three boys, my age or thereabouts. I've become a target, irrespective of my crime – it no longer matters, people are dead. They don't stop, but I hear the boys' laughter until they're out of sight. I already know what it is; the sickening smell noticeable before anything else.

Regardless, I take off my jacket and look at the damage; the brown shit stain against the denim blue. There's a paper bag on the floor, exploded and covered in the leftovers. I carry my jacket until the next street where I find a bin and hastily stuff it inside, trying not to touch the splatter of brown. I'm left standing in my blue-and-white-striped dress, the one Danny had wanted me to wear for him – the one I was wearing when I saw him with his children. I shake the memory away, too uncomfortable to remember in its entirety.

In spite of it all – the gossip, the brick through the window, the bag of shit, the looks and the insults – there remains one inexplicable truth, a certainty beyond all reason or logic, beyond law or opinion, right or wrong: I loved him. And that was my mistake. With love, there is always grief – someday, somehow.

57

NOW

I feel my body slip down the wall, landing with a thud against the cold hard floorboards. My head hits the door frame and a sudden sharpness of pain radiates through my body, my teeth knocking together with the force. I don't open my eyes – there is nothing worth seeing.

The sense of betrayal and my own stupidity are overwhelming, the years of decisions and avoidance that should have led me elsewhere echoing in the cold darkness of regret. How could I have been so stupid?

I can hear voices, muffled and indistinct – it sounds like they're coming from another world, strained and strangled shouts breaking through the fog of concussion. I open my eyes slowly, scared of what I'll see.

At first I can't work it out; a blur of pushing and shoving, the back of Nick's head hitting the wall, Connor punching him, Nick running into him. They haven't noticed me moving, slowly sitting up and watching it all unfold. Why are they fighting? I can't make sense of anything. I back away into the flat, using my feet to push myself along the floor.

I can hear noise coming from Nick's bedroom – Bear barking from behind the door. I look around, squinting through blurred vision, desperately seeking inspiration – anything that will help me.

I scramble to my feet and my eyes fall on the table by the door and the award sitting on top, the solid pillar of crystal. I pick it up, feeling its weight in my hand. I try to compose myself, to slow my breathing and focus. I hide behind the wall so that I can just see the landing beyond and the chaos that's unfolding.

Nick's bleeding but I can't tell where from, blood pouring from somewhere on his face – his nose maybe, or his cheek. Connor is stood facing him, his back to me.

"What the fuck are you doing?" he asks Nick breathlessly.

They stand looking at each other, a brief stalemate. I lock eyes with Nick and something passes between us, an acceptance that there is no other way out. I don't have time to question the instinctive need I feel to help him – perhaps with hindsight I'll consider it more of a survival instinct, eradicating the bigger threat – I take two hurried strides forward and smash the towering column into the back of Connor's head, as high up as I can reach. His head meets my swing with more resistance than I'm prepared for; I feel a tear in my shoulder after the sickening crunch of his skull.

I drop the award, glass shattering everywhere, and I retreat to the doorway clutching at my shoulder. I watch him fall to his knees with a thud against the hard floor, blood pouring from several gashes on his shaved head; the blood cascades down, pooling in the creases of his neck then staining his white T-shirt. His body sways, reaching out for the bannister. Nick looks at me and, for a fleeting moment, he is just Nick – I want to run to him, to not ask the questions I need him to answer because I know they'll change everything. But the reality is it's already changed, the damage irreparable. He swings back his arm then hammers his fist into the side of Connor's swaying head, a single resounding punch.

The stairs creak under the pressure of Connor's body falling down them, heavy and lifeless, and the loud thuds of various different bones connecting with the wall on the way induces a fresh wave of nausea. I feel numb, unable to process my surroundings or make sense of the situation – everything feels oddly unreal. I'm covered in a thin layer of cold sweat and I'm shaking violently, unable to control my trembling limbs. Dizziness comes in waves and I hold onto the door frame to try to steady myself – the room is spinning. I want to make sense of it all but I don't think it's possible.

Nick holds onto the bannister while watching Connor's lifeless body by the back door, the narrow beam of light from the windowpane bathing him in a soft golden glow. Nick wipes the blood running from his nose on the back of his forearm, smearing it in a red stain which matches the one on the floor beneath his feet. I look at Nick, hunched over and breathing heavily, but he doesn't look at me. He looks suddenly broken; a man held together by a purpose that's unravelling fast.

My mind flits between my options which seem alarmingly sparse – I could run past Nick and over Connor, hoping he's dead or at least incapacitated, then out through the studio. Or I could retreat into the flat, shut the door and lock myself in, call for help or shout from the windows. I'm scared I'll fall if I try to run – my body no longer feels under my command – but I'm scared I'll be trapped if I shut myself in, at the mercy of a man whose life I have somehow ruined.

As I'm weighing up my options, unable to commit to either, Nick stands up straight then walks silently down the stairs. I flinch as he passes, no longer sure of who he is or what he's capable of, but it's as though he doesn't even realise I'm there. He reaches Connor and crouches down, placing two fingers on his neck. He seems to wait for a long time, checking for a pulse that isn't there, then he slumps down onto the floor, his back against the wall and his head in his hands.

I stand holding onto the door frame, still needing something solid to grip. I watch him as he slowly realises the enormity of the situation, seeing the emotions I feel reflecting back at me. What have we done? What have I done?

After a while he slowly gets to his feet, looking down at Connor before looking up at me.

"I need to explain," Nick says. "I need to explain everything."

He stays stood at the bottom of the stairs, Connor's body lying behind him. I don't move, too afraid to say or do the wrong thing.

"I'm going to come up," he says. "You don't need to be scared of me."

I back away into his flat then quickly worry I've trapped myself in and move back out again, onto the landing where splatters of blood glisten against the floorboards. Nick watches me, his hands held up in a gesture of submission.

"Erin, listen to me. If I wanted to hurt you I wouldn't have stopped Connor."

I hadn't comprehended why Connor had let go of me, and the thought of Nick being the reason fills me with so many conflicting and confusing emotions that all I can do is shake my head. Questions rise quicker than I can make sense of them, rushing through my mind in disarray. I feel as though anger is permeating my core and changing who I am, the physical pain of betrayal flooding through my veins. How can he expect me to sit and listen to what he has to say?

He walks up the stairs, each footstep purposefully light, each movement carefully managed so as not to spook me. I feel as though he's preying on me, stalking ever nearer until he's close enough to pounce.

"Stop!" I say. "Don't come any closer."

I don't know why I say it, I have nothing to enforce my command, nothing other than the guilt and remorse I'm counting on him feeling for whatever he's involved in.

He stops, holding up his hands. "I just want to talk."

"About what?" I shout. "What could we possibly have to talk about?"

"Don't you want to know why?"

I don't want to admit it – to him or myself – but I feel it; a burning need to know. If I don't have the answers it will eat away at me over time, the uncertainty haunting me with endless possibilities I'll never be free from; I know this from experience. Every day for the past fifteen years I have asked myself why he did it – why Danny felt he had no other option but to kill himself and his family.

Did he think I'd betrayed him? Did he find out his wife had? Was it planned? Was it because he'd lost his family or his job, his reputation or respect, or because he'd lost me? I'll never know. I have never handled uncertainty well; with the absence of facts I have a tendency to invent my own narrative which is almost always worse than any truth could be. I need to know. I need the truth.

I take a deep breath, deflated. "Yes. Tell me why."

I move away from the door, my resoluteness carrying me. I sit down on the top step and look at him, waiting for the answers.

"Shall we go inside?" He looks over his shoulder at the lifeless body of Connor by the door.

"No. Here. Tell me here."

He sits down on the step he's standing on, turning sideways to face me. He's no longer bleeding but the red stains remain, smudged under his nose. He takes a deep breath and begins.

"My wife was Megan Miller," he says.

And just like that, it all makes sense.

58

FIFTEEN YEARS AGO

I sit on the train opposite a woman with a baby. She's feeding him a bottle but he keeps craning his neck over towards me, smiling. I smile back, enjoying the simple pleasure. She doesn't know me, there are no preconceptions or misconceptions; I am just a girl on the train. At the next stop, she gets up and hoists the baby onto her hip, smiling as she leaves.

I'm soon joined by a middle-aged man in a suit who sits down and pulls a newspaper from his bag. He opens it, shaking out the creases. On the front cover there is a full-page photo of Danny, Melissa and their children, stories still surfacing despite the passing of time. Underneath the picture, the caption reads:

Daniel Miller, 44, ploughed his family into a lorry in suspected murder-suicide.

I look at the picture they've used – the same one most of the papers ran with in the weeks and months following the incident – they're standing on the coastal path, their backs against the sea.

Danny's wearing a white short-sleeved shirt with beige

shorts, a pair of sunglasses tucked into one of his pockets. Melissa's trying to hold her hair out of her face, the wind whipping it in every direction. She looks pretty. She's wearing a long white dress, the hem lifting in the breeze. Eva is beaming at the camera from under a straw hat, a fluffy pink cat clutched in her hand. His other daughter looks serious, her long auburn hair pulled back into a ponytail. Danny's arm is draped over her shoulder, his face caught mid-laugh. It couldn't have been taken long ago, perhaps the summer we began our affair. He looks happy.

I read the paragraph underneath:

Shamed teacher Daniel Miller, 44, drove his car head-on into a lorry in a suspected murder-suicide plot. Miller was teaching at Moorwells School in Norfolk until his arrest in October last year. He was accused of having an affair with one of his students. Daniel, his wife Melissa, 41, and their youngest daughter Eva, 9, were killed instantly. Megan, 13, survived the crash but spent several months in intensive care.

59

NOW

T he sound of her name hits me hard, the weight of it palpable after all these years. I think about her, but I never speak her name; she remains a sulky thirteen-year-old in my mind, unaffected by the passing of time or the consequences of that day.

"She died three years ago. Overdose," he clarifies. "It wasn't the first time she'd tried it. She'd been sectioned a few times and was in and out of hospital. We'd tried everything; every counsellor and antidepressant possible. But it was like she didn't want to be helped. She was always slightly out of reach."

There's a sorrowful tone to his voice that speaks of his pain, an internal struggle to say the things he's kept hidden until now. I'm trying to listen to his words but they're competing for space in my head with my own questions; my own confusion.

"She hated you. She blamed you for everything."

I look away, ashamed.

"Do you know what she remembered about that day? About the crash?"

I look at him again, waiting for the answers to questions I've had for so long.

"Her mum had asked her dad to come over to try to work things out. They were driving to the beach – somewhere no one would know them. Then when they were on the bypass she turned to him and told him she was the one who reported him."

So he knew. He knew it wasn't me. I try not to react.

"She turned to Meg and her sister and told them she loved them."

My stomach turns, the disturbing reality becoming clear.

"Then she reached across to the steering wheel and pulled their car into the path of a lorry."

My hand is at my mouth, catching the cry that is desperate to escape.

"Meg tried to find you a few times. She needed to know you'd been affected by it, that your life wasn't easy."

I almost laugh at the absurdity of it – of course I've been affected by it, it defines my life, and had she have found me she would have realised that. I wonder whether it would have been enough, whether it would have changed the outcome for her.

"When she died I felt a sense of responsibility. To be honest, I think I just needed something to focus on, to give my life meaning again – a purpose. For so long my life had been about taking care of Meg, it was all I knew. So I paid for a private investigator to track you down, and when he found you living here I moved to be near you, to watch you."

The thought sends a chill down my spine, the realisation that he's been watching me to determine whether my life has value or meaning, to decide whether I'm too happy or acceptably sad.

"When I saw where you lived I felt sick – all that time, while Meg was suffering from the implications of an affair you'd had, you'd moved on and landed on your feet. It felt like I'd be betraying Meg if I just walked away."

I'm shaking my head, bewildered, trying to come to terms

with the information as it sinks in layer by layer. How overwhelmingly wrong he'd been to measure my happiness by wealth. My head is pounding, a lump swelling on the side.

"I know," he says, "I know now that it wasn't like that."

"Who is he?" I ask, gesturing to Connor's body.

Nick looks at him for a moment before turning back to me. He looks sad, guilty eyes wet with the trace of tears. They'd been friends at some point – I'm sure of it.

"When I was younger I was arrested for possession of cocaine. I'd started using it a few months before and it was beginning to spiral. I had to appear in court and, to avoid prison, I agreed to attend a rehabilitation programme. I had to go twice a week for a year. That's where I met Meg, and it's where I met Connor. I never touched drugs again and neither did Meg, but Connor never intended to stop using – he breached the order after six months and he's been in and out of prison ever since.

"A few years ago he turned up on our doorstep needing cash. We tried to help him get clean but he wasn't interested, he was just looking for his next fix. Meg always felt sorry for him, always made excuses for him. She gave him some cash and he ended up back in prison a few weeks later. That's where he was until a few months ago. He tracked me down and turned up at the studio. He didn't know about Meg. He thought a lot of her."

I can feel the pieces of the jigsaw beginning to fit together.

"So you gave him drug money to attack me?"

"No. I didn't pay him, and it wasn't my idea."

"But you went along with it."

"It was never meant to go as far as it did. He was supposed to scare you, that's all. To give me a chance to step in and get to know you."

We sit in silence for a while, letting the revelations settle. The tragic irony of it all dawns on me; that he saved me from a situation he'd created. It had felt like serendipity, finding something beautiful in the aftermath of such trauma. I realise now it was actually his way of luring me into trusting him; the Good Samaritan.

"Did you ever tell him to stop?"

"Yes, after the day at the beach. That's why he came here this morning, he didn't agree. I told him you were already paying for what you did..."

I interrupt, anger rising to the surface. "What I did?" My voice breaks with rage. "What did I do, Nick? I was fifteen and I fell in love."

"With a married man," he says calmly.

"I was a child! And those were his loyalties, his promises, not mine!"

For the first time, I realise I believe in what I'm saying; I believe in my innocence. In the face of being told I'm to blame, I realise the unfairness of it. I'm not blameless, but nor was it my fault. I didn't initiate the affair. I didn't betray my spouse. I didn't steer the car into oncoming traffic.

Nick doesn't say anything for a while, his head resting against the wall. The throbbing in my head is getting worse, waves of nausea making the room spin.

"Meg believed you were to blame."

"And you? What do you believe, Nick?"

"I..." He pauses, sighing. "I felt such crippling guilt after she died..."

I don't say anything at first, refusing to feel any sympathy for this man I thought I knew.

"I trusted you," I say. "I came to you when I was scared."

The memories come flooding back to me, the times when I have felt safe with him: his studio, his flat, the beach, the reservoir...

"I know."

"You told me to go to the police."

"Because I knew you wouldn't."

I rub my neck, rolling my chin around on my chest to try to ease the stiffness.

"I feel disloyal to my wife for how I feel," he says. "I couldn't blame you the way I wanted to. The way she did."

I try to look in his eyes, searching for some truth, but the outline of Connor's body behind him is luring me away. Nick follows my gaze, taking in the man who was willing to kill me for him – or for his own twisted sense of justice.

"He shouldn't have hurt you like he did."

"So broken ribs weren't part of your plan?"

He shakes his head. "No, he was just supposed to scare you."

"Was it you watching me? Or him?"

"No, I wasn't watching you. And he shouldn't have been either. The day at the reservoir – when I saw him – I told him to stop. But he wouldn't listen."

"And the letters, whose idea were they?"

"I didn't know anything about them until you told me."

I try to process the information, to make sense of something that feels like a dream.

"Why now, Nick? Why wait until now?"

"Connor showed up a few weeks ago. I don't think I would have done anything had it not been for him."

"It's easy to blame a dead man."

"I'm not blameless. I wanted to scare you. I wanted you to suffer. Except, when I found out you were already suffering it didn't give me the satisfaction I'd hoped for. I know how it sounds but I can't lie anymore."

"I'm sorry my shitty life didn't make you happy."

"*I'm* sorry. I wanted you to suffer the way Meg had, to know what it felt like to live with that kind of pain. But once I got to know you…" He sighs heavily. "You've shut yourself off from everyone you care about, to live with a man who doesn't care about you – and I still don't understand why."

"Because of what happened!" I shout. "Because I fell in love for the first time in my life and a family died as a result. My dad was harassed for doing nothing. And for what? A few months of happiness? It's not worth it!"

He lets his head rest back against the wall, looking up at the ceiling.

"I know about your mum," he says. My stomach turns. "I know she killed herself. I know it must have seemed like you lose everyone you love."

"How do you know about my mum?"

I didn't find out until I was a teenager, perhaps thirteen or fourteen. Dad had always protected me from the truth, telling me she'd had a heart attack. It made me sad, especially the thought of Dad carrying the weight of that by himself. I was almost two when it happened, but Dad had always been my main carer, Mum often too depressed to make it out of bed. I felt sorry for her, unable to clear the darkness to see the light in my dad. When I found out about Danny, disturbing thoughts surfaced from time to time – *it's too much of a coincidence, I must be at fault somehow* – but no one else has ever suggested the link before. It feels particularly cruel that Nick has.

"The private investigator did a background report."

He looks ashamed and I can only hope that that feeling lives in him until the day he dies, haunting him with the choices he's made.

"I hope my life story made good reading."

"Your mum was depressed, like Meg. That's not good reading, it's just very sad."

He puts his head in his hands and takes a deep breath. I watch as his shoulders rise and then fall, deflated.

"I took no pleasure in any of this," he says. "I was trying to make up for the ways I'd failed her when she was alive; I couldn't always be the person she needed."

"You're not responsible for her suicide."

I immediately regret saying something that would offer him any comfort – it's more than he deserves – and yet I can't help but feel a part of me softening, empathising with him in his turmoil.

"Not directly, no. But I was her husband, I should have been able to keep her safe."

"From herself?"

"I wasn't there," he says, and it's obvious he's carrying the kind of guilt that doesn't understand reason or logic.

The rain has returned outside, fast and heavy, and it's accompanied by thick grey clouds that have left us with little light. It feels very apt.

"What now?" I ask.

Faced with Nick's revelations my mind has barely had time to process the body that lies behind him, or the fact that I'm partly responsible. I know it was self-defence – I have no doubt that he would have killed me – but the thought of reliving everything to the police, of bringing up the past and tying it in with the present, feels unbearable.

"Go," he says.

"What?"

"Go. Leave town."

"I can't just..."

"Why? No one knows you were here."

"But why would you... why?"

"I couldn't help her. But perhaps I can help you. You deserve better."

My mind flits back to that day in his flat, talking to him about John. *You deserve better.* Then the day at the beach, sat in the café as he looked at my bruised wrist. *This isn't okay.* It all seems like a lifetime ago.

"What will you do?"

"He's a known druggy, the police will believe me if I tell them he came looking for money and got aggressive when I asked him to leave."

"But my fingerprints will be on the…"

I look behind me to the shattered glass that lies on the floor, the award in pieces, covered in Connor's blood.

"I'll clean up first. I'll make it right."

"I don't think you can ever do that."

Tears begin to fall. It all seems so desperately unfair – the betrayal, the consequences to a mistake I made as a child, the heartache so poignantly painful; an echo of the darkness that came after Danny.

"Please don't cry," Nick says.

"I trusted you!" I'm shouting, the numbness of the shock wearing off, replaced by sheer panic. "And now look." I gesture to Connor's body. "Oh my god, oh my god."

"It's okay."

"It's not okay, nothing about this is okay. He's dead! We killed him!"

"No, I killed him. And it was self-defence. Hey." Nick tries to catch my gaze, to anchor me. "We did what we had to do, okay? Now you need to pull yourself together. You're stronger than you believe."

I put my head in my hands and sob, screaming into the palms of my hands. It must be a dream, it must be a terrible dream.

"You'll see how strong you are, when you have no other choice."

"I can't just walk away."

"Yes, yes you can. And you will. Now go."

His voice is calm but firm and in that moment, if nothing else, I am grateful to him for taking control, for pushing me away. I wipe away my tears and pull myself up onto shaky legs. Why is it always the case; you have to summon the most strength when you feel at your weakest? It seems so profoundly unfair; a fundamental flaw in mankind. As I get to the step where he sits he takes my hand.

"It was real," he says. "I felt it."

I wish he wouldn't play to my emotions – I feel vulnerable, my defences weakened. I use all my resources, everything I have left, and I let go. I don't stop to acknowledge the body and I don't look back to say goodbye. I walk straight through the studio and out into the greyness of the day, my dad's voice cutting through the chaos in my mind. 'You know, Erin, you can never judge a man by how he acts at his best. You have to see him at his worst; at his weakest. You have to watch him try to overcome adversity, then you'll see him for who he really is.'

When I get inside the car, I reach into my bag for the cheque from Ray. I look at it for a while, my fingers tracing the outline of his signature, holding onto the belief he has in me. *Follow your heart.* I think of my dad, the man who raised me through his own grief and then guided me through mine. I put the cheque back in my bag, start the engine and drive away.

60

NOW

The sea comes into view. The clouds have cleared to allow the horizon to sink seamlessly into the vast expanse of blue. I pull over, parking on double yellow lines; it doesn't matter, I won't be here long. The ground is damp from the rain but the sky shows no memory of it, it's as clear as the sea beneath it. I take the letters and the cheque and rip them into tiny pieces until there is nothing left to make sense of. Then I walk down the road to the nearest bin and toss them inside.

The sun is bathing the headland in a soft golden glow, the cliffs casting long shadows on the beach. I take in the places I haven't seen for so many years – the places that still feel like home. A memory surfaces; the last time I saw my dad all those years ago. 'The thing is, no matter how many thousands of miles they travel, they will always return to the beach where they hatched.' I watch the sea as the waves roll in, crashing against the rocks and sending splashes into the air. I hold out my hands to catch them, listening to the roar of the waves welcoming me home.

THE END

ACKNOWLEDGEMENTS

It has been a joy to be part of the wonderful team at Bloodhound Books: Betsy, Fred, Tara, Ian, Abbie and Hannah – thank you so much for all your knowledge, support and guidance. Thank you also to my editor, Morgen, for your endless patience and reassurance. Your input and advice have been invaluable.

I am indebted to my first readers: Nicki, Abby and Beth. Thank you for taking the time to read my manuscript and encourage me to believe in it, and for the many, many discussions throughout the whole process. Your support is appreciated more than you know.

Mum and Dad – thank you for reading me books as a child that ignited a spark. For everything you've done and for everything you continue to do, thank you from the bottom of my heart.

To my husband – the best partner I could wish for – thank you for your unwavering support, tireless positivity and heartfelt encouragement. You are the reason I was able to follow my dream.

Finally, to my children – thank you for making every day an adventure. I am so immensely proud of you both.

A NOTE FROM THE PUBLISHER

Thank you for reading this book. If you enjoyed it please do consider leaving a review on Amazon to help others find it too.

We hate typos. All of our books have been rigorously edited and proofread, but sometimes mistakes do slip through. If you have spotted a typo, please do let us know and we can get it amended within hours.

info@bloodhoundbooks.com